Praise for *Sunday's Child*
"A witty, wonderfully poised, poignant, self-pityless book."
– *The Gazette*, Montreal

"Written with exquisite style, perfect pace and unusual elegance . . . always engaging, it is a genuine tour de force."
– *The Hamilton Spectator*

Praise for *Buried on Sunday*
"Phillips' prose has the cool sparkle of champagne, a deft blend of malice and understanding." – *San Francisco Chronicle*

"Phillips offers an urbane view of the gamut of human foibles and the shenanigans of fate." – *The Gazette*, Montreal

"Scrumptious entertainment . . . Phillips makes some shrewd and wise observations about sexual and social choices."
– *Booklist*

Praise for *Working on Sunday*
"[Phillips] offers diversion, good humour, some entertaining scenes, a few pungent *aperçus* and a sideways glance at the human condition." – Carol Shields, *The Globe and Mail*

Praise for *The Mice Will Play*
"A pleasing, light romp reminiscent of an Oscar Wilde parlour play, with hard truths veiled in happy façades . . . Phillips has managed to give his work his own stamp while reviving a genre—the parlour farce—that's been dormant for too long." – *The Globe and Mail*

Praise for *No Early Birds*
"Phillips . . . works like a composer: the merry tune in the treble clef is so catchy, it takes a while to notice the bass notes are building. But build they do . . . toward a common human reality and depth." – Joan Barfoot, *Quill & Quire*

A Voyage on Sunday

by Edward O. Phillips

The Geoffry Chadwick novels:
Sunday's Child
Buried on Sunday
Sunday Best
Working on Sunday

Other novels:
Where There's a Will
Hope Springs Eternal
The Landlady's Niece
The Mice Will Play
No Early Birds

Edward O. Phillips

A Voyage on Sunday

A Geoffry Chadwick novel

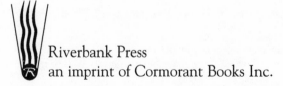

Riverbank Press
an imprint of Cormorant Books Inc.

**Canada Council
for the Arts**

**Conseil des Arts
du Canada**

ONTARIO ARTS COUNCIL
CONSEIL DES ARTS DE L'ONTARIO

The publisher gratefully acknowledges the support of the Canada Council for the
Arts and the Ontario Arts Council for its publishing program. We acknowledge
the financial support of the Government of Canada through the Book Publishing
Industry Development Program (BPIDIP) for our publishing activities.

Printed and bound in Canada

National Library of Canada Cataloguing in Publication Data

Phillips, Edward, 1931-
A voyage on Sunday / Edward O. Phillips.

"A Geoffry Chadwick novel".
ISBN 1-896332-18-8

I. Title.

PS8581.H567V69 2004   C813'.54   C2003-907265-7

Cover and text design: John Terauds

The Riverbank Press, an imprint of Cormorant Books Inc.
215 Spadina Ave., Studio 230, Toronto, Ontario, Canada M5T 2C7
www.cormorantbooks.com

for K.S.W. and J.J.T

I always love to begin a journey on Sundays, because I shall have the prayers of the church, to preserve all that travel by land, or by water.

Jonathan Swift, *Polite Conversation*, Dialogue 2

I

I have always detested travel. Leaving home for any but the most urgent personal or business reasons must surely be one of life's more dispiriting experiences. To begin with, I always overpack, convinced that the plane will hit an air pocket just as the stewardess is handing a Coke to the passenger seated next to me, with the result that all the sticky fluid will land in my lap. Without a backup suit in my luggage I will be confined to a hotel room while the local dry cleaner tries to salvage my trousers. I need extra socks because the ones I am wearing might develop holes, extra underwear in case the local food or water should render me suddenly incontinent, extra shirts and ties lest the popular restaurant's *table d'hôte* slide from my fork with damaging results. I need a bottle of scotch the way an infant needs a security blanket, plus a whole range of medications and analgesics, nostrums I would never take at home, fearful that the second I check into a hotel my head will begin to pound or my heart to burn.

Finally there is the unknown and ominous hazard of other travellers, every one equipped with a life story of singular banality he is eager to share: the romance of working for General Foods, the saga of a used car dealership, the epic struggle of installing aluminum windows. If the He is a She the tale is often supplemented by photographs carried in the same roomy reticule that also holds knitting and a romance novel. When I read *The Canterbury Tales* at college, under the guidance of a professor with hair in his ears and none on his head who chuckled away at Chaucer's humour and humanity, I remember thinking how relieved I felt that I did not have to ride to Canterbury in the company of those long-winded pilgrims. The hazards of travel vastly outweigh the benefits.

The question might legitimately be asked as to why I was standing at the rail of a ship enveloped in dank, dark Caribbean air, looking down at a tin roofed embarkation shed and watching the last few passengers burdened with carry-on luggage trying to negotiate the gangplank. Why indeed? Explanations are never easy and seldom brief, but I will attempt to be both. To begin with, I had recently retired. More precisely, I had retirement thrust upon me, as Shakespeare might have said. Richard Lyall, senior partner of the law firm Lyall, Pierce, Chadwick, and Dawson, sat down at his burnished mahogany desk one morning, reached for a file, and died. It was an enviable death, no pain, no warning, no loss of dignity. He looked as though he had nodded off for a catnap prior to an important meeting. His death affected the remaining partners more than we could have imagined. Sober, fair, deliberate, he had been a solid foundation on which our possibly more histrionic talents had rested. Without him we were cut adrift. Christopher Pierce had long been under siege from his wife to move out to British Columbia where the grandchildren were already in school, while Michael Dawson decided to lower his high blood pressure by spending time on the golf course.

Having neither grandchildren nor golf clubs, I could have continued to work. Offers came from a couple of law firms, and I confess to being momentarily tempted. Not yet sixty-five, in good health, and with several decades of experience under my belt, I carefully weighed the pros and cons before deciding to step down. So accustomed had I become to the rhythm of my own firm I felt apprehensive about having, at this point in my life, to adapt to others. There were dozens of young lawyers out there, hungry for work, and I certainly did not need the money. What finally tipped the scales was my belief in leaving the party while it is still merrily in progress, before the evening has wound down to tired guests, empty glasses, overflowing ash-trays. I held with the old vaudeville dictum: "Always leave 'em laughing," and chose to pull out while I was still ahead.

My secretary withdrew from the easy job of dealing with mail and telephone calls to the far more arduous task of full-time grandmother. We held a lunch at one of the local private clubs, all leather armchairs and threadbare oriental rugs. Pre-dictable chicken was served, unsurprising speeches were made, unobtrusive tears were shed; and the firm of Lyall, Pierce, Chadwick, and Dawson ceased to exist.

Enter Audrey Crawford. The English-language community in Montreal is small, and news about its residents travels faster by word of mouth then ever it could on the Internet. Within a few days of my retirement lunch Audrey telephoned, ostensibly to wish me every success in my new venture, as though I were about to climb Mount Everest. Whenever I hear Audrey's voice on the telephone my guard goes up. By now it has become a reflex because she always wants something: my money, my time, my attention. To give her credit, she sets an excellent table and never stints on liquor. But she is always on the hustle, usually for a cause of such unimpeachable worthiness I feel like the Grinch for turning her down. Yet I always do, on principle. I will not allow myself to be manipulated by heterosexuals.

"Geoffry darling, I wouldn't have dared ask you before now as I know how busy you have been, but could I beg a little of your time—now that you have a bit more of it—for a small project I have in mind. It's for the library . . ." Her voice trailed off momentarily, allowing the worth of the undertaking to sink in. "I know the major renovations have been completed, but the building is desperately short of funds for new acquisitions. And the landscaping is far from finished."

Our local library, a source of pride for the community, had recently undergone a major overhaul. What had been essentially a nineteenth-century institution had to gear itself up for the twenty-first. A great deal of local interest and involvement had been generated, not surprisingly. What cow, next to those scrawny beasts that roam unchecked throughout India, could be considered more sacred than a library? The very word induces a respectful hush. Whereas a great many people have turned their backs on the church, these same apostates fall to their figurative knees at the portals of a library. Even those who can barely pry themselves from the TV screen long enough to take a pee will pay lip service to the need for access to books. To raise funds for the institution shimmers with the aura of a holy cause, combining the best features of the New Jerusalem and the Emerald City.

But Audrey plus the library remained a lethal combination. "What is the project?" I asked warily.

Seizing the opening, Audrey pushed her way in. "We thought it would be great fun to put on a play, in Queen Mary Hall, proceeds to go to the library. We plan to make it a gala evening, wine and canapés during the intermissions, and a raffle after the final curtain. We'll charge a good price for the tickets, say fifty dollars a head."

"That's a pretty hefty price for amateur theatricals. Most of the people I know would gladly pay fifty dollars to stay home."

"Geoffry Chadwick, don't be such an old stick. The idea is to have a good time, not wear a hair shirt!"

"I suppose you'll be putting on a comedy, with the actors constantly in motion, clearing their throats, making faces, telegraphing the laughs?"

"I don't think comedy is such a good idea," she replied, "not for inexperienced actors. Comedy requires professionalism, and we will have to make do with amateurs."

Audrey had a point. Amateur groups can do a better job of *Oedipus Rex* than *The Importance of Being Earnest*.

"Do you have a play in mind?"

Audrey paused just a moment. "We were thinking seriously about *Hedda Gabler*. Ibsen can always draw an audience."

"I see. Hedda is a very demanding role. It's been played by the best. Do we have someone here in Westmount who is up to tackling such a big part?"

Audrey gave a deprecating little laugh. "We'll hold auditions. I'm sure we'll find someone. I thought I might read for the part myself."

The coin dropped. Audrey was masterminding this fundraising scheme so she might have the opportunity to play Hedda Gabler. By turning the evening into a benefit for the library she was concealing her ego behind a smokescreen of philanthropy.

Audrey knew enough not to push too hard. "Think it over. This Wednesday we are having our first committee meeting at my house over tea. Come around four if you can. There will be heaps of good things to eat, and if you don't want tea the bar will be open. Do try to make it."

As I replaced the receiver I found myself amused by Audrey's energy and determination. She could easily sit down at

her Empire desk and write a cheque for the library well in excess of what the projected evening might raise. Not only does
Audrey have pots of money in her own name, she married a
hugely successful man. Her wedding to Hartland Crawford
seemed more like a merger than a marriage. Whereas at some
weddings the guests take home a small slice of bridal cake or a
basket of sugared almonds, the guests at Audrey and Hartland's
union each received a certificate representing one share of
Crawford Enterprises Limited. I still have mine; its value has
increased tenfold.

I have known Audrey since college days and can remember
she had a run at acting. Many young people do. Taking a turn
onstage used to be a rite of passage, like a Sweet Sixteen party,
acne, or buying your first condoms, an experience most of us go
through and leave behind. I never went onto the stage, but I
have always disliked the spotlight. Audrey, however, was in-
fected by the acting virus at private school, where she played
Romeo and St. Joan, and carried the infection on into university, where she appeared as Lady Macbeth, Goneril, and Lady
Bracknell. I suppose she was all right; I don't really recall.
What I do remember is that she wanted to study acting in New
York, but her mother wouldn't hear of her darling daughter
becoming a common strolling player. Prejudices dating from
earlier centuries still lingered, and actresses were still thought
in some quarters to be no better than they should. I suppose if
Audrey had wanted to be an actress badly enough she would
have managed, but marriage happened to her, and the acting
career went into the closed file.

I telephoned my friend Elinor Richardson. How a homosexual in late middle age ended up keeping company with a
widow some years his junior is one of those mysteries that

perhaps should not be probed too deeply. As I said, explanations are seldom simple.

"Am I speaking to Elinor Richardson, the grandmother who still likes a good time?"

"The very same. Have you missed me?"

"Like a front tooth."

"Seriously, Geoffry, I was just about to call you. I ran into Audrey Crawford in the supermarket, and she put the arm on me to work on a play, *Hedda Gabler*, to be staged as a fundraiser for the library."

"She just called me for the same reason. Are you going to read for a part?"

"Good heavens no! Although Audrey did suggest I might try out for Juliana Tesman."

"That's a huge compliment," I snorted. "It's years since I suffered through a performance of *Hedda Gabler*, but isn't Juliana the husband's old aunt?"

"I suppose. But you must remember, Geoffry mine, that under the magic of makeup even I can be made to look old."

"You'd have to look like the woman who escaped from Shangri-la, the 'most old woman in the world.' Audrey is going to play Hedda."

Elinor paused to digest that one. "You have to be kidding. Audrey has three or four years on me. She's got to be sixty if she's a second."

"She is. We were at college together, and I'm sixty-three—a strikingly handsome and well preserved sixty-three I grant you—but I can remember when Audrey turned twenty-one. I was twenty-four."

"But Hedda Gabler is around thirty. How will Audrey manage to sustain the illusion? Queen Mary Hall isn't that large."

"I venture to suggest she will cast the play with her contemporaries, if she hasn't already. She claims there are to be auditions, but I wouldn't bet the rent. When she archly suggested she might read for the part of Hedda I realized this was to be the theatrical equivalent of publishing your own book. The big question is: are you going to get yourself involved? Remember, Audrey won't take yes for an answer. She could sell sand in the Sahara."

"I've been asked to tea on Wednesday, for a sort of informal committee meeting. I may volunteer to help out with costumes, or props. What about you?"

"We'll see. I don't mind doing something so long as I can work on my own, nothing that reeks of togetherness. What are your plans for this evening?"

"It looks as though I will be playing grandmother. Jane is still not too pregnant to get around, and Michael has to go to Quebec City for a conference. I told Jane I'd mind the kids for a couple of days so she could tag along. I'd ask you over for a meal, but I know how you feel about small children. Better beans and bacon in peace than cake and jelly in chaos."

"You speak in metaphor. Will Jane be home by Wednesday?"

"She should be. We might grab a bite after the meeting at Audrey's."

"Why not. I'll call you before then."

"Please do. I'll be hungry for grown-up voice. I quite enjoy *Sesame Street*, but Barney sucks, as the young say today. À *bientôt, chèr.*"

The April day couldn't seem to decide whether it wanted to be pissy or just plain awful, but the wet snow had temporarily abated and I needed to walk. Dressing for this kind of weather is always a problem. We were no longer in the depths of winter, nor had this particular April given any indication of delivering the sweet showers that bring May flowers. Zipped into galoshes, a collapsible umbrella tucked under my arm, I set out for the nursing home where my mother now lives.

I wanted to think about the two recent phone calls. Fundraising must be for the twentieth century what the Crusades were for the Middle Ages: an opportunity to be militant in aid of a worthy cause. Whether liberating the Holy Land from infidels or holding an auction to raise money for a dialysis machine, the participant is prepared to sacrifice time, energy, and money in pursuit of a nebulous but worthwhile goal.

These days Jerusalem is invaded mainly by tourists wearing sunglasses instead of visors and carrying cameras rather than broadswords, but the drive to raise funds continues unabated, especially during a decade of governmental penny pinching. In principle I could endorse Audrey's efforts to raise money for the library, if only her colossal ego did not block the view.

I have never been a great supporter of amateur theatricals. Novice actors tend to underestimate the intelligence of the audience and fall back on a stock variety of vocal tricks and gestures to make sure we get the point. Another difficulty I encounter when attending performances by amateur groups is attempting to connive at the fiction that the persons on stage really are the characters they attempt to portray and not people I meet at Christmas cocktail parties or know by sight from the bank. For me the curtain is not a fourth wall, the raising of which permits me to observe the lives of those onstage without their appearing to notice that I am lurking out there in the dark. To watch those dusty draperies slide open is to be made embarrassingly aware that I am but a few feet away from a group of nervous people, some of whom I know, trying to remember lines, cues, and blocking while attempting to cope with costumes tried on for the first time at the dress rehearsal.

On the other hand, were Elinor to be working on the production I would find that a considerable inducement to participate. We could laugh at the absurdities, groan over the indignities, and have ourselves a high old time. Perhaps the best course of action would be to hang fire until the meeting at Audrey's on Wednesday.

As the robin flies (I have never seen a crow in Westmount) the distance from my apartment to Maple Grove Manor is not far. I said good afternoon to the receptionist, who always looks at me as though I had come to rob the place, and stepped onto the elevator, fortunately empty. One of the residents, a man in his late eighties with hair combed across his scalp like a bar code, tends to hang out in the lobby. Starved for male companionship, he buttonholes me, often following me onto the elevator, where he proceeds to tell scurrilous jokes usually involving travelling salesmen, farmers' daughters, nuns, darkies, and red-skins. I am not a prude, but vulgarity presupposes intimacy; and I don't even know the man's name. When he dies a cluster of attitudes will die with him, and perhaps the world will be no worse off.

Mother has positively bloomed since moving into the nursing home. At first I was hugely reluctant to dislodge her from the apartment where she had lived since my father died, but she decided the move would be best for all. Whereas she sat around the apartment all day, drinking vodka, chain-smoking, watching TV, and seldom if ever changing out of her robe, now she has her first drink of the day at four P.M. and puts on clothes to be wheeled down to the dining room for dinner at five-thirty. (One of the many terrors of old age is the mealtimes imposed on the elderly.) Mother doesn't seem to mind the early dinner hour, fortified as she is by a few belts of vodka she bribes one of the nurses to buy for her. She no longer seems to mind that the dining room is a no smoking area. In her apartment smoking a cigarette was a way of passing time. She has never knitted a stitch in her life, one of the many non-accomplishments for which I admire her. Now she is surrounded by activities, nods off at lectures and readings, plays three cards at bingo, refuses to have anything to do with crafts, and has discovered the small library, although with her short attention span one book can sustain her for days.

Recently Elinor and I, armed with Mother's power of attorney, went on a shopping spree and bought her armfuls of new clothes, all easy to pull on or zip up, everything cut to add bulk to her almost anorexic emaciation. This afternoon she wore a long, wraparound skirt, meaning she did not have to wear pantyhose, and a blouse with Byronic sleeves under a bolero. The resident hairdresser had cut her fine hair short, so short in fact she looked like one of those women who collaborated with the enemy, but it was tidy. The woman had also encouraged Mother to wear the palest of lipsticks so as not to contrast too sharply with her translucent skin. Mother now looks the way Peter Pan might have looked had he lived to be ninety.

Since it was shortly after four when I entered her room, Mother had already poured her first drink. She doesn't fool around: a large shot of vodka in a plastic tumbler (she has been known to drop things), a small splash of water, and it's happy hour. Ice kills flavour and dilutes the drink. To her credit she keeps a bottle of scotch on her dresser just for me. Mother does not mind drinking alone, but prefers to hoist in company. Unfortunately all the other residents are too fragile to keep up with her, and the nurses can't drink on the job.

"Geoffry, what a pleasant surprise. I'm amazed you decided to venture out on such an unpleasant day."

"Couldn't stay away, Mother." I leaned through the haze of cigarette smoke to kiss her, Montreal fashion, on both cheeks. "Actually it's messy underfoot but not cold."

"Pour yourself a drink, dear."

Four P.M. is a bit early for me to start knocking them back, but I made a dumb show of pouring a scotch, making it weak. "What's new at the zoo?" I asked.

"That extraordinary man, Mr. Barlowe, I believe—he sits around in the lobby—told me the most perplexing story. He followed me onto the elevator to finish it. It seems a travelling salesman stopped at a farmhouse and asked for a bed for the night. 'I'm sorry,' the farmer was supposed to have replied, 'but you'll have to share a room with my son.' 'I'm sorry too,' replied the commercial traveller, 'because I think I'm in the wrong story.'"

I laughed politely. What else could I do? But I quite failed to see the inconvenience of sharing a room with a young man.

"I think old Mr. Barlowe is getting a bit dotty."

"Could be, Mother. Guess what. I've been asked to work on a play, a fundraising scheme for the library."

"Do tell. I hope you're not going to act. It's such bad form to display oneself in public."

"No chance of that," I replied, nursing my drink. "I may do something about promotion, although how does one promote Audrey Crawford as Hedda Gabler?"

"Is Audrey going to perform? I would have thought her a bit too old. Your father and I once saw *Hedda Gabler*. I was so impressed. To think a woman of those times would have the courage to walk out on her husband, especially when she has just learned her son has such a dreadful illness. Top me up, will you, dear?"

I reached for her tumbler. "It was most affecting," she continued. "After the matinée your father and I went out for dinner, to the Plaza, or was it Longchamps. I think it must have been the Plaza . . ."

And she was off, happily not remembering but reinventing the past, a past where skies were always blue, men chivalrous, women modest, servants polite, and dogs friendly. Who am I to edit this harmless fantasy?

After a while she ran down. I finished my drink, declined a second, and stood. "Time to push off, Mother. You'll be heading down for dinner soon."

"I'm glad you're going to work on the play, Geoffry. Now that you are retired you must make an effort to get out and about. The more active you remain, the longer you will postpone moving in here."

"That's a thought," I muttered as I kissed her goodbye. The persistent Mr. Barlowe was lurking by the front door as I stepped off the elevator. He wasted no time on preamble.

"Did you hear the one about the travelling salesman?"

"I'm sorry, but I think I'm in the wrong story," I repeated briskly, annoyed that he had been bothering Mother with his bad jokes.

"You've heard it?"

"Do you know something, Sir? When a group of scientists carbon dated that joke it was found to be two thousand and seventy years old."

"Carbon dated? Now that's a good one." And off he shuffled, chuckling happily to himself.

I pushed my way outside thinking the old are self-protective, like teflon pans. Did I want to live that long? Not having a ready answer I hailed a cab. Snow had begun to fall thickly, and the prospect of another scotch, my book, a spot of TV, and my own company seemed very appealing.

II

When I last visited Audrey Crawford she and Hartland lived in a Scottish baronial house high on the hill near the Westmount Lookout. I supposed it could be called a mansion, were that word not so pretentious, so three-storey-detached at a good address seen from the perspective of semi-detached bungalow in the suburbs. The Crawford house had been built at a time when servants were taken as much for granted as twice-daily mail delivery and milk brought to the door by a horse-drawn wagon. Changing times, values, and priorities have turned many of these elegant edifices into real estate white elephants, especially for those whose children have moved away. Wisely, Audrey and Hartland sold to a family from Hong Kong who believed that their civil liberties, not to mention their immense fortune, would be more respected in Canada. The Crawfords moved off the hill into a house on a quiet avenue just above Sherbrooke Street. By any but the most affluent standards the new house would pass for a mansion: three floors, generously proportioned rooms with high ceilings, and several working fireplaces.

By nature prompt, I was the first to arrive, having only a few short blocks to walk from my building to Audrey's new house. While she went to answer the door I studied the tea—enough to feed a college football team—spread out on the long dining room table. Dominating the display sat a sandwich roll.

Someone, I doubt it had been Audrey, with steady hand, sharp knife, and infinite patience had with surgical precision reduced a loaf of white bread to a long, thin strip. This was then coated with what looked like cream cheese into which chopped walnuts, glazed fruit, and goodness knows what all else had been mixed. The thin slice of coated bread was then rolled, secured, chilled, and set on a platter waiting to be sliced. That kind of labour-intensive food is not meant to delight but to intimidate, and I took note.

The new arrivals turned out to be people I knew, Frank Wilkinson and Jeremy Baker. They had both been to university with the rest of us, Jeremy a couple of years ahead of me, Frank one year behind. Tall, greying, elegant, and terribly grand, Jeremy ran one of the more prestigious antiques stores in the city. Much of his stock came from people like Audrey, couples moving into smaller houses and simplifying their lives. I have been told that regardless of the piece, its great age or excellent quality, Jeremy manages to suggest it has been unearthed at the Salvation Army. Whenever he deigned to buy an object, no doubt at a fraction of its true worth, the seller ached with gratitude. He wears the kind of expensively tailored suits whose cuff buttons actually unbutton.

Frank Wilkinson no longer lived in Montreal, having become a costume designer of international repute. I remember him as a teenager, in rapture after seeing the gowns designed by Gilbert Adrian for Jean Harlow, Myrna Loy, Greta Garbo glittering on the giant screen. From adolescence he understood that he had to design clothes, not pedestrian outfits to be worn to business meetings or cocktail parties, but gowns to be seen on stage, on screen, on floats, in pageants, in any situation where exaggeration seemed normal. His niche turned out to be opera, and his *Carmens*, *Toscas*, *Don Giovannis*, and *Der Rosenkaveliers* have been enshrined in a coffee table book the size of a coffee table. Handsome in a shopworn kind of way, Frank has the look of a man who has awakened once too often in a cheap motel room beside someone whose name he can no longer remember. He was the first young man with whom I seriously fooled around, back in the days when sexual longing surrounded us like a nimbus. We have been friends ever since.

Frank greeted me warmly, Jeremy as though I had just asked him for a handout. We were exchanging the usual greetings when a new arrival came into the foyer. Elsie Connors, another emeritus from college days, was the kind of woman my mother would have described as "not quite top drawer." Elsie Dawes, as she had been before her marriage to Dennis Connors, came to parties wearing white angora sweaters with rhinestone jewellery, matching earrings, necklace, and bracelet. Tight skirts showed off the figure she could have turned to advantage as a model, had her parents not thought, as did Audrey's, that a life of standing upright in the public eye meant a private life spent flat on one's back. When a young man placed a hand on the backside so tantalizingly displayed, she slapped his hand away and called him "fresh." Like the rest of us, she married, and in the fullness of time Dennis Connors achieved prosperity in the hardware business. He also died, leaving her a wealthy widow. Still pencil slim, Elsie has never quite succeeded in shedding her angora image. She mixed synthetic fabrics with real, a silk blouse with a polyester suit, just as she wore costume jewellery along with the genuine thing: large fake pearl earrings surrounded in brilliants to complement the collar of authentic braided pearls with a diamond and ruby clasp. Coro faced off against Tiffany, and we all dropped our eyelids in silent disapproval.

Elsie compensated by having what everyone agreed was a heart of purest gold. If her bangles were only ten carat, her heart was an unalloyed twenty-four, making her a frequent member of any committee convened for a worthwhile cause. Casually dressed in slacks and a large, bulky sweater, she admitted to having just come from the dentist; her still frozen jaw left her disinclined to speak.

Seated at the head of the table, Audrey poured tea and urged us to eat. I avoided the alarming roll, opting instead for tiny sandwiches made with asparagus tips and some filled with chopped egg salad. Flanking Audrey at the head of the table sat Frank across from Jeremy who, when not eating with quiet voracity, leaned on his elbows, the tips of his fingers pressed together. After a sip of tea Audrey launched right into the reason for the meeting, to discuss a production of *Hedda Gabler* as a means of raising funds for the library. The budget for acquisitions failed to encompass the large quantity of new publications coming onto the market. Merely to maintain the magazine and periodical subscriptions remained a steadily escalating cost, and this was only one of many areas where extra funds could benefit. She paused to slice the sandwich roll and to let her words sink in. The subtext fairly shrieked. Anybody who was unwilling to support a fundraising effort for the library would probably be prepared to burn books in the main square, if only we had one.

Two more women arrived, one with a low centre of gravity who wore a parka on which a Remembrance Day poppy was still pinned, the other with her Labrador retriever which was persuaded with some difficulty to remain in the vestibule. They tiptoed in with the kind of self-effacement guaranteed to draw attention, then made rather a pantomime of refusing tea.

Audrey resumed her place and her discourse. Our committee did not want to repeat the mistakes of those who had organized the art auction.

"What went wrong?" I asked. "I didn't attend the auction."

Briefly Audrey went on to explain an auction had been held in Queen Mary Hall, our community auditorium. Local artists were persuaded to dust off works they had been unable to sell and to donate them to the cause. The organizing committee, of which Audrey was not a member, had considered the occasion a resounding success, although by the time the open bar, buffet table, flowers, and string quartet—all considered necessary to put the buyers into an expansive mood—had been paid for, the committee found itself in the red. "Never mind," they had announced, burnishing the silver lining, "the good will and publicity generated for the library were well worth going a few hundred dollars into the hole."

Audrey wanted no miscalculations with our undertaking. The play was to go into rehearsal next week. Auditions were not yet completed, but she herself had been chosen to play Hedda. (Why was I not surprised?) Jeremy was to play her husband, George Tesman, and Elsie Connors had been cast as Thea Elvsted. To imagine Elsie as the ingenue could be no more of a stretch than accepting Audrey as Hedda or Jeremy as her middle aged husband. Judge Brack had been awarded to Alan Howard, a local television personality who had jumped from the CBC before he had been pushed. He was also going to direct. That took care of the major roles.

Audrey toyed with her malachite beads, chosen to set off a hunter-green crepe blouse. With her old-gold hair, full but still shapely figure, suspiciously taut skin, and artful makeup, she was living proof that high maintenance and strong determination, along with stacks of blue chips, can discourage the aging process. The next issue was that of the stage crew. Elinor Richardson, unfortunately unable to be with us this afternoon as her daughter would be late getting back to Montreal, had agreed to help dress the players and look after props. Frank Wilkinson had graciously agreed to design costumes for the women, and Audrey's little dressmaker was going to run them up. Here Audrey paused to give Frank's hand a squeeze; he smiled on cue. I suspected Audrey's little dressmaker charged by the stitch, but I knew we were dealing with flexible bookkeeping.

"Geoffry, I thought you might help sell advertising," said Audrey, addressing me for the first time.

"You mean you want me to go from shop to shop in the neighbourhood, requesting people to place ads in our program? Or—worse still—telephone around, interrupting innocent civilians at work or play to solicit ads? No! An unequivocal no! A no that does not mean 'maybe if you coax me,' but negative minus." Frank Wilkinson laughed out loud.

"However," I continued, "I may have a counter proposal. What kind of program do you wish to hand out at your fifty-bucks-a-seat soirée? Photocopied sheets listing cast and crew, a nickel and dime job—or a substantial booklet, with perhaps an engraving of the library on the cover? If so," I went on before Audrey could cut me off, "I think I can call in some favours and get us a handsome program free, gratis, and for nothing. I am working on the assumption that the more freebies we can manage, the greater the profit for the library."

"That is an excellent suggestion," announced Mary Browning, one of the late arrivals, whose black Labrador had moved from the vestibule to under the table, noisily gulping the chicken salad sandwiches she passed it. "I'll try to scare up some local advertising. I have to give Hamlet his daily walk, so I may just as well visit local merchants." Apparently Mary Browning and her dog came as a team, like a knife thrower and his sequinned target or the magician who saws through his frangible partner in tights. Lucille Beauchemin, Mary's friend, had shed her parka and tucked into the tea. She volunteered to act as stage manager.

Ever aware that a satisfied guest is a compliant guest, Audrey suggested we graduate from tea to a drink. Over scotch I moved into a corner with Frank.

"I'm glad you're going to be working on the production, Geoff." (People who call me Geoff have known me a long time.) "We can use a dash of common sense on this undertaking. I've seen many a production of *Hedda*, but never one quite so long in the tooth. I know the role of Hedda is a pit stop between Juliet and Mrs. Malaprop, but Audrey is just plain too old."

"It had occurred to me," I said, "but we soldier on. How come you are designing the production?"

"Audrey cashed in some chips. She did me some favours when I was starting out, and I owe her a few. As a matter of fact I'll enjoy working in the nineteenth century. I just did a production of *Nabucco* for the Seattle Opera, and I'm fed to the teeth with breastplates and chic little slave outfits."

"Are you in Montreal for a while?"

"In and out. Eileen hasn't been well, and I like to look in whenever possible. Now that my parents are dead I'm the only family she has left."

Frank's parents were really bad news, his mother a foolish, bothersome woman who never knew what she was going to say until she had said it, his father a retired military type who brushed his hair straight back from his face and wouldn't go to the corner store without wearing his regimental tie. They had no idea of how to deal with a sensitive boy and, like my own parents, raised their only son to be a gentleman. For Mr. and Mrs. Wilkinson a true gentleman lived in a state of constant denial. A gentleman said no to everything that could be accused of giving pleasure: unusual food, bright colours, spontaneous behaviour. Gentlemen never laughed out loud, or wept in public (big boys don't cry), or gave vent to anger, or admitted to love, that most seductive of unruly emotions.

Fortunately Frank had an Aunt Eileen, whom I got to know as she was a friend of my mother's. Every insecure youngster ought to have an Aunt Eileen, an adult in whose company you are never clumsy or stupid or perverse. Aunt Eileen never said, "Look but don't touch." She offered second and third helpings without a sigh and a remark about a hollow leg. She kept a chest of drawers full of old clothes to be used for the sole purpose of dressing up. She also took Frank to the movies, over his parents' strong objections, because she claimed she did not like to go alone. At once Frank fell under the spell cast by the silver screen, a lifelong enchantment for which there is no known cure. Those young people raised on television as just another household appliance, like a stove or a vacuum cleaner, will never understand the thrill of entering a movie palace. To step into a lobby designed with all the skewed glamour of an operatic set was to enter a world where everything was possible. Those mock Egyptian temples, Spanish plazas, rococo palaces run amok suggested life held limitless options. Seated in the dark of the theatre while Tom and Jerry slugged it out, Judy Garland sang, Rita Hayworth danced meant being, quite literally, beside oneself. It was at the movies that Frank fell under the spell of Gilbert Adrian, perhaps the most gifted designer of women's clothing for the screen; and the rapture he experienced over "Gowns by Adrian" made him realize that he wanted to be a designer, a goal from which he never deviated.

Whenever he is free Frank comes to Montreal to visit his aunt, now an old lady. I always enjoy Frank when I see him. We go back a long way, which counts for something; and he brings with him a breath of theatrical glamour, almost as if he were an ambassador from a country I know only from the newspapers.

Frank lit a cigarette. I know Audrey tolerates smoking, as she was once a heavy smoker, but Mary began to cough and Lucille gave Frank a look that would have withered cactus. My instant, unguarded reaction was to tell them both to fuck off, even though I do not smoke myself. Common sense and my upbringing suggested otherwise, and I motioned to Frank to step outside for a breath of air.

Once on the wrong side of the door, Frank inhaled deeply. "If the booze doesn't get me the smokes will."

"Either that or you will die from death," I suggested. "So will I for that matter."

"Have you ever noticed," he continued, "how the people who have given up cigarettes, caffeine, cholesterol, and empty carbohydrates for carrot juice and oatmeal muffins think they will live forever? You may postpone dying for a few years, but is that really living? It must be, as the papers love to promote that denial-as-fun lifestyle."

"What I really love to read," I said, "are those Cheerful Charlie columns that encourage you to have a rollicking sex life at ninety-five. The good news is that you don't have to wear a condom. The bad news is all the rest. At ninety-five I hope to be under a tasteful granite stone, not clanking my hipbones against someone who has had both hips replaced."

Frank laughed out loud. "Do you suppose there is money to be made from a *Joy of Sex* manual aimed at geriatrics? Ten positions you should avoid. How to turn a kiss into mouth-to-mouth resuscitation. How to distinguish hyperventilation from passion. Orgasm is not a stroke. With a video spin-off and an 800 number. All major credit cards accepted."

We were still chuckling when Audrey opened the door. "There you are! I thought you had decamped. Frank, you are welcome to smoke inside. I hate to think of you huddling out here like the homeless."

"Frank was getting the evil eye from publicity and stage management," I said. "As a matter of fact, Audrey, I should be moving along. May I use your phone?"

A call to Elinor assured me her daughter had returned from Quebec City, meaning Elinor was free for dinner. I called a cab and offered Frank a lift to his aunt's apartment.

"You might think of settling Eileen in Maple Grove Manor," I suggested. "Mother loves it, and you would be spared the worry about the apartment and making sure she has suitable care."

"You have a point. It is a concern. Having her in a nursing home would spare me a lot of anxiety. Thanks for the ride."

"Will you be in town for the play?"

"Wouldn't miss it. Maybe we could get together: lunch, a drink?"

"Love to. Now that I'm no longer punching a clock I have time to spare."

I gave the driver Elinor's address, and we pulled away from the curb.

I met Elinor shortly before Christmas. She and I work out at the same health club, but we met officially at Audrey Craw-ford's annual Christmas party. Elinor sang carols; I did not, but then I never do. According to the way I was raised I have turned out to be a very poor sport, meaning I do not allow myself to be bullied or cajoled into playing bridge, singing carols, driving into the country for Sunday lunch, or making my spare room available to billet out-of-town choristers, most of whom would have a much better time cruising the showers at the YMCA.

Elinor and I were both at sixes and sevens. Her husband had recently died, as had my friend. I hesitate to use the term "longtime companion" because we had known one another only six years; and the word "lover" suggests heavy breathing, rumpled sheets, fooling around in the shower, and Homeric battles. We collided and separated, only to meet again in late middle age. Patrick and I had enjoyed a brief fling during the Sixties, when casual sex had become a cottage industry and people were too busy making love to make war. We had six wonderful years, and then he died. Elinor experienced an almost parallel situation, having remarried her divorced husband. The second marriage was the good one, and then he died. Elinor and I were both beached at a time when we had planned, if not to set sail into the golden years, at the very least to pick up a pair of oars and row in that direction.

We liked each other at once, and a series of unforeseen and unrelated incidents combined to throw us into one another's company during Christmas week. She learned that I was gay, which bothered her not all. She also learned that I had once been married, which she founded mildly curious. And when a mixture of stress and alcohol sent us into a companionable embrace, all of those months of celibacy began to make themselves felt.

Having sex with a woman is not unlike riding a bicycle. You never forget how, even though you may choose to ride a motorcycle. And I have to admit that Elinor and I have a novel relationship. We have both known a number of men, although Elinor feels a little bit naughty about talking double digits. If I could even begin to remember everyone I got it on with I would be dealing in the high threes or, were I completely honest (never a sound policy in matters sexual) spilling over into four. It seems like another life lived by another person. I had slept with nobody since Patrick died. Now if I don't sleep with Elinor I sleep alone. And I enjoy a wonderful sense of freedom, no longer in thrall to the itchy demon that tells me if a man has good legs, a round bum, a handsome profile, or eloquent hands, I have to find out if he is available. It is a lesson I took an inordinately long time to learn, but as I once read on a trivet from Pennsylvania: "Too soon old. Too late smart."

Elinor lives in a small townhouse in the western end of Westmount. Like the owner, the house has style that does not flaunt itself. Handsome traditional furniture sits on rich orientals which in turn rest on floors sanded and Varathaned to the colour of fine tobacco. She owns a handsome collection of still-life paintings, "dead nature" as the French like to call the genre. I prefer the English nomenclature, for still-life is a kind of painting I have always enjoyed. In a culture obsessed with what it owns, what could be a more suitable icon than a series of objects, lovingly rendered, for public display. The house is refreshingly free of clutter, Elinor's reward to herself for having raised two children as a single mother. After two decades of compulsory chaos she has embraced an undemonstrative sense of order. A neat freak myself, I find her house welcoming and comfortable. We embraced warmly, not having seen one another for three days.

"I've come to take you away from all this," I declared.

"To the clean, pure life I've always wanted? To a world where people no longer whisper my name? Pour yourself a drink." Elinor had prepared a drinks tray on her dining room table. "I'm afraid I started without you. I had a long talk with Audrey earlier this afternoon, when I phoned to say Jane had been held up and I couldn't leave the children. After I had been alternately cajoled and strong-armed—you know Audrey —into looking after props, she laid a heavy burden on my bent shoulders. As you know, perhaps the key prop in the action is a brace of duelling pistols which had belonged to Hedda's father, General Gabler. She uses one of them to shoot herself at the end of the play."

"I fail to see your problem," I said as I sat in a wing chair. "Do you have a coaster or a napkin for my glass?"

"How well trained you are," she said as she placed a small brass dish on the mahogany occasional table beside my chair. She kissed me on the forehead. "You can come back."

"I hope so. As I was saying, doesn't every Westmount family, at the very least those above Sherbrooke Street, own a brace of duelling pistols, along with swizzle sticks, a Stilton cheese scoop, and button hooks?"

"Would that it were that simple. Hartland has a pair of revolvers that belonged to his father, who was an officer in World War I. But revolvers are more wild west than provincial Norway."

"*Hedda Gabler* at the O.K. Corral?"

We shared a quiet laugh before I had a sudden idea. "Did

you ever know the Parkinson family? The old man died only last week. I didn't go to the funeral, but it seems *le tout* Westmount turned up for the service at St. Luke-the-Apostle, followed by an S.R.O. reception at the Lord Elgin Club. You know how I dislike crowd scenes, and Parkinson was a mean old bugger, bought himself respectability by donating heavily to local charities and hospitals. He also built up quite a remarkable collection of antique weapons. I wonder if the collection includes duelling pistols."

"Geoffry, you're a genius!" exclaimed Elinor. "But isn't it perhaps a bit soon after the funeral to intrude upon the family with such a request?"

"I know the son, Robert. We were at law school together. As I couldn't get to the funeral, I paid a visit to the funeral home. Why don't I give him a call?"

"Well, if you don't think it would be an intrusion . . ."

I didn't. As I dialled the number I wondered in what kind of shape Bob Parkinson would be so soon after the burial. Bob is the last of the big-time drunks. Unlike today's high-minded, clean-living, politically correct, post baby boomers, for whom anyone who has two drinks and a dividend should join AA, I still make the distinction between a drunk and an alcoholic. A drunk drinks to have a good time, not to exorcise demons. Drunks do not pour vodka into their morning orange juice and hide bottles in the linen closet. They wouldn't dream of attending meetings of support groups that didn't offer a well stocked bar. They can go for weeks as normal social drinkers until an occasion arises that needs to be properly celebrated.

For Bob Parkinson, the death of his father, a stingy, sanctimonious old curmudgeon, merited a celebration. Now the old man's considerable fortune would go to Bob and his sister June.

A professional virgin, she takes after her father and wouldn't say manure if she had a mouthful. Not Bob. When I arrived at the funeral home in the late afternoon I could see at once he was hardly prostrate with grief. In fact, he was obviously over-refreshed and cross with the funeral home as the director would not permit an open bar at the other end of the room from the coffin, fortunately shut.

"Thanks for coming, Geoffry," he said, squeezing my hand. "Would you care for a small drop?" From his inside jacket pocket he produced an elegant silver flask with his monogram in gothic script.

I shook my head. Rather than slide into the platitudes of grief I explained the prior engagement must prevent my attending the funeral.

"Not to worry," he exclaimed, giving me a matey clap on the shoulder. Taking a swig from the flask he put it away, then leaned forward. "Did you hear the one about the guy who moved to another city and decided he needed a checkup? So he found himself a doctor who did all the usual stuff—the stethoscope, the ECG, grabbing his nuts—then pulled on a rubber glove and lubricated the middle finger. 'I'm going to examine your prostate,' he explained. 'Please bend over the table so I can insert my finger.'

'If it's all the same to you, doctor,' said the patient, 'could you insert two fingers? I'd like a second opinion.'"

Having recently undergone that particular examination I was more amused than I let on; however, funeral homes are not the ideal venue for standup comedy.

I dialled Bob's apartment. The answering service suggested another number, which I called.

"Bob, it's Geoffry speaking. Geoffry Chadwick."

"Chadwick, you old squaw fucker! What's on your mind?"

"I've called to ask a favour. In your father's collection of weapons, is there by any chance a pair of pistols, duelling pistols, say late eighteenth century?"

"There sure is."

"A dedicated group of local citizens is putting on a production of *Hedda Gabler* to raise funds for the library, and we were wondering if we might borrow the pistols to use in the play. Naturally you'll be given a pair of complimentary tickets."

"You can have the guns on one condition."

"What's that."

"That I don't have to go to the goddamned play. I'm up at Father's house right now. Want to drop by and pick them up? I'll give you a drink."

"Sure thing. I'll be right over."

I returned to the living room. "Elinor, I just spoke to Bob Parkinson and he's not exactly keening and moaning. He wants me to come over now and collect the pistols. Shall I strike while the iron is hot, to coin a phrase?"

"If you wouldn't mind. The pistols are the only item in the play that has me worried. Everything else I can find locally. Look, if you're delayed we can send out. I'd be happy with a peanut butter sandwich if I knew we had weapons for the production."

A pistol in the hand is worth two in the museum. I called a cab and went outside to wait in the street. Mayfair Crescent lay at the top of a large hill dignified with the name of Westmount Mountain. It was my first trip up the hill since Audrey's Christmas party. The taxi drove past houses in which I had once lived or visited regularly with that freemasonry accorded to children and their friends, so long as they behaved.

Little appeared to have changed, yet I knew that if I rang familiar doorbells, unfamiliar faces would open the door.

The cab turned onto Mayfair Crescent, a street that by itself contributed a large part of municipal real estate revenue, and pulled to a stop in front of a Victorian house that looked more like a movie set than a family residence. Few would have been surprised to see a large, misshapen creature shambling down the wide oak staircase into the forbidding front hall. A fireplace in the inglenook glowed with an electric fire, lumps of red glass lit from beneath. The face of the grandfather clock showed phases of a jolly, smiling moon, the only spot of cheer visible on the ground floor carpeted in deep reds and curtained in dark greens. Glints of silver and the occasional gleam of polished brass could not beat back the specific gravity of heavy furnishings suggesting a joyless opulence. The life lived in this house must be one of high seriousness unleavened by frivolity. I hoped I would not have to tarry.

The front door had been opened by a housekeeper from Central Casting, black hair parted in the centre and tugged back into a bun above a severe black dress, possibly a uniform but more likely mourning for her late employer. Her angular features expressed disapproval, and when Bob bellowed downstairs that he'd be down as soon as he had taken a leak, the ends of her tightly compressed mouth turned down even further.

When Bob finally came down the stairs, one hand grasping the bannister for support, I could see he had been drinking. Once a truly handsome man, after the fashion of a Thirties matinee idol, he had become mute testimony to the dispiriting truth that a dissipated life leads to a dissipated air. A cross-hatching of tiny veins covered his cheeks, and he had acquired the soft, spongy look of someone whose body retains fluid.

From past encounters I knew he would reach a certain level of inebriation and then level off, so that further drinking did not show. He ushered me into an oak panelled room dominated by an enormous rolltop desk which he had evidently been rummaging through.

"Just sorting through the old man's stuff," he began as he poured us both a drink. The large silver tray, on which sat a bottle of scotch, Waterford tumblers and water jug, and a circa nineteen-thirties chrome ice bucket, had been polished to a soft satin sheen. Alfred Parkinson may have inhabited a time warp, but it had been well maintained.

"Cheers, Bob. Are these the pistols?"

On a marble topped table lay a mahogany case with brass fittings in which lay two pistols on a bed of faded blue velvet. I know nothing about firearms, but these weapons, with their curved, carved handles and long, gleaming barrels looked as though they truly might have belonged to General Gabler.

"They certainly look like the real thing," I continued. "I know they will be well taken care of. I will ask the stage manager to take them home after each performance, and the day after the play closes they will be returned to you. I promise."

"Not to worry. I don't want them. Now that the old boy has kicked off I no longer need to rob banks." Bob roared with laughter at his own joke. "And I'm glad to help out the library." He flopped into an armchair with armrests carved in the likeness of heraldic lions. I sat more gently in the matching chair.

"I'm pleased for you, Bob, and for June. Now, if you will excuse me, I have a dinner engagement." I rose to leave.

"Sit down, Geoffry;" he gestured me back into the chair. "I'm bored with going through the desk. The old man kept every goddamned grocery bill."

As I had feared, picking up the pistols was turning into an episode. I studied the painting of ruminating Highland cattle on the far wall and wondered how soon I could pry myself away. Bob lay back in his chair and smiled, half closing his eyes and running his tongue over already moist lips. "You're looking good, Geoffry."

"It's a trick of the light, that and polyfilla."

Bob gave a throaty chuckle. "You sell yourself short, kiddo. Would you like to go upstairs?"

"Upstairs? Whenever for?"

"Don't be dense, Geoffry. I thought we might have a go, for old times' sake."

I sat upright, mildly aghast. Bob was hitting on me. To be sure, we did have it on a few times, back in the Sixties, but everyone was getting it on in the Sixties. Whatever one may have done during that indecorous decade ought to be expunged from the record. Bob and I had enjoyed the most casual kind of sex; I stopped seeing him because a night with Bob meant a major hangover the next morning. For thirty years we hadn't even alluded to our past escapades, and now he wanted me to go upstairs in this haunted house and recapture the rapture.

Sensing my hesitation he rose to his feet. "Come on, Geoffry, it won't hurt a bit."

Trying to keep it light I assumed a mock serious expression. "I'd love to but I can't. I've taken a vow of chastity, to the Moon Goddess. I can't have sex until the next full moon—and we are only in the first quarter."

Bob leaned over and put his pudgy hands on the arms of my chair. "Bullshit!" A blast of alcoholic breath enveloped me. "I don't have anything nasty, if that's what you're thinking."

"But I do. I have chlamydia. I can never have children."

Bob laughed and exhaled more fumes. "Come off it, Chadwick. You're behaving like goddamned Snow White."

"I never have sex on a day that ends in Y, and—and 'My heart belongs to Daddy.'"

"Sure it does." He gave my leg what was meant to be a friendly squeeze just above the kneecap. The sudden pressure caused me to jump and spill my drink into my lap. "My, my, we are skittish, aren't we. Here, let me get you another."

As he crossed to the silver tray I stood and mopped my trousers with a handkerchief. I remained standing, as I preferred to be a moving target. If having sex with Bob Parkinson was part of the deal for borrowing the pistols then Hedda Gabler would have to stab herself to death. He had two free hands, but I was encumbered with a full tumbler. Without ceremony—heavy drinkers are seldom subtle about sex—he placed his hand on what used to be called my private parts and gave a friendly squeeze. I suppose he meant to turn me on, but again he miscalculated and ground my balls together.

"Jesus Christ!" I exclaimed with a mixture of rage and pain. "That will do. Kindly keep your hands to yourself!" Still trying not to spill my fresh drink I ducked behind the armchair. As I belong to the pre-drugs generation, I have known more than my share of drunks. Thwarted, they can turn mean. I would far rather have sex with the Creature from the Black Lagoon than with Bob Parkinson in his present state of disrepair, but he was not about to be put off.

"You didn't used to be so goddamned coy. And that was back in the days when you were a whole lot cuter than you are now."

I realized he had meant to offend me because he felt slighted by my refusal, but with age comes the ability to accept truth. Bob was right; I wasn't very discriminating back then. If it stood still long enough I would gladly give it a bonk. And I certainly was cuter, an arch way of saying thirty years younger. I fought down the caustic reply I wanted to make, something to the effect that back then he didn't look like the Michelin man. Instead I tried to temporize.

"Look, Bob, I mean nothing personal. We have both changed. It would be a mistake to play the tape backwards. Let's not spoil the good times we had by trying to turn back the clock; which reminds me, the grandfather clock in the front hall is still on daylight saving time. Now I really must go."

Bob glared at me with such intense dislike in his bloodshot eyes that for a moment I thought he might take a swing at me. Instead he lurched over to the makeshift bar, poured neat scotch into his tumbler, and took a large swallow. Then, as if he were on a videocassette played in slow motion, he paused and carefully put down his drink. His knees appeared to buckle as he sank slowly onto the oriental rug as if sinking into water. So easily did he slide down that he could not have hurt himself. I checked his breathing, slow, deep, regular, and turned his head slightly to ease the flow of air. Nothing to do but let him sleep it off. For a moment I thought of alerting the housekeeper, but she would probably want me to help get him upstairs to bed. There were limits to my goodness.

Instead I picked up the case holding the pistols and let myself out the front door. Bob had not said I couldn't take them, and if he wanted them back he would have to find them first. But that was tomorrow's problem. Of the two drinks Bob had poured me one had gone into my lap and the other sat untasted on the table beside my armchair. The drink I had barely touched waited for me at Elinor's, and I did not tarry in getting back to her house.

III

If Heaven is an eternity of cast parties after a successful opening night, then Hell must be a dress rehearsal that lasts forever. To be sure, I was spared the worst of the agony as I only had to watch from a seat in the back of the hall. Elinor had been sucked into the performance as if by a giant vacuum cleaner, her diligence and dedication appearing more like vices than virtues in her present situation. "Ask Elinor" had become the all-purpose panacea whenever problems arose, as they tended to do in clusters, like grapes. She also let drop that she understood the rudiments of stage makeup, a skill acquired during her earlier days as a parent. Naturally she had been pressed into service to make up everyone but Audrey, who was doing her own *maquillage*. The unfortunate Elinor had become the de facto stage manager, operating around the incompetent Lucille Beauchemin, one of those fluently bilingual people who has nothing original to say in either language.

During an earlier rehearsal the unglamorous Lucille had demanded to know whether the director intended to bring *Hedda Gabler* into the twentieth century and make a statement about a woman imprisoned in society and trapped by men. Alan Howard looked faintly puzzled and explained that if he could persuade the actors to learn their lines and remember where they were supposed to stand, then that would be statement enough. In reply Lucille tossed her head, an incomplete gesture as she had no neck, and stomped off. From then on her interest in the production dwindled.

During the first intermission Elinor sneaked out to confer with me. "How you find Audrey?" she asked.

"It isn't difficult. She seems to have staked out a claim on downstage center."

Elinor smothered a laugh. "Wicked creature, that's not what I meant. What kind of performance is she giving?"

"You tell me. You've been coming to rehearsals. I get the feeling she is in the wrong play. Her approach is far too declamatory. When she discovered Aunt Juliana's bonnet on the chair you might have thought she was Hecuba surveying the ruins of Troy."

"Over and above the fact that you sound like Statler and Waldorf from *The Muppet Show*, I'm afraid you are right. The director has tried to convince Audrey she can let the character develop slowly before the audience. She doesn't have to tell us everything at once. Alan has tried to get her to tone it down a bit; they've had some real dustups. At the moment they're barely on speaking terms."

"One thing I will say for Audrey," I observed, "she knows her lines. Here we are at the dress rehearsal, and three of the players are still carrying scripts, including Elsie who has one of the principal parts."

"I know. That's the price you pay for dealing with true amateurs. Alan has suggested more than once that an audience paying fifty bucks a seat might legitimately expect a cast to be word perfect. He rounded on Elsie, but she dissolved into tears. I was astonished. Do adult women still cry when confronted by their shortcomings?"

"Whoever accused Elsie of being adult? But since she is nearly Audrey's age one can almost believe the two of them were at school together—the Gestapo Finishing School."

Elinor laughed out loud. "I must be off. Thanks for coming, Geoffry. Even a small audience makes a difference to the performers." She gave me a broad wink. "I'll do something really nice for you."

"You've already done that. This time I'd like you to bake me an apple pie."

"How about rhubarb, with no sugar? Catch you at the next intermission."

I watched Elinor hurry down the aisle and through the door into the backstage area. Even when working she wore a skirt, having grasped the essential truth that something happens to a woman's backside after fifty that is not enhanced by trousers that cling. The curtain had remained open during intermission so that Alan, costumed as Judge Brack, could run through his instructions to cast and crew. I suppose one of the advantages to a play like *Hedda Gabler* is that the set does not change from act to act. Most of the furniture onstage had come from Audrey's house, further shattering whatever faint illusion the partially prepared actors had managed to sustain. How many times have I sat on that sofa or in that high backed armchair, my highball resting on that small round table. When Elinor had asked Audrey whether she was apprehensive about lending her good living room furniture lest it be damaged, Audrey had airily replied that she would simply have it all refinished and reupholstered. To quote a well-worn adage: "Money cannot buy happiness," but it can certainly cause a great many unhappiness-making problems to disappear.

Central to the plot of the play is a porcelain stove, of the kind much favoured in nineteenth-century Europe. North America has always preferred cast-iron stoves, small and fat for heating, wide and capacious for cooking. There being no porcelain stoves outside museums and private collections, a cast-iron Quebec heater sat stage right balanced by the battered upright piano that ordinarily sat on the floor of Queen Mary Hall. The overall effect was eclectic and not unlike that of many Westmount drawing rooms, furnished as they are with a mixture of good family pieces supplemented by odds and ends picked up at auctions and garage sales, like living rooms in a city under siege.

Frank Wilkinson came to sit beside me just before Act II began.

"I thought Audrey looked pretty good in Act I," I said, "thanks to you."

"A housecoat is easy to design," he said. "The A-line hides a multitude of sins. The biggest problem was persuading Audrey to wear a wig. Hedda would never have worn her hair in an old-gold bubble, à la Loreli Lee. What poor old Audrey doesn't realize is that when she's onstage her hair looks like a wig and the wig looks like her own hair. And I'm not going to be the one to tell her."

The house lights had gone down, but there appeared to be some confusion behind the curtain, now drawn closed.

"You'll like the gown I designed for the next two acts," Frank continued. "I stayed away from the bustle; Audrey's got a big enough ass as it is. I put her into a short, ruched train; the effect is slimming. I also gave her wide cuffs on a fitted sleeve; they draw attention to her arms and away from her waist, not so slender as it once was, like mine, I'm afraid."

After much audible whispering and a number of muffled thumps from behind the curtains, they parted to reveal Audrey standing stage left near a pair of French doors opening into a void. According to the program, it is afternoon. One had to take the time of day on faith, as the harsh overhead lighting washed out any reference to chronological time.

Frank was right. Audrey did look well, the long, layered skirt in bands of ochre and burnt sienna with its short train making her look both taller and more slender than did the fashions of today. She was going through the motions of loading one of the pistols, borrowed with blessings from Bob Parkinson, who had obviously forgotten our little contretemps when he awoke the next morning. A loud retort came from backstage, where a stagehand had fired a starter pistol on cue to simulate Hedda's shooting at Judge Brack. It was difficult to follow the scene, not that I really minded, as Frank kept up a running commentary. Since I go to the theatre about as often as I go to church, I generally sit still and keep quiet, just as I had been trained as a child. Perhaps in both places I feel a bit like an interloper and fall back on silence as protective colouring. Frank belongs in the theatre and feels no need to pretend a false reverence.

"I find it difficult to buy the story that Audrey-slash-Hedda and Elsie-slash-Thea went to school together," he began, "unless they went to reform school. Good program, by the way."

"Glad you like it," I said. "I cashed in some favours and leaned on a friend in the printing business, for the sake of the library, *ça va sans dire*. To my astonishment he brought them in on time, which makes them about the only aspect of this production, aside from the gowns, that is ready. Audrey thought there ought to be a synopsis of the play, in case parents brought their children."

"At fifty clams a seat? She's dreaming in technicolour. Who would want to subject their children to *Hedda Gabler*, unless they'd done something way out of line, like robbing a bank or blowing up the power station. We're a long way from Super Mario Brothers or the Ninja Turtles."

A woman sitting three rows ahead turned and glared in our direction. Frank is not easily intimidated, but the appearance of a new character onstage temporarily captured our attention. Eilert Løvborg, played by a youngish lawyer named Grant Bar-lowe, strode onstage as though he owned a controlling interest in the building.

"What a prick!" whispered Frank. "Truly in love with himself. I'm sure he practices safe sex and wanks off in front of a full length mirror. That way he remains faithful to the love of his life." Frank's whisper carried further than most people's speaking voice.

"I'll have to take your word for it," I said. "I go out of my way to avoid aging boomers."

"Good thinking," said Frank with a chuckle. "Audrey in-sisted on doing her own makeup. Her idea of making herself youthful is to outline her eyes until she looks like Elsie the Borden cow on Prozac."

Frank and I broke into the laughter of shared malice. The woman sitting ahead of us turned around, skewered us with a look, and hissed, "Would you mind!"

Frank stood. "Time for cigarette—and I know how it all ends." My bum was sore and I wanted to stretch my legs, so I followed him outside, where I found him leaning against the balustrade contentedly puffing away.

"I'm surprised nobody has turned *Hedda Gabler* into an opera. It cries out for musical treatment. Hedda would be sung by a dramatic soprano; Thea Elvsted by a lyric coloratura. Eilert Løvborg would be a tenor, with a light sound, not one of those spaghetti and meatball belters. George Tesman would be a baritone and Judge Brack a bass. The libretto could easily accommodate an aria for each character, and Hedda would have a high old time with a kind of mad scene when she burns the manuscript in the stove."

Frank had already finished his second cigarette when Elinor joined us.

"Frank thinks the play would make a good opera," I said. "Pity I'm not a composer."

"You're right," said Elinor, "but our immediate concern is to bring it off as a play." She ran a hand over her short pageboy, which sunlight turned the colour of old pewter. "Do you have any telling comment about the production so far?"

"Two acts down and two to go," I replied. "I'm trying not to think about having to sit through it tomorrow night."

"It's going to be a long evening, for all of us. Alan has just asked me to be prompter. I seem to know the play better than most of the actors." Elinor threw up her hands. "The sum of the parts is infinitely greater than the whole. Anyhow, I think it's about time for Act III, and I know you gentlemen don't want to miss a single second." She put a hand on Frank's arm. "I have to hand it to you, Frank. Your gowns are sensational, so good in fact they make the rented costumes look tatty."

"Thanks, Elinor. I hope Audrey isn't too upset that her costumes are upstaging the others."

Elinor smiled. "She's learning to live with it. Now, in we go, single file, and no talking in line."

Obediently but reluctantly we followed her inside.

As the hall was nearly empty, Frank and I chose seats far distant from the termagant who had chided us about talking. Frank was not about to keep silent, and his comments helped the time pass more quickly.

"Audrey is such a control freak," he began, "I would have thought her a natural to play Hedda, which is to say all she has to do is play herself. If, as has been suggested by too many directors, you have to rummage around in your button box of experience to find analogies for the part you're playing, Audrey has spent most of her life going to *Hedda Gabler* school."

"You're right there," I said. "I was once at her house for dinner. It happened to be maid's night out, and she asked me to clear away. Since I had brought two bottles of excellent wine, I felt I had paid my dues. If she wanted me to clear, I said, she would have to pay me the minimum wage for a full hour, not prorated. Somebody else jumped up and volunteered; you know how people love to be used. So do I, but not at the dinner table."

Frank gave me a long, complicit look, and we both turned our attention to the stage. Jeremy/George Tesman was explaining to Audrey/Hedda how he had found the lost manuscript quite by chance. Jeremy's haughty, supercilious manner was not inappropriate for Hedda's professor husband, given that he was thirty years too old.

"Maybe I'm carping," I began, "but I find these heavy handed theatrical coincidences a little hard to swallow. What would have happened if George Tesman had not found the manuscript?"

"The play would end a lot sooner and we could all go home." With a little sigh Frank hunkered down in his seat and, *faute de mieux*, watched the action onstage. I am a lawyer, not a behavioural scientist, but I wonder if we do not all have a deep, subconscious pool of gestures and postures that untrained actors employ onstage. Dejection is a deep slouch, drunkenness or fatigue a lurching stagger, anger a toss of the head that threatens whiplash. Hands are never still. Features twitch.

Only someone with real stage experience understands the pull of immobility. For an amateur production you need an amateur audience, or else battalions of relatives and friends.

The moment had come for Hedda's big scene where she burns the lost manuscript in the stove. Fire regulations forbade a lighted stove, with the result that the door to the Quebec heater had been placed upstage and we had to imagine flames and smoke. Audrey's performance was so exaggerated, so over-the-top, that I shrank from looking at the stage. Granted, the lines are almost impossible to deliver with a straight face: "I am burning your child, Thea. I am burning your child!" But I could hardly bear to watch. I felt embarrassed both by her and for her, and wished she was not going to put herself on display for the community at-large and her friends in particular.

The last pages of the ill-fated manuscript were fed into the stove, and the closing curtains muffled Audrey's attempts at maniacal laughter.

"Now for two cigarettes," said Frank, "one on either side of my mouth."

I rose and followed him outside.

Elinor arrived in hot pursuit. "Geoffry, I know what I'm going to ask is way beyond the call of duty, but would you mind terribly coming backstage for a minute and telling Alan the play isn't too dreadfully awful. If Frank should try to tell him it's okay he'll know its a lie. Frank is in the business. But he might be tempted to believe you, and he could use a bit of a boost."

"You mean you want me to behave like the holy fool and tell lies we would all like to believe?"

"Not quite. I just want you to think of a couple of bits you liked about the production so far."

"Like the closing curtains? And the huge relief at having to sit through only one more act?"

Elinor formed a circle with her hands. "As I gaze into my crystal ball I do not see an apple pie but an apple pie bed. I see many meals with my mother at which you are present. I see a birthday card saying 'Happy Birthday, Geoffry'—and tucked inside a season ticket to a series of organ recitals at our local Anglican church. Now, are you coming backstage?"

I followed Elinor down the aisle past a series of bronze plaques honouring worthy citizens who are no longer with us. The stage in Queen Mary Hall is little more than a large speaker's platform equipped with rudimentary lighting equipment and a set of curtains. The wings on either side of the stage are tiny, obliging the actors to change in another part of the building. They must sneak along a passage leading from stage left to a side door of the auditorium. In order to conceal the actors from the audience a makeshift screen had been erected consisting of chenille bedspreads hanging from a rope and looking not unlike the Monday morning wash. Elinor assured me they were only temporary, hung for the dress rehearsal and to be replaced with something less unsightly for the actual performances. Experience has taught me that few things in this mutable world are more permanent than a temporary installation.

Alan Howard had the easy, breezy manner of someone accustomed to dealing with the public. Whenever we speak I always get the feeling he would be more comfortable if there was a microphone between us.

"Oh, hi, Geoffry. Three acts and you haven't bolted? Elinor must have something on you." He smiled to reveal teeth that reminded me of Scrabble tiles.

"Not at all," I lied glibly. "It's years since I last saw the play.

The costumes are excellent. Audrey looks sensational. So does Elsie."

"Costumes are not the performance," he observed with a wry smile. "Elinor, would you do something for me? Stand behind the curtain so we can get the lighting right. I want to play out the final suicide behind a scrim," he explained, "so that the audience sees Hedda put the gun to her head in silhouette."

"I see," I said lamely. The idea itself was novel and, if done properly, would be effective. Every director wants to bring something fresh to a play that has been staged countless times. The idea of watching Hedda prepare to shoot herself while the actors downstage carried on business as usual had true dramatic potential, but I felt dubious about Audrey playing the scene with the required restraint. The emotions she had unleashed when burning the manuscript would have been more appropriate in the amphitheatre at Epidarus than in the confined space of Queen Mary Hall. But my mission backstage was to reassure the director, not to utter gloomy caveats.

"It ought to be really effective," I added. "Can you light her so that she will appear as a shadow figure?"

"I think so. You're standing too close to get the right effect. It ought to work from the auditorium."

I was just about to return to my seat when Audrey came through the makeshift passage to the stage. "Geoffry!" she cried as though I had just returned from the moon. "I didn't realize you were here." She thrust out both her hands, which I felt compelled to reach for in return. I won't kiss you because of my makeup. Are you enjoying our little production?"

"Very much," I fibbed. I don't think God will punish me for the lie, as it was well meant. "And you look wonderful. Frank has really done you proud."

Audrey did look particularly handsome. In Act IV, Hedda is in mourning for her husband's aunt, and Audrey had changed into an elegant black silk gown with a high neck and long sleeves. The gown made her look taller and more slender, if not younger. She was playing the role of leading lady to the hilt, striding about the stage, flipping her short train, striking attitudes on and around the sofa.

"If you have nothing better to do after the rehearsal," she began, every inch the affable star, "then perhaps you and Elinor might like to drop by the house for a drink."

"Sounds good, Audrey, but I'll have to check with Elinor. She'll have some mopping up to do, and there will probably be a meeting with the stage crew."

"Well, I'll be in my dressing room. Do drop by."

I smiled and moved toward the stairs. Audrey was bound to be riding a post-performance high, and having just negotiated four acts of her Hedda I didn't feel up to Audrey continuing the performance as your friendly neighbourhood leading lady. I made my way back to the auditorium where I saw Frank sitting near the back.

"Aside from that, Mrs. Lincoln, how did you enjoy the play?" he asked as I sat down.

"The oldies are the goodies," I said as the house lights went down. The curtain did not open immediately. "Audrey is having a little 'at home' after the show. Are you going?"

"Probably not. I promised Eileen I'd drop by and tell her about the rehearsal. What was all the fuss with the electricians?"

"Special effects. We're going to see the suicide in silhouette, behind a scrim."

"As my sainted old mother used to say, 'There's nothing

like a nice suicide to cheer up a dull afternoon. I hope the prop man manages to get the firing cue right."

The curtains parted on Act IV, the shortest and most focussed. Frank said little, whether from interest in the action or a late afternoon slump I couldn't tell. George Tesman and Thea Elvsted settled down to decipher Eilert's notes for the burned manuscript, and Hedda moved upstage into the alcove. From the mahogany case Audrey lifted one of the pistols and held it to her temple. Backstage someone fired the starter pistol one more time, and Audrey, now no more than an outline behind the scrim, reclined on a couch, carefully, so as not to crush her gown. Alan as the judge delivered the closing line: "Good God! People don't do things like that!" and the curtains closed to scattered applause from the sparse audience.

"All right, everyone," called Alan reverting to his role as director, "before you change we will rehearse the bows. When the curtain first opens, Audrey will be alone on stage. After her solo bow the rest of the cast will come on one by one: George Tesman, Thea Elvsted, Eilert Løvborg, me, Aunt Juliana, and the maid. If there is enough applause we will all take another curtain call during which Audrey will step forward, bow, and return to the line. Okay, let's walk through it."

"Good idea," said Frank, now relieved of the obligation to stage whisper his comments. "Nothing brands a production as high amateur more than watching the actors straggle out to take their bows. Very un-cool."

The curtains opened to reveal Audrey, every inch the star. Putting her sixty-year-old knees to the ultimate test, she plunged into a deep curtsey that in itself was worth a round of applause. One by one the others walked onstage, Jeremy as though about to deliver a sermon, Elsie as if somebody backstage had just copped a feel, Alan with the assurance of someone used to the spotlight. The curtains closed, then opened to reveal the actors in a row, awkwardly holding hands, like worshippers in a New Age church. We all applauded as loudly as we could. Audrey stepped forward to take her solo bow, but something happened. From the back of the hall I couldn't see just what, but suddenly Audrey pitched forward off the stage to land heavily on the floor of the auditorium where she lay, inert.

In the ensuing noisy confusion Elinor had the presence of mind to insist Audrey not be moved until an ambulance arrived. I located the nearest telephone and dialled 911. As luck would have it the ambulance arrived promptly, and a barely conscious Audrey was lifted carefully onto a stretcher and dispatched to the nearest emergency ward. Elinor rode with her to the hospital.

The excitement and the rehearsal over, the actors sat dejectedly about, too apathetic to change out of their costumes and remove the stage makeup. Hanging over everybody's head, as if suspended from a giant dirigible, was the question of what would happen to tomorrow's performance if Audrey was seriously hurt.

Alan took charge. "I suggest we all go and change, then meet back here for a conference. Geoffry, I hope you'll stay."

"Certainly, although there's not much we can do until we hear from Elinor."

Frank had gone back outside to smoke. "Well, well," he said as I joined him. "Death by costume. It looked to me as though she stepped on the hem of her gown as she curtsied, and the tension pulled her forward as she tried to stand. I should have thought to warn her. Professional actors and singers learn to cope with the long skirts, trains, capes, wigs, and the like."

"I imagine if Audrey can't go on we will have to cancel, or at least postpone the performance. We don't have understudies. By the way, did anyone think to tell Hartland that his wife took a nosedive?"

"Not unless Elinor called him from the hospital."

"I'll do that now," I said. "Are you going to hang around for a while?"

"Naturally. All this drama is far more interesting than the play itself."

After begging a quarter from Frank I went to the telephone. "Mr. Crawford, please. Geoffry Chadwick speaking."

At Hartland's insistence we all ended up at the Crawford house for drinks and a conference. Hartland had gone straight up to the hospital to learn Audrey had sprained her wrist and suffered a concussion. Otherwise she appeared to be all right. She was to remain in hospital overnight for observation; if all went well she would be free to go home tomorrow. No question of her being able to perform.

Hartland drove Elinor to Queen Mary Hall with instructions to bring everyone back to the house for drinks and a meeting about how to proceed. Since I know my way around the bar, I was pressed into service. Frank volunteered to help.

"You read about messages being pushed into empty bottles which are then thrown overboard," he said. "Months later they wash up on distant beaches and people are amazed. Doesn't anyone realize the ultimate message in a bottle is the liquor itself?"

"Food for thought," I replied as I poured a rye and diet ginger ale for Elsie Connors, a scotch and Coke for Lucille Beauchemin. To pour Coke into good scotch was not unlike spreading caviar on Oreos, but *"chaqu'un à son goo."* Once again we found ourselves seated around a dining room table on which platters of cheese and pâté had been set out by the staff. I love the idea of staff. What I dislike is the idea of strangers living in, listening, watching, prying. Ease and comfort are a high price to pay for privacy.

Elinor repeated what she had learned from the doctor, notably that Audrey would be in no condition to perform. Alan suggested that one of the other actors, Elsie perhaps, could step into the part, carrying a script, while someone else read Thea's part. The logical person would be Elinor, as she probably knew the play better than the actors.

Elinor opened her green eyes wide and quashed the idea. "There are limits to my dedication," she announced. "I did not want a part in the first place, and I'm not about 'to go out there a youngster and come back a star.' This isn't 42nd Street. Fifty dollars is a good deal of money to pay for a play reading in costumes, and," here Elinor allowed herself a smile, "who will volunteer to tell Audrey that somebody else is going to take her place?"

Subdued, nervous laughter rippled around the table.

"If I may make a suggestion," I began, "let us postpone the play until Audrey is better. Either that or refund the money. Now, our immediate problem is tomorrow night. How do we contact all those who have bought tickets? Not everyone will see a notice in the paper or hear an announcement on the radio. A great many people will still turn up. The wine is bought and the catering paid for. The waiters have been hired for the evening. We have the items in place for the raffle. What I propose is that we set up a wine bar, serve the food—much of which is ready to go and won't keep—and hold the raffle."

"Good idea, Geoff!" barked Hartland, a man who looked as though sent by Central Casting to play a retired military officer. "But I have a better idea. We'll offer them a refund, but those who accept are disqualified from the raffle. Don't say I said so—but most of the people I know won't weep if they don't have to sit through four acts of bloody Ibsen." Hartland had a manner that did not invite contradiction; furthermore, we were all drinking his liquor and eating his food.

"If the rest of the cast is game," suggested Elinor, "we could postpone the production until the fall. By then Audrey will be back on her feet, and with the added rehearsal time the performance will be more polished."

Alan and Frank both came down on Elinor's side, and by the time Hartland suggested another round of drinks, the issue appeared to be settled. To be sure, the items up for raffle were not too shabby: a 35-inch television with VCR, a weekend at the Château Frontenac in Quebec City, a return flight to Vancouver, and a Caribbean cruise. All Hartland had to do was make a few phone calls, *et voilà*—a list of prizes.

As Hartland had predicted, the ticketholders were not in the least disappointed at being faced with wine and canapés but no play. They arrived to find the chairs in the auditorium neatly stacked against one wall and a moveable chalkboard at the entrance announcing the performance had been postponed. The well-heeled audience, not one of whom asked for a refund, arrived full of martinis and highballs. They fell upon the foodstuffs as if just off a raft from Cuba, drank the wine as if the liquor board were on strike, and applauded heartily when Hartland climbed onto the stage to conduct the raffle into which he had insisted on entering the names of the cast and crew as a gesture of thanks for their time and effort.

He began by craving our collective indulgence and assured us our tickets would be good for the performance, whenever it was rescheduled. Nobody seemed overly curious as to when. Next he read a brief message from Audrey, apologizing to everyone and wishing us all a happy and prosperous summer. Then with his own personal brand of pompous chivalry he invited various drab ladies in uneventful clothes to come up on stage and choose a number from the punch bowl holding the raffle numbers. The stellar prize was beyond doubt the Caribbean cruise, and when Hartland read out the name of Elinor Richardson, the cheers and applause were mingled with groans of disappointment.

Only after the last of the wine had been drunk and the remaining bits of food polished off did the crowd begin to peel away. The evening was generally pronounced a huge success, although by the time the wine and catering had been paid for I suspected there would be hardly enough funds left over to buy the library a subscription to *TV Guide*. But, as I had known all along, the fundraising angle was no more than a pretext for a vanity production of *Hedda Gabler*. I was about to observe to Frank, pouring himself the last of the wine, that pride comes before a fall, but decided it would be deficient in charity.

Besides, I could not help feeling a grudging admiration for Audrey; she had managed the unusual trick of upstaging herself.

IV

There are no free gifts, just as there are no permanent waves, wrinkle-free sheets, or lifetime guarantees. When Elinor was handed the envelope representing her prize, she in turn handed it to me to slide into the inside pocket of my jacket. Only after she, Frank, and I had returned to her house for something to drink that wasn't wine did she get around to slitting open the envelope and examining the contents. Faces do not really fall, certainly not a face like Elinor's with its prominent cheekbones; but her expression turned suddenly from sweet to sour.

"Shit!" Her sibilant whisper drew out the *sh*. "The cruise has to be taken within the next six weeks, and that is just the time Jane is expecting her baby. I can't leave. She is counting on me to move in and take charge."

"Isn't that a pain in the wazoo!" said Frank from behind a cigarette and a highball. "But there must be some fine print we can invoke. You're a lawyer, Geoffry."

I reread the agreement. "Seems pretty airtight. Obviously the reason Hartland was offered a cruise as prize is that late spring is a slow time and space was available. There is a choice of three dates and two ships, but they all fall within the next six weeks. No cash equivalent, by the way."

"This calls for another drink," announced Elinor who had been too busy organizing the raffle to grab a glass of wine. "Isn't that a bummer." She picked up the brochure. "A suite no less:

two beds, sitting area, bathroom with tub and Jacuzzi, large cupboards, and a window instead of a porthole. I could live with
that." She tossed the folder onto the coffee table. "It could have
been so pleasant." She reached over and took my hand. "You,
me, and the bounding main."

"You were going to take me along?"

"Who else? And you really should go. It would be a shame
not to use the ticket."

"I don't fancy a cruise on my own," I said. "All those widows from New Jersey. I'll be besieged. It's not vanity, I assure
you. Godzilla could get dates on a cruise ship."

"Take someone with you," suggested Elinor. "The ticket is
good for two people. I don't want you running around unchap-
eroned."

"Take me along," said Frank with a laugh. "I'm clean, cheerful, honest, hardworking, and I don't sweep under the rug."

"What a good idea!" exclaimed Elinor, turning to Frank.
"Can you get away?"

"As a matter of fact I think I can," he replied. "I'm in Santa
Fé for July and part of August, but for the early part of the summer I'm flexible."

"Well then, it's settled!" she stated. "You two go off and enjoy the cruise, while I stay home and scrub and keep house for
my son-in-law and grandchildren—but don't feel guilty." She
laughed. "That's the problem with having kids. By the time
they're fit to live with they're living with someone else."

We were all feeling a bit euphoric from drink and the knowledge that the play was on hold for a while, perhaps for good.
The feeling was not unlike that of having just written the last
exam. If I had any misgivings they were swept away by the
energy of the moment. I would have preferred to travel with

Elinor, but going with Frank, whom I had known for many years, seemed like a reasonable trade-off. We all had another drink and sent out for pizza. I assured Elinor that once she was free of her grandmotherly duties the two of us would take a trip. We laughed and joked, ate pizza with our fingers and drank beer, and believed the world to be a pretty good place.

That was until the next morning. I won't go so far as to say I was hungover, but I felt a heaviness of spirit, a kind of twentieth century *accidie* made up of equal parts scotch, wine, more scotch, pizza, beer, a late night, and the jolting realization I was committed to spending a week with someone I did not know as well as I would have wished. I could hear Elinor moving around the kitchen; the telephone rang and she answered, but I postponed getting out of bed. As things stood, Frank and I were going on a cruise together sometime during the next few weeks. That meant we would be spending a full week in one another's company, sleeping in adjacent beds, eating meals together, going ashore together, having our pre-dinner drinks together. His clothing would be hanging next to mine, his toothbrush and razor jostling mine for space on the shelf above the hand basin. It had taken me a while to get used to sharing with Elinor, a tidy and organized woman. I knew nothing about Frank's personal habits, and found myself reluctant to investigate. I do not enjoy togetherness, except with someone I know well. And although I had known Frank a long time in chronology, we had only met as adults in social situations. Did I want to spend a week cheek-by-jowl with him? Not much.

Is there life before coffee? My bladder prodded me out of bed, and I made my way downstairs to confront an alert Elinor. I know it is not morally wrong to be cheerful in the morning, but sometimes I think it should be.

She poured me a mug of fragrant black coffee. "I'm really sorry I can't go on the cruise with you, Geoffry. It would have been a lovely holiday, but I just can't leave Jane. Still, I'm glad you're going. I'll be up to my neck in housekeeping and babies, so you might just as well be on a ship. And Frank just called to say how delighted he is with the idea of the trip. He even tried to persuade me to come along and he'd book himself another cabin; but I can't. He'll be company for you, and good company too, I'll bet dollars to doughnuts. He'd like you to call him at his Aunt Eileen's when you are awake. He's really excited."

Elinor looked at me quizzically. "What's the matter, Geoffry? You seem awfully quiet."

"I'll be better and brighter after my coffee," I said, contracting my face into a smile. Surrounded, trapped, cornered, I found myself caught in that most fragile yet tensile net, somebody else's self-esteem. How could I tell Frank I did not want to travel with him? Now that I was retired I could no longer use that all-purpose excuse of prior commitments at the office. Elinor too seemed delighted with the idea of giving two friends a holiday, the whole seasoned with a dash of self-sacrifice. I could disappoint her, but I would prefer not to. What had seemed such a wonderful idea late last night now took on the aspect of summer camp, where every function, including the most private, is done in company. How often have I heard the truth shall set us free. Unfortunately truth is not unlike one of those volatile, unstable gases that can incinerate everything in its path. For all my misgivings I could see no way out, short of surgery or suicide. Never had I felt more sympathy toward Louis XVI and Marie Antoinette than I did at that moment. Monarch Cruises had become my personal Varennes.

The information package that accompanied the tickets for

the cruise recommended that non-American citizens carry a passport. One of the last services my now retired secretary did perform was to badger me into renewing my passport. Surely the activity most divorced from reality we regularly undertake is to have our picture taken, sitting immobilized in front of a lens so that one second of our lives can be recorded to give us legitimacy for the next ten years. Medicare cards, drivers' licences, security passes, and passports all require photographs for purposes of identification. If anybody—nurse, immigration officer, security guard—looked carefully at the photograph and again at the subject, how many people would be denied surgery, access to their jobs, or the right to enter the U.S.A.

It has been suggested that if you look like the photograph in your passport you are not well enough to travel. Such was certainly the case with me. I opened the small, navy blue booklet, emblazoned with the lion and the unicorn, to be confronted by a likeness that made the picture of Dorian Gray appear positively flattering.

I have never been what one would have considered handsome, but at the very least I could pass muster. For a small surcharge the photographer offered me colour, thereby compounding the error. In black and white my hair looked silver, not gray; my eyes pale and interesting, not washed-out blue. True, I still had the hair, and the eyes still functioned without glasses, except for reading. But whether in colour or tones of gray, the somewhat bony, angular face had succumbed to the pull of gravity. Everything seemed to be slipping, the skin under the hairline, under the eyes, under the chin.

I go to a gym, not as often as I should but frequently enough to keep my conscience from carping. Always tall and thin, I have not put on weight so much as redistributed what is there.

I am not overjoyed with the result, but gravity overcomes us all. The brochure promoting the ship showed a swimming pool on one of the decks; but no horses, tame or wild, could drag me into public scrutiny wearing trunks. Besides, the pool in the photograph swarmed with children, cause enough to give it a wide berth.

The tropics in June would be warm, but the brochure promised air conditioning. I had a closet full of summer-weight clothing; Montreal in July can get pretty steamy, although nothing I owned struck me as suitable for the *Blue Horizon*, the ship on which Frank and I had finally agreed to take Elinor's cruise. I owned no short-sleeved shirts exploding with flowers, nor T-shirts with slogans. (I should have been a taxidermist. I'll mount anything.) My lightweight slacks came in shades of tan, olive, navy, not canary yellow, burnt orange, shrimp, or madras. Shorts did not enter the picture, as I have reached the age when the less flesh on public display the better. A body over sixty wants a life of its own.

The longer I studied the brochure, a large, glossy production more like a fashion magazine than a tour guide, the less I thought of the whole undertaking. "Monarch Cruises presents its flagship: the *Blue Horizon*!" Everyone in the carefully posed photographs enjoying small, airbrushed epiphanies—lingering over drinks in the cabin, smiling at the steward in the dining salon, leaning casually against the rail in full evening dress—looked at least half my age. Posed in groups of two, four, six, or eight, they came in pairs, like gloves: one male, one female. No dashing single men marred these tableaux; no mysterious unattached ladies lurked in the background. Frank and I would make up a couple of sorts, but I felt certain we would turn out to be marginal. The more I studied the shiny pages with their infinite promise of pampering, cosseting, spoiling, the more I wished I could stay home. To be sure, whenever I have to travel I have the same uneasy feeling. The day before the flight I would gladly climb the steps of St. Joseph's Oratory, all one hundred and one of them, on my knees if only I could unpack my bags and stay put.

To back out now was out of the question, so I went to visit Mother. After going through the pantomime of pouring myself a scotch, I sat in one of the armchairs she had brought with her from the apartment.

"I do hope you are on the port side, Geoffry," she began. "I remember your grandfather saying, 'Port out, starboard home.' You'll bake on the starboard side."

"I'm not too worried, Mother. The ship has air conditioning, and I'm not a civil servant sailing to India."

"I once sailed to England on the *Empress of Canada*," she said. "They served bouillon on deck mid-morning. Your father insisted I drink it, but I always found it terribly salty. Craig used to stride about the deck, breathing deeply, while I lay huddled under a rug. I didn't much care for shipboard life; the constant motion made me drowsy. And way too much food—always with the same people at table. Most tiresome." She paused for a swallow of vodka and water. "Never mind, dear, I'm sure you will have a lovely time."

"I'm sure I will," I said without much conviction.

One of the few things I remember from Sunday school was an English girl with shiny red cheeks and prominent teeth who told us the story of Noah and the Ark. She kept insisting the Ark was not large, not at all like the *Queen Mary*. The more I thought about Noah and his motley crew the more I realized conditions must have been pretty close and smelly. That voyage must surely have been the cruise from Hell. In spite of air conditioning, bars on every deck, and full service in the cabin, I wondered whether life on the *Blue Horizon* would be noticeably better. True, I wouldn't have to shovel elephant dung overboard, but Frank and I would be sharing a cabin, a bathroom, a life. I would be obliged to converse with strangers at meals. There would be no single space on that entire giant ship I could call my own.

I knew I was carping. Most people would be delighted at the prospect of a week in the Caribbean on board a luxury ship. There is no record of Noah's having taken a dinosaur aboard the Ark. Perhaps I would be the resident dinosaur on board the *Blue Horizon*. Time, to quote the well-worn saw, would tell.

The *Blue Horizon* was scheduled to sail from Puerto Rico, not Fort Lauderdale. Frank was to fly in from San Francisco and meet me on the ship. Only when I received my itinerary did I realize that getting from Montreal to San Juan would absorb most of Saturday. In order to make the flight to Atlanta I would have to be up at the crack of dawn. Not even the hoary joke—I was up at the crack of Dawn, and Dawn loved it!—could make me smile when I thought of the alarm going off at 5:45 A.M.

As I drank my coffee on Saturday morning, I packed the last few items I hoped would not crush in transit. Joan Crawford recommended packing with tissue paper, but she also scoured the bathroom whenever she checked into a hotel. I am not Joan Crawford, so I folded my clothes carefully and trusted to fate. The doorman called to say the limousine was waiting. Once settled into the back seat, I put myself into a kind of

suspended animation, like a chrysalis. I shuffled through the line
to check in, handed over my luggage, passed through customs,
and headed for the departure lounge, all the while operating on
about fifteen per cent of my total consciousness. Travelling by
plane is unnatural, and though I do not fear for my safety, I find
airports dehumanizing and faintly humiliating. Luck was on my
side, as there was no one I knew in the departure lounge, so I
was spared having to grind out early morning chat until we
boarded the plane.

How many people of my age had their idea of Atlanta in-
delibly shaped by *Gone With the Wind* and all those old movie
sets going up in flames while British Vivien Leigh demonstrated
true American pluck. I have seen photographs of Atlanta
today, a large American city with the inevitable cluster of tall
buildings at the core. Yet the Atlanta of the movies, no more
than a jerrybuilt set, has a far stronger grip on my imagination.

Nothing had prepared me for the airport. With not too
much time to make my connection to San Juan, I had to ride
a metro to the departure terminal. A train? In an airport? Civilization as I knew it faltered. Hardly had I opened my magazine
when our departure for Puerto Rico was announced. The
flights from Montreal, otherwise unmemorable, were my first
exposure to what was to be a week of cast-iron smiles. On the
video screen a stewardess, smiling grimly, led us through safety
procedures. Another attendant with wraparound teeth served
me a plastic tray of food well protected from the passenger by
layers of impenetrable plastic wrap.

I must have dozed off, as a voice announced we were beginning our descent to the San Juan airport. With the change
in time zones, the afternoon was comfortably advanced as we
coasted to a stop on the runway. We had been told there would

be a ship's representative to greet us. What I had not expected was a cluster of uniformed young people waving signs with the legend "Blue Horizon" and chanting the name of the ship as if it were a mantra. In due course all passengers from the plane destined for the ship were herded into a line with me at the front. Not a few passengers had taken out cigarettes and lighters so they could smoke the second they left the terminal building. Rumpled from two long flights, holding a carry-on bag and a raincoat, I felt more like a refugee than a tourist.

"This way please!" called a young woman, her face tense from smiling, and the long line of passengers began to shuffle toward the exit into the damp heat of a Puerto Rico afternoon. A child cried; all those with cigarettes lit up and inhaled greedily. After the cool spring air of Montreal the change of atmosphere came as a shock, and by the time we had been shepherded onto buses, like so many schoolchildren on a field trip, I felt sticky as well as wilted. The drive from the airport to the pier does not show off San Juan at its best, and we all felt a surge of relief to see the immense white hull with the words "Blue Horizon" emblazoned across the prow.

As a non-American citizen I was steered toward a side wicket in the embarkation terminus, a long, low cinder-block shell that was hot, sultry, unwelcoming. I handed in my ticket and passport, and was then instructed to board. Once I had negotiated the gangplank to be met with a frigid blast of Arctic air conditioning, a uniformed steward glanced at my ticket and ushered me into an elevator. After a ride of several floors, the doors opened and I followed my guide down a carpeted corridor to my stateroom, or suite.

The room turned out to be as promised: two roomy single beds, a desk, a dresser, as well as the seating area furnished with a loveseat and two armchairs grouped around a table, everything in tones so studiously neutral as to be invisible. On a tray sat the obligatory fruit basket, oranges, apples, bananas, one kiwi fruit, and one bunch of grapes. A large window offered a view of the derelict pier. Cupboards were ample, drawers plentiful, and the bathroom shower drained into a tub equipped with the advertised Jacuzzi.

No sooner had the steward left in a blaze of smiles than I ducked into the bathroom to take a pee. The first hurdle to overcome was a sign on the wall above the toilet which read: "This toilet is connected to a vacuum sewage system. Please do not throw into the toilet anything other than ordinary toilet waste and toilet paper." Serenely confident of following instructions to the letter, I took a pee, then flushed. For a brief, terrified moment I thought I had wrecked the appliance. With a deafening, sucking roar, like that of Lake Ontario going down a drain the size of Toronto, my modest discharge disappeared. After the turbulence had calmed down, leaving the bathroom unnaturally silent, I felt relief I had not been wearing a toupee, contact lenses, dentures even, as surely they would have been snatched from my head, my eyeballs, my jaws to be dispatched to a part of the ship well below the waterline. I emerged from the experience like Coleridge's Wedding-Guest, "A sadder and a wiser man."

I hung up my coat and began to unpack my hand luggage when a knock sounded at the door. I called out "Come in," and the door opened to reveal a young Indian or Pakistani barely into his twenties.

"I am John, your butler," he announced with solemnity as he tugged at the waist of his maroon pea jacket. "It will be my pleasure to serve you."

"Good afternoon, John. Is there any sign of my luggage?"

"I will bring it as soon as it arrives on board." He dropped his voice at the end of the phrase to underline his dedication. "Is there anything you would like in the meantime?"

"Yes, could I have two more pillows. And perhaps you'd better bring an ashtray. My cabin mate smokes."

"Right away, sir." He backed out the door as though taking leave of royalty.

I felt a nameless apprehension. A cabin steward is a cabin steward, a butler is a butler, and never the twain shall meet. Whatever the young man claimed to be, he looked far too young to have had much experience in doing anything.

Another knock at the door announced the arrival of my suitcases, accompanied by much obsequious body language. When John finally oozed back through the door, the bags sat randomly on the floor in the seating area. I had asked him to lift the heaviest case onto the bed, but so absorbed had he been in his role of dedicated retainer that he ignored my request, all the while reiterating his pleasure in being able to serve. Before I unpacked, I took a shower. How good it felt to rinse off the grime of travel. A ship's newsletter announced that dress tonight would be casual, also that there would be open seating in the dining salon. There was still no sign of Frank, but my clothing in the cabin would announce my presence on board. The deck plan in our cabin (stateroom sounded too old-fashioned and suite too pretentious) told me the Blue Lagoon Bar was on the Sunshine Deck, the level above mine. I walked up one flight of stairs and into a room shimmering in shades of turquoise, all variations on the colour of suburban swimming pools.

I headed for a table in the corner, flanked by large windows, a lovely spot no doubt when at sea but at the moment looking down on the corrugated tin roof of the embarkation shed. It took me a while to get the waiter's attention, as the party at the next table, Middle American the way Mount Rushmore is rock, were grilling him about where he was born. His dark skin suggested somewhere in the Caribbean, but with the dogged persistence that passes for friendliness, they insisted on finding out which island, the name of his town, and how long he had been working on the Blue Horizon.

Finally he disengaged himself and took my order, a double Glenlivet, water, no ice. He did not smile. Neither did I. The tumbler arrived so filled with ice that I would have been obliged to remove some cubes in order to drink. It was my first experience of trying, on a ship catering largely to Americans, to order a drink without ice. Regardless of the waiter's request the bartender begins by plunging the glass into a tub of chipped ice. Not having smiled at the waiter nor having expressed an interest in his brothers and sisters, I had no compunction about sending back the drink.

As I sipped my whiskey I discreetly studied the other people in the bar. By now the party at the next table had gone noisily down to dinner. Many of the couples, always couples, had the wilted look of people still waiting for their luggage. They all looked roughly half my age except for those older people who must have been parents. One couple in their early forties was seated with a single woman, presumably somebody's mother, a female fighting the good fight against the inroads of time, and losing. Her white-blond hair, crimson lipstick, and artificial nails made her look more predatory than alluring. When the husband crossed to my table and asked me to join them I made my excuses: because of travel I hadn't eaten all day and was just on my way down to the dining room. Some other time. I smiled, a *Blue Horizon* smile in which the mouth spreads to expose the teeth, but the eyes are not engaged.

I rode the elevator down from the Sunshine Deck, past the Calypso, Meridian, Florida, and Granada Decks to the Fiesta Deck, a.k.a. Number Seven, where the dining salon was located. Like most of the ship's decor, the dining room had been done up in a manner suggesting Art Deco, with touches of Shopping Mall Modern, in muted secondary colours of mauve and beige. Having identified myself as being alone, I was shown to a table for eight, four of whom spoke only German. After a few stiff pleasantries which informed me they were from Hamburg and part of a tour, I gave up the unequal struggle and began to converse with two women to my right, obviously mother and daughter.

"Where you from?" demanded the older of the two.

"Montreal."

"We're from Chicago. You married?"

"No."

"You travelling alone?"

"No, I'm with a friend, but he hasn't arrived yet."

"He must be flying in from San Francisco. Word is that sailing will be delayed because of a late flight from the West Coast."

"Is that right?"

The polite preliminaries having been disposed of, she then went on to tell me that she had just rediscovered her daughter who had been put up for adoption as an infant. The mother did not elaborate, but marriage seemed to be a preoccupation. Curious about her birth mother, the daughter had hired a private investigator to track her down; and here they were, travelling together so they could really get to know one another.

The bonding extended to their hair and clothes, modified pinafore dresses with puffed-sleeve blouses, their hair gathered at the crown and cascading untidily down their backs. The daughter did not look young; the mother did not appear particularly old. They both had pinched, tired faces and too much mascara. Once I had expressed my pleasure in seeing them so happily reunited the conversation petered out. Across the table the German group talked with animation. The food could not be faulted, nor could it be called outstanding. Names on the menu showed more originality than the preparation: supremes and croustades, terrines and blanquettes. It was food uncomplicated by love or gratitude. As soon as I politely could, I excused myself and returned to the cabin to find no trace of Frank.

Faute de mieux, I set off on a tour of inspection. Since we were still in port, the casino was closed. Small matter, as I do not enjoy gambling. On another deck, in a lounge called The Sheltering Palms, a few couples danced to a combo playing their instruments directly into microphones as if for the hard of hearing. In the ship's theatre, The Tropicana Room, a show was in progress. Six young men and women danced and sang their way through a musical tour of the Caribbean, their voices miked to the level of distortion. I watched them for about twenty minutes, long enough to realize that not all young hopefuls make it into the national company of *A Chorus Line*.

I wandered outside and leaned on the rail. By now the terminus was floodlit, and late passengers trickled up the gangplank. I strolled around to the port side. Across the harbour at the next pier another cruise ship, *Empress of the Isles*, was preparing to sail. A clone of the *Blue Horizon*, she loomed, white, immense, multi-tiered, with a heavily miked calypso band playing on the sun deck, the music clearly audible across the water.

A couple about my age leaned against the rail, she in turquoise stretch pants, he in a Hawaiian shirt dotted with flamingoes. "Doesn't that music make you want to dance?" she asked.

It didn't, but I agreed it was very contagious.

"Where you from?"

"Montreal."

"You get a lot of snow this winter? We're from Wisconsin. We get lots of snow, too."

"At least that's one thing we won't see this week," I suggested.

"That's right." They moved away. "Have a nice evening," she called over her shoulder.

As I retraced my steps to the starboard side I passed the windows of the Blue Lagoon Bar. The party that had sat near my table before dinner was back, all drinking something pink that must have been mixed in a blender, each tumbler topped with a tiny paper parasol. Would I go in for a highball? Maybe later.

I stood at the rail looking down at the discoloured roof of the embarkation terminus. Uncompromising floodlights exaggerated the drab ugliness of the scene: the cracked concrete paving, the forklift trucks not parked so much as abandoned, the scruffy vegetation clinging to life between periods of drought and downpour. I felt isolated rather than alone. To be by myself is never a hardship; however, I am accustomed to being in control of my surroundings. At the moment I was quite literally trapped in an environment whose sole *raison d'être* was to provide a good time. Not to undergo a wonderful time seemed almost like a breach of contract, a failure of trust. I felt not unlike a completely healthy person occupying a bed in a hospital, a bed I neither needed nor wanted. Moreover, I was preventing some needy soul from receiving health care to which he was entitled.

I regretted Elinor had decided not to come on the cruise. The two of us could have made our own good time, ignoring the other passengers unless we met someone truly congenial. The irritating part is that Elinor herself was now sorry about having been suckered into grandmotherhood. Her daughter had already borne two healthy children without a problem, so there was no reason why she could not have hired someone reliable to keep house while Elinor enjoyed her prize. What about the father? Was he totally helpless? As the day for departure drew steadily closer I could tell Elinor regretted her impulsive generosity. She wanted to come along, but Frank had already arranged his schedule around the cruise. When I suggested booking a single cabin for Frank so she could share her prize cabin with me, she began to vacillate. She really should stay to look after the grandchildren. By then I would gladly have scrapped the whole undertaking, torn up the tickets, and gone to the movies. But that would have left Frank high and dry.

Elinor and I had dinner the night before my flight and tried terribly hard to make the best of what we both knew to be a bad deal.

"It's only for a week."

"Time passes so quickly when you're on the go."

"It's going to be awfully hot at this time of year."

"In most cultures a mother tends a daughter giving birth."

"There are plenty of cruises to choose from. We'll take one in the fall."

And so forth and so on. The lines were so interchangeable I can't remember who said what.

Perhaps I might have that highball now. We were only an hour or so from midnight, and the gangplank was still down. A sudden surge of passengers from the terminus suggested the delayed airplane had finally landed. As I looked down I saw a man who could well be Frank. From my vantage point on the topmost deck, I was a long way from the pier, but there was something familiar about the walk, the crisp salt-and-pepper hair. Overcome by a surge of something like relief, I took the stairs down to the cabin to be there when he arrived.

From his combination of jollity and exasperation I could tell Frank had enjoyed a few drinks on the plane.

"Jesus H. Antichrist!" he began as he entered the cabin in the wake of a smiling steward. "*Quelle* effing trip! Somebody on board suffered a heart attack and we had to make an emergency landing in Kansas City. And the food! Fortunately they had the good grace to serve it in small portions." He tossed his overcoat onto the bed. "At least we don't have to wear seat belts on a ship."

With a bow the steward withdrew.

"God! Do I need to pee!" Frank put down his hand luggage.

"Do you have any moving parts that might come loose?" I asked. "Bridgework? An ear trumpet? A St. Christopher medal? We have a vacuum toilet, and when I say vacuum I mean the suction from outer space."

I waited a moment for the sudden roar followed by a "Jesus Christ!" Frank burst out of the bathroom. "You weren't kidding. It nearly took the buttons off my jacket. Let's have a drink."

"There's a mini-bar under the TV."

"Mini-bar my ass. I brought liquor with me."

I couldn't help laughing out loud. "Didn't you read your shipboard instructions? No liquor is to be brought on board by passengers."

"Screw that!" retorted Frank. "That's how these cruise out-fits make their money. They give you all the food you can eat and all the towels you can use, then sock you for drinks at three-fifty a shot. No thanks." From his carry-on bag Frank took a forty ounce bottle of scotch and poured us each a drink.

"We'll have to hide it," I said. "There's a safe in the closet, but it's designed to hold jewellery and travellers' cheques, not bottles of whisky."

"I'll wrap it in dirty laundry and stow it in the back of the closet. That ought to discourage prying eyes."

Chuckling over Frank's flagrant disrespect of the ship's rules, I raised my glass. "Cheers!"

At that precise moment the ship's whistle gave a blast that must have been audible in Florida. The faintest suggestion of vibration indicated the engines had started up. Another ear-damaging blast, part scream, part explosion, pierced the night, no doubt startling everybody on board and jolting awake those who had retired early. Almost imperceptibly the roof of the embarkation shed began to move away. From the cabin window I could see a narrow strip of turbulence between the ship and the pier. Without fanfare we were under way, a departure shorn of the trappings of transatlantic crossings: no tugboats, streamers, bagpipes, waving crowds, men in Homburgs, women in furs and orchids. No glamour. We simply moved away from the pier and headed out to sea.

I glanced at my watch, which read twenty minutes past midnight. Officially it was Sunday morning, but it still felt like Saturday night as I had another drink while Frank unpacked.

He was hungry after a day of airplane meals, but neither of us felt up to tackling the midnight buffet. Instead I rang for the butler, first hiding the bottle of scotch under the bed. John made rather a production of greeting Frank and insisting on what a pleasure it would be to serve him. We could barely interrupt this litany of dedication in order to ask for a tray. I reminded him about the extra pillows and ashtray.

No sooner had he closed the door than Frank exploded. "Is that lady from Lahore our cabin steward?"

"Butler. He calls himself a butler."

"Butler my buns! He's still wet behind his coffee-coloured ears."

As I was to learn over the next few days, much of the food on board was filling but not satisfying. Cocktail sandwiches, tiny quiches, little cakes, and petits fours are not much of a meal, but Frank was too tired to care. So weary was he in fact that he fell into bed without bothering to remove the shirt in which he had been travelling all day. Butler John had still not delivered the extra pillows I needed for my back—Frank had taken a saucer to use as ashtray—so I folded the quilted bed cover into a sort of bolster. By the time I slid into bed and turned out the light, Frank was fast asleep.

Soothed by the faint vibration, I soon grew drowsy. We were underway.

V

The following morning I peeked through a crack in the drawn curtains to see an overcast sky above an expanse of cement-gray water. Frank slept soundly; so far I had not heard him snore. When I rang John to bring coffee I reminded him about the extra pillows I had requested. This occasioned a veritable dance of self-effacement which I cut short as I did not want him to disturb Frank. A newsletter listing the day's activities had been slid under the door. I found the document almost depressing. Beginning with mass in the library at 7:00 A.M., not a moment of daylight was without a program, were the idle passenger so inclined. Lectures on where to shop and what to buy; classes on crafts, materials included; movies; dance and fitness instruction; tai-chi; and bridge lessons were listed with times and places, like courses in a bulletin for summer school. Should all else fail, there were closed-circuit programs on the cabin TV. It was almost enough to make one want to jump ship.

Frank floated slowly up to consciousness. "I dreamed I sailed the seven seas—in my Maidenform bra. Are we there yet?"

"We're at sea, if that's what you mean. There's land in the distance; I think it's the Dominican Republic. Not what I expected, but then what is. Coffee?"

"Please. But first I have to risk a pee in that killer toilet. Should I rope myself to the bed?"

By now Frank had shed the shirt he had worn to bed and

pulled on a robe. As a youth he had been rail-thin. Age had filled him out, but he seemed really quite trim for a man of his years.

"Is it okay if I shower?" he called from behind the door.

"Go ahead." I poured myself another cup of coffee and settled down in the seating area with a magazine. Frank did not waste time, and in a matter of minutes he had showered and shaved. While he was dressing I did the same. So far we were managing not to crowd one another, a good omen.

By now the scanty supper was letting Frank down, and he was hungry. I have no real objection to eating breakfast, so long as I don't have to make any effort. Lazy about food at the best of times, I would rather skip breaking my fast than cook it. A card left on our desk, printed to resemble an invitation, indicated we had been seated at table number seven, second seating, naturally. My idea of hell on earth, or at sea, would be early supper with a dining room full of children. Breakfast however was open, and we rode the elevator down to the dining-room deck and found our way unaided to number seven.

Staff on the *Blue Horizon* turned out to be a miniature U.N. The *maître d'hôtel*, a very grand Greek, was born to intimidate those passengers who seldom ate out, except at fast food restaurants. He and I locked glances, played chicken for several seconds, then he smiled the *Blue Horizon* smile as he handed us each a breakfast menu. Our overly friendly waiter came from the Philippines, as he was quick to point out. When neither Frank nor I volunteered our country of origin, he asked to know. I couldn't tell whether this overriding curiosity was ship's policy or simply his way of ingratiating himself with two passengers who were old enough to know the score. Good looking, in a boyish, crew-cut fashion, he identified himself as Peter. He smiled with his eyes. The bus boy, considerably older than the waiter, was a darkly handsome Hungarian whom both Frank and I checked out over the menus.

"If we could only clone him," whispered Frank, "then we could each have a go."

"I don't shit where I eat, if you catch my drift."

"Perfectly. Are you going to have toast? Hot or cold cereal?"

"Sounds a bit menopausal," I replied. "Perhaps I'll go for the eggs benedict, the ultimate holiday breakfast."

"Not a bad idea," agreed Frank. "Egg yolks over egg yolks, and diets be damned!"

Since we were the only passengers from table seven who had ventured down to breakfast, we were at the mercy of the chatty Filipino, who began to badger us with questions about life in Canada, while the saturnine Hungarian glowered in the background. I did not wish to be rude on our first meeting, but I detest being grilled over breakfast. What is the weather like in Canada? Do we get a lot of snow? How much are waiters paid? How much of one's salary goes for rent? We were rescued by the maître d' who came to ask if everything was all right. He also gave our waiter the laser look, and Peter disappeared in search of fresh coffee.

"Christ!" said Frank. "I hope every meal isn't going to turn into Twenty Questions."

"Possibly, but there will be four other people to take up the slack."

"A terrifying prospect. If all else fails, we can eat in the cabin."

We both mopped up the last traces of egg yolk and Hollandaise with toast, just to make sure the arteries were properly coated. By then it was time to return to the cabin to collect our life jackets. Because of the late departure, lifeboat drill was to be held at 10:00 A.M. A well-scrubbed, flaxen-haired young woman was making up the room with great economy of movement. I asked if I might have two extra pillows. She smiled and hurried down the corridor. By the time Frank and I had fitted ourselves into life jackets, she had returned with the pillows. So much for our butler and his mission to serve. I wrestled with the seductive temptation to make generalizations based on racial stereotype, a struggle in which the politically correct Geoffry Chadwick went down in defeat.

Frank and I, bulky in our vivid orange life jackets, surveyed one another.

"It's not sable, darling, but it floats." Frank struck an attitude in front of the mirror. "Has it occurred to you that this cabin, this entire ship has far more mirrors than it needs? Everywhere I look I see myself, usually at the most unflattering angle. And don't let's talk about the bathroom. I've seen bits of myself in there I didn't even know I owned. Now, where do we go so we won't drown?"

"Our deck foregathers in the casino, one deck up."

Due to the late departure, the casino had not opened. Apparently it could only operate while we were at sea. According to the activity bulletin it was supposed to open this evening at nine. What a depressing sight it was, all the slot machines covered in canvas bags, the gaming tables draped in drop cloths, the chairs stacked against one wall. Almost as depressing as the room itself were the other passengers. Average age: forty; origin: middle America; average weight: twenty to fifty pounds more than necessary. Several of the couples had brought their children along on the cruise, and, overstimulated by the sense of occasion, they filled the room with their unwelcome presence.

"This will be my first and last time in the casino," I said to

Frank. "What is gambling but a tax on stupidity?"

"J'agree. But where did all these children come from? Surely there must be some sort of maritime law against children on board. In case of shipwreck, women and children last!"

"That's a holdover from the *Titanic*," I said, "and am I ever sick of the *Titanic*. I know it was terribly sad, like the Children's Crusade or the Battle of Culloden. But it happened. The ship sank. People drowned. Enough. Who today laments the *Empress of Ireland*, the *Andrea Doria*, all those ships at Pearl Harbour. If I see one more movie, documentary, or musical re-creation of the *Titanic* I'll—I'll sing 'Nearer my God to Thee' in the talent show."

Frank placed a hand on my arm. "Geoffry, dear Geoffry, aren't you overreacting just the teeniest bit?"

"Perhaps." Suddenly we both dissolved into laughter, the shared laughter that excludes all others. As two older men travelling together, conservatively but expensively dressed, we had already drawn glances. Now we found ourselves at the centre of a not wholly generous scrutiny, fortunately broken by a ship's officer with a bullhorn compelling our attention.

Instructions were simple. At the sound of the emergency signal we were to proceed at once to our cabins to don life jackets, then report to the stations we had been shown on deck. The crew would be there to give instructions on boarding the lifeboats. The whole exercise reminded me of fire drill at school. Neither Frank nor I uttered a word, unlike several of the overweight men whose loud asides and self-conscious bravado made the officer in charge difficult to hear. Instead of shutting up their husbands, the wives giggled encouragement. In a case of real emergency they would probably panic and rush the lifeboats. I found myself disliking them intensely.

Dismissed by the officer in charge of our section, Frank and I returned to the cabin to leave our life jackets, then ventured out on deck. A flight of steps, currently being scrubbed by a small, swarthy man in a white jumpsuit, led down to the pool deck. The pool itself was open to the sky, but the entire area was enclosed by large windows in the process of being hosed down by a tall, blond man in a blue jumpsuit. The ship's brochure had boasted that its pool was filled with salt water, at the moment vaguely murky and filled with children. The urine content must be staggering. At one end of the area stood a bar, its canopy covered in a thatch-like material which must have measured up to fire and safety standards. Rows of reclining deck chairs, bands of vinyl wrapped around an aluminum frame, circled the pool. Frank dropped into one and gestured that I sit beside him.

"That's my wife's chair," said a man's voice. I turned around to look at the speaker, a middle-aged man in boxer trunks whose waistband was stretched to the limit by a belly covered in dense, matted hair.

"The chair was empty. How can you claim it belongs to your wife?"

"That's her towel."

I looked around to see a towel, one from two large stacks of identical towels, tossed carelessly over the back of the recliner.

"The towel itself is hardly distinctive. It could be anybody's towel. Where's your wife?"

"Having her hair done."

"You mean to tell me that while your wife is on one of the lower decks, having her hair done, that nobody is to sit in this chair because she happened to throw a towel over the back?"

"That's the way it's done," he rumbled ominously.

"Not where I come from. In Canada it is a backside, not a towel, that holds a seat. When your wife returns I will be happy to relinquish the chair. Far be it from me to come between a man and his helpmeet. In the meantime, while your wife is under the dryer I am sure you will have no objection to my using the chair."

He shifted belligerently, enough to make him lose one of his sandals.

"You know something," said Frank. "This so-called recliner is not very comfortable. Shall we take a turn around the promenade deck?"

"Why not."

After struggling to our feet we climbed two flights of stairs to the Sunshine Deck on which the promenade, a rectangular walkway, circled the ship. Many of the recliners lined up against the rail were already occupied by sunbathers naively believing their sunblock would protect them from tropical rays, no less lethal for being shrouded in haze. A few people jogged, isolated in their private world of Walkman headsets. A couple speed walked, their pendulum elbows swinging in unison. As we passed the ship's gymnasium, visible through full-length windows, we could see passengers stationary-bicycling with grim determination. Another walked the treadmill, striding nowhere with immense purpose beside a woman doing penance on the Stair Master, all this intense activity at variance with the underlying idea of a relaxing cruise.

The two of us kept a brisk pace, more brisk on the leeward side of the ship as wind off the water was strong. With mutual accord we paused to lean against the rail and gaze out, as sailors have for centuries, at the mesmerizing sight of the wake, turbulence turning the stripe of water cerulean in marked contrast to the flickering gray ocean stretching unbroken to the horizon.

"I had no idea it was so windy," said Frank. "It's windier than a fashion shoot. My hair must be a total disaster."

I ran my hand over my own head in an ineffectual attempt to smooth my hair down. "You know something? Those lifeboats look quite large when seen up close, but I don't much fancy bobbing around the Atlantic in what is at best an overgrown rowboat."

Frank nodded his head. "And I won't even have my mink coat to keep me warm, like Tallulah Bankhead in that Hitchcock movie. *Lifeboat*? 1944, if I remember correctly."

"At least we wouldn't have U-boats chasing us, only sharks. That was a good movie. I loved the way Bankhead managed to keep her long bob looking neat, day after day adrift at sea." I chuckled. "My favourite line was when the men suggested using her diamond bracelet as bait for fishing. 'Do you suppose they'll bite?' asks one of the men. 'Why not?' replies Tallulah in that inimitable baritone. 'I did.'"

Frank laughed out loud. "My favourite Bankhead line comes from a play I saw her in one summer on Cape Cod. It was a completely forgettable bit of summer stock fluff, except for one good line. One of several men supposedly in love with her accuses Tallulah of not being serious. 'Not serious!' she growls. 'I'll have you know at Vassar they called me the Ibsen girl.'"

We both laughed before I spoke. "You just said it out loud. You said the bad word: I-B-S-E-N! Just for that you'll have to buy me a drink, for penance. What do you say to three times around the deck, then into the Blue Lagoon for a well-deserved bloody mary."

"Suits me." And the two of us set off. Our three turns up, we headed into the bar and to what I had come to think of as my table. I had begun to revise my estimation of Frank as a travelling companion.

At first I had been frankly apprehensive about sharing my life for a week with someone I knew only superficially. Yet when I studied the other passengers I realized how fortunate I was to have Frank along. We shared a point of view, a sensibility, that of the gay man in his sixties. Our credo was to put a comic spin on discomfort. We did not long for spousal benefits or time off from work so we could attend our lover's father's funeral. We preferred to be discreet about our orientation, and this absence of candour allowed us to be spectators with the best seats in the house.

There was nothing remotely effeminate about Frank. With his salt-and-pepper hair trimmed short, he looked more like a banker than a man associated with the stage. Like me, he chose clothes of conservative colour and cut. His face now looked lived in. North America worships the smooth, untroubled look of innocence, with the result that lines and furrows necessarily suggest experience. If your parents have wrinkled foreheads and heavy lines bracketing the mouth, chances are you will, too. However we still like to think of creases and pouches as visual records of unhappy love affairs, binges, bouts with drugs or alcohol, and chronic unhappiness. Frank had the kind of *beau-laid*, ugly-handsome looks that suggested a wealth of experience. I am sure he has been around the track a few times. Most gay men have. I am also certain that women must find him irresistible, even moreso as he does not come on to them. Humour, experience, diffidence can get a woman's attention far more quickly than the standard testosterone tactics, unless of course the woman is sixteen, a biker, or a refugee from a Southern Gothic novel.

Acerbic on the surface, Frank was basically unflappable; he demonstrated the capacity to deal effectively with a crisis. Just as important, he was prepared to stand aside while someone equally competent solved the problem. Many people feel compelled to rush in, give instructions, contradict others, and block the view. Watching Frank in action at those tedious rehearsals, I could observe him cope. Perhaps that particular ability is a necessary survival skill for working in theatre, a chaotic environment at best. In an earlier century Frank might have managed a Wild West show, a travelling circus, or an itinerant opera company. He would have been able to keep the balls in the air, jolly along the employees, scrape together the payroll, outwit the Indians before they became Aboriginals, and get out of town ahead of the creditors.

I would not accuse Frank of being dishonest. Rather, he demonstrated an intense pragmatism, survival skills at their most basic. Unlike Robinson Crusoe, who had only a man Friday, Frank would have contrived to have a man for every day of the week, including Sunday. His trick was not to be ruthless but to stay focussed. His honesty lay in being true to himself. Although I have known Frank for a long time, I was beginning to realize I did not know him as well as I had thought. To be sure, our meetings in the past had been brief, social occasions, where nothing too serious ever came up. Then again, did Frank really know me? Whether or not he did, I was beginning to realize he would be a good companion for the trip. Not least of his qualities was his ability to salvage something droll from the most unpromising situations. Finally, nobody who claimed Jean Harlow—she of the razor-sharp delivery, spectacular hair, and Adrian wardrobe—as his favourite movie star could be all bad.

Some years ago, before the Caribbean cruise had become a

working-class prerogative, like disability pensions or trips to Disney World, I took a cruise with my lover of the moment. Much to my surprise, the cruise had been his idea, although in retrospect I cannot imagine anyone less suited for life on a ship. James Ralston was his name, and James was what he liked to be called. Were one to slip into Jim, Jimmy, or J.R., he managed to look vaguely offended, as though protocol had been breached. On his own he was about as outgoing as a barn owl to which, with his round, steel-rimmed glasses, he bore an uncanny resemblance. He made few demands as a lover for the simple reason that he was a self-sufficient man. He made no claims that I could not comfortably meet. At times I would have enjoyed more of his attention than he was prepared to give, but wisely, perhaps, I did not insist. More than one relationship has foundered because a partner demanded the other take notice once too often. Much as I abhor domestic violence I cannot avoid the subversive feeling that when a man is slapping his wife around she does have his full attention.

James and I sailed to the Caribbean from New York City. It was a good way to begin a cruise, as we had two full days on board to unwind from the lives we had left behind. The further south we sailed, the more balmy the weather grew, and by the time we arrived in the Caribbean we were rested up and tuned in for the experience. James came fully prepared for shipboard life. Along with a briefcase filled with files, he had packed a tome on the economic history of the West Indies along with a biography of John Maynard Keynes. James's idea of casual dressing was to wear a white or blue business shirt opened at the neck, with the cuffs folded back twice. He splurged on a pair of prescription sunglasses so he could read on deck and sent away for one of those Tilley Endurable hats that makes the wearer look like a stand-up comic at a country fair.

James had been to the Caribbean before, on his honey-moon, but the marriage had ended some time before I met him. "I don't know about the fauna, but the flora looks carnivorous," had been his observation. At first he did not want to sit at a table with strangers, until I persuaded him that we might find conversation drying up as we faced one another three times a day. Furthermore, I did not intend to watch him read his way through meals. He compromised on a table for four, and we ended up with another couple about our age from New York City. Whatever fun I had on that cruise was due to Chuck and Doris. New Yorkers are different from other people: smart, quick, contemporary, wry, and funny. Doris had James pegged in a second. "Just turn him to the wall, honey, and come ashore with us," she had suggested on our third morning at sea. I took her advice and left James, happily tucked away in the library, the least-visited room on the ship.

What a wonderful time we had bouncing around Puerto Rico in an antique tour bus, fuelled no doubt by gasoline with an octane level higher than that of lighter fluid. Chuck and Doris were blessed with the ability to see the comic possibilities of inconvenience. G.K. Chesterton once said something to the effect that an adventure is an inconvenience rightly considered and an inconvenience only a missed adventure. Laughter and anger are two sides of the same medallion, and with my New York friends the toss always landed laughter side up.

James steadfastly refused to join in, more than content to wave us off as we rode the tender into Sint Maarten to buy per-fume and walk in the warm white sand until our feet swelled. He joined us for the day trip to Caracas because he wanted to see the statue to Simón Bolívar, but for the rest of the trip he

was an inert presence, like certain gas molecules we studied at
school. The air conditioning in the ancient bus broke down
and we all complained loudly, except for James who suffered in
silence. He wore the expression of the saint in a Baroque painting
who is about to be beheaded or shot full of arrows. That night
in the lounge he danced one dance with Doris before excusing
himself to go down to the cabin and read. Disloyal though it
sounds, I had a better time when he wasn't there.

It would have been easy to dismiss James as dull, only he
was not dull. He simply did not need other people around in
order to be content. When he found himself in company, he
felt no obligation to scintillate. He was a good listener, but few
people on a cruise want to unburden themselves at serious
length. Yet in his own quiet way he had a good time, while I
was grateful for Chuck and Doris. We exchanged addresses and
made plans to get together in New York, in Montreal. Then
Chuck died suddenly and Doris moved to Phoenix to be near
her children. We telephoned back and forth for a while, but
time passed. Now we exchange a note on a Christmas card.
Even were we to meet again I know we could never recapture
the euphoria we shared on the ship. You can't go home again.
Unfortunately you can't go away again, either. Just as time
blunts grief it also erases happiness, and perhaps it is a better
idea to seek out new experiences than attempt to recapture
those that have passed into memory.

James and I continued to see each other for a while after
the cruise, but the experience had not brought us closer. I had
already read the writing on the wall when, to my astonished
relief, his firm asked him to set up an operation in Vancouver.
We parted friends, and promised to get together soon, very
soon. Then I learned he had married again, and to my surprise

I realized I was pleased with the news. He really was better off with a wife than with a series of random lovers. And I knew he would never stray. Sex generally involves another person, and James was far too self-sufficient to want that kind of interruption very often. I sent the newlyweds a silver tray for which I received a conventional thank-you note on one of their informals with Mr. and Mrs. James Ralston in raised script. A line had been drawn through the printed name, and "James and Shirley" written above it in ballpoint pen. That was the end of that. He was my lover and it is Doris with whom I still keep in touch. Perhaps there is a moral to be drawn, but I have to confess I am not quite sure what it is.

There are worse ways to hammer away at your health than by drinking a bloody mary at noon while watching grim-faced people jog past the window. I am sure Frank and I were shaving years from our lives, albeit those at the least interesting end. The pleasantly taciturn waiter had been replaced by a bouncy girl with a ponytail, who asked "you folks" what we wanted. We asked for bloody marys without Tabasco. I happened to glance over to the bar just in time to see the bartender reach for the Tabasco bottle. I realized he did not listen attentively to any of the waiters when they gave their orders.

I went to stand at the bar. The bartender refused to look at me. "Excuse me," I said in that aggressive way that demands attention, "but I asked for no Tabasco in my drink. Last night I asked for no ice and got a tumblerful. In future, please pay attention to the waiter." I did not smile; neither did he. But he began the bloody marys from scratch. After less than a day on board it was becoming increasingly clear that people were there to serve just so long as you did not deviate from a certain norm. Most people today do not smoke, so my request for an ashtray in the cabin went unheeded. Most people prefer iced drinks, so to request a drink without ice failed to register. I did not mind the bartender being surly; in fact I rather welcomed it. But I damn well wanted the drink I had ordered. Were I to complain to an officer the bartender might well lose his job, and I did not want his dismissal on my conscience. Sometimes it is better to take arms against a sea of troubles.

After the customary "Cheers!" and raising of glasses, Frank settled himself comfortably in his chair. "You know something, Geoff. Elinor is in every respect a remarkable woman, but I never had you pegged as moving in that direction."

I smiled. "Neither did I. The whole thing just sort of happened. There was a man in the picture; Patrick was his name. I'm surprised you didn't meet him. I certainly didn't keep him hidden."

"Schedule, I guess. So often my visits to Montreal are in and out. Where is he now?"

"He died, of a stroke. Have you noticed nowadays that when a gay man dies of something that is not AIDS-related, you feel obliged to add a footnote? Elinor had been recently widowed, and the two of us were thrown together last Christmas. She was burned out of her sublet apartment, so I let her live in Mother's place, which I had kept on while Mother tried out life at Maple Grove. One thing led to another, and now we seem to be an item." I laughed. "A great many people I used to know are shaking their heads, you may be sure."

"Does she know about your—shall we say—variegated past?"

"Elinor is a liberated woman, which means she has an independent income. She understands the score, insofar as a straight woman can appreciate what a gay man of my age has been through. She knows I have had male lovers, but I haven't been too specific about numbers."

"A wise decision. Don Giovanni kept lists, and look what happened to him. Do you miss the old life?"

"Less than you might think," I replied. "I'm too old for it now. The mere idea of going to a bar filled with people one third my age all dancing to music loud enough to cause hearing loss. Need I go on?"

Frank laughed. "And even if you do find someone who has a fixation on older men, what do you talk about after the fact. These days, ten years equals a generation gap, twenty years a different era, and thirty years another century."

"You're absolutely right. Elinor and I come from the same space, as the young say today. We share the same values. We saw movies when they were considered relevant, not camp. We learned good manners, those little courtesies that ease the friction of intimacy. We do not wallow in self-examination. Elinor is not the kind of woman who stands naked in front of a full-length mirror meditating on life, love, longevity, and cellulite. I do not stare into my own eyes while shaving and wonder where I went wrong."

"You don't?" asked Frank with mock astonishment. "That's how I begin my day, every day. Do you love her?"

I paused a moment before answering. "Yes, I do love her. I cannot honestly say I am in love with her, but love, as I understand it, lasts one hell of a lot longer. 'Love' is a choice of the mind; 'in love' is an act of the heart. You know what I mean. Being 'in love' has sent generations of women into the arms of the wrong man, meaning someone from a different postal code. Am I being very pedantic?"

"Not very, just a little," replied Frank with a smile. "But I understand your point. If only we could fall in love with the right man, how simple our lives would be."

It was my turn to smile. "Do I hear the jaded voice of experience?"

"You do. Shall we have another pop before lunch?"

"By all means. Are we going down to the dining room to be served at our table, or shall we stand in a long line at the Coral Reef Cafe so we can schlep our buffet lunch to a formica table next to a family-values man with three petulant children."

Frank leaned back, placing his hands together so only the tips of his fingers touched.

"I'd say the dining room."

I signalled for the waitress.

VI

Elinor,

I will no doubt be home, safely or otherwise, before you receive this letter; but I will send it air mail and hope that one of the more enterprising locals does not steal the stamps. I particularly wanted you to see the personalized stationery delivered to the cabin, my name in print across the top of each sheet: a whore's dream of elegance. As I write, Frank is taking a shower and I am sitting at the desk, a highball within reach. Frank brought a bottle of scotch on board, in defiance of regulations. Naturally the ship makes big money on drinks. When I asked what we will do when the liquor runs out, his answer was that he never travels without a roll of duct tape. In answer to my puzzled query he said he will buy liquor when ashore and duct tape it to his leg to smuggle on board. America sait faire.

Tonight's dinner has been designated as semi-formal, meaning some of the male passengers may rise to a tie, and several of the women will wear a frock. Remember frocks, puffed sleeves and sweetheart necklines? The dress code on board, if such it may be called, is studiously ignored by roughly half the passengers, who flaunt their beer bellies and cottage-cheese legs in outfits that would never have made it past the Hays office. The dressmaker bathing suit may have been matronly, but it hid a multitude of imperfections.

Today we anchored off a resort near the Dominican Republic for those who wanted to water ski, snorkle, or play golf, leaving the ship uncrowded for the rest of us. Neither Frank nor I indulges in that sort

*of thing, so we slept away most of the afternoon. Tomorrow we tie
up at Barbados, where this letter will probably be mailed. On the map,
Barbados seems much closer to northern South America than to
southern North America, so heaven knows when the letter will
arrive. I wish you were here sharing the experience first hand. Frank
is a most agreeable companion, I have to admit; but your presence
would have added a touch of respectability, even if we were travelling in what used to be called sin. Two single men travelling together
raise heavily pencilled or plucked eyebrows. Time to close.*

Wish you were here,
Geoffry

By the time Frank and I, both wearing ties, prepared to face the
dining room and meet our table companions for the rest of the
cruise, we were both a bit drunk. We did not stagger, or slur con-
sonants. Our voices remained modulated and our conversation
free of the more vulgar expletives. Yet we both experienced the
slight shift in reality, a warm, pleasant feeling that hints at more
possibilities than simple sobriety could ever conjure up.

It turned out to be just as well, as we were in for a jarring
surprise. After riding the elevator down to the restaurant deck,
crowded with couples laughing and giggling with the slightly
grim determination of those intent on having a good time, we
entered the dining room. Only two empty places remained at
our table, but before I had a chance to take in the four strangers, my attention was captured by a woman seated with her
back to the entrance. Something intensely familiar about her
almost caused me to stop walking. Then, as if sensing our approach, she turned, and there sat Elsie Connors.

"Surprise!" she called out gaily. "Welcome aboard! I've just been telling our table about the two most attractive men in Montreal."

"Good evening, Elsie," I said lamely. "Good evening," I repeated to the others.

"Good evening," parroted Frank. "Actually, I live in San Francisco."

By now the waiter had appeared to pull out our chairs, and we sat.

Still smiling in triumph over her coup, Elsie proceeded to make introductions. "Geoffry—and Frank, this is Susan."

The young woman in her early twenties could barely conceal her disappointment that the two single men at the table were old enough to be parents. "And this is Darlene—and Brad," continued Elsie relentlessly. Frank and I half rose and shook hands across the bowl of freesias, real I was relieved to notice. "And you know me, Elsie!" she concluded coyly.

Fortunately the waiter wasted no time in handing us menus, which provided a temporary distraction.

"What brings you to the *Blue Horizon*, Elsie?" asked Frank in a neutral voice.

She gave an arch little laugh. "When I heard that Elinor had won the cruise I got the idea it might be fun to tag along, as I would already know someone on board. Then I learned she couldn't go and that you and Geoffry were using the prize. I had to confess I liked that even better, so I booked onto the ship."

"Bring me a double scotch on the rocks," I said to the waiter.

"Make that two," added Frank.

While perusing the menu I also studied my table mates. Elsie wore a pink sun dress with a bolero jacket, the left shoulder of which displayed her collection of scatter pins, tiny jewelled insects. I suspect the jewels were real, but they still looked terribly Forties, as did her armful of silver bangles. Was she here to poach on Elinor's territory, or did she have her eye on Frank? Time, as they say, would tell.

Susan was a standard, government-issue, American beauty: regular features, smooth skin, good teeth, glossy brown hair, and clear eyes devoid of expression. I had a feeling that if I looked directly into her eyes I could probably see the back of her head. She turned out to be from Wisconsin, as good a place as any, and admitted to be travelling with her aunt and uncle; but they had preferred the first seating for dinner. Darlene, an angular brunette on the far side of forty, had the look of a woman who knows the score. She had large brown eyes, artfully made up, which she kept trained on Brad, a man also in his mid-forties with the bland good looks one sees in recruiting posters and glossy ads for mid-priced cars. It was evident they were travelling together and equally evident they were not married.

Our drinks arrived, the adult equivalent of a security blanket. As I examined the menu, a formality really, as I almost always order the veal, I had rather a bad attack of What-the-hell-am-I-doing-here. I suspect Frank suffered the same or similar symptoms, but we refrained from looking at one another.

"Well," began Elsie, our orders taken, "are we all going ashore at Barbados tomorrow?"

"I'm going with my aunt," replied Susan without much enthusiasm. "She wants to take a tour of the island, but my uncle wants to stay on the ship. I guess I'll have to go."

"I'm sure you'll have a grand time," exclaimed Elsie, sounding not unlike a social director. I was seeing a side of Elsie

heretofore concealed, that of a take-charge organizer, the kind
of woman who masterminds corn roasts and Easter-egg hunts.
True, I had most recently seen her when Audrey Crawford was
much in evidence, the queen of taking charge. Yet I could not
stifle a feeling of dismay at the prospect of fending off Elsie for
the next five days.

Our Caesar salads arrived with much ceremony and creamy
dressing, few croutons, and no anchovies. Frank suggested a
bottle of wine and asked the busboy to send the wine waiter.
Sasha arrived at our table wrapped in a mantle of lush moodi-
ness. He proffered the wine list as though it were a First Folio.
When the wine arrived and Frank had performed the ritual
motions of smelling the cork, then inhaling the fumes from a
splash of wine in the glass itself, once he had actually taken a
sip, rolling it around his tongue as though he had just brushed
his teeth before pronouncing it satisfactory with a curt nod, the
waiter prepared to pour. Elsie said she really shouldn't, but just
this once; Susan said nothing but shifted her position slightly
so the waiter could reach her glass; Darlene said isn't this nice;
and Brad said why not. The last to be served, Frank ended up
with less than half a glass and ordered another bottle.

"Here's to a wonderful trip!" toasted Elsie, raising her glass,
"and to our generous host." She reached across the table to
touch glasses with Frank and flashed him a smile that telegraphed, to me at least, that he was her principal reason for
taking this cruise. "We're all going to the show after dinner,"
she continued between sips of her bouillon. "I hope you and
Frank will join us," she added, making Frank appear an after-
thought.

"I don't know, Elsie. "I spent about fifteen minutes in the
theatre last night, and I still have ringing in my ears. I've heard

it said that if it's too loud, then you're too old. That may well be true, but I would like to end the cruise with my hearing intact."

"Oh, but you must come!" insisted Elsie. I was beginning to wonder if perhaps she, too, had a quart of something concealed in her cabin. "We'll sit near the back."

"How come I didn't see you on the plane flying down from Montreal?" I asked, pointedly changing the subject.

"I came down early, to visit friends in Lauderdale before coming on to San Juan. I was looking for you all over, but it is a large ship."

"Yes, isn't it," I remarked with some satisfaction. The very bulk of the vessel might help to insulate us from Elsie.

The main course arrived. No matter what the chef does to veal, it always tastes the same, bland and unthreatening. Our table companions were drinking Frank's wine as though the French vineyards were under siege. He ordered a third bottle. Wine on top of whisky is not always the best idea in the world, but discovering Elsie Connors at our table had set off any number of alarm bells, drowning out those which sounded more weakly against mixing grape and grain.

Darlene and Brad said little, but managed to suggest they had climbed reluctantly out of bed in order to dine and could hardly wait to get back to the cabin. Like most gay men, I find heterosexual heat very boring. Having come to terms with my orientation at a time when, as the saying went, "The only thing worse than going to bed with a dead woman was going to bed with a live man," I had become adroit at concealing my interest. To observe the searing eyelocks Darlene applied to Brad, the hand brushing, leg rubbing, pantomimed kisses, and excessive solicitude over passing the butter and inquiring after the entrée suggested to me that the romance would not outlive the cruise. When two people in their forties behave like sixteen-year-olds in the grip of a first crush they are headed for a colossal blowup the second reality intrudes on the erotic idyll. The first ray of pragmatic daylight will shrivel the emotion the way a sunbeam destroys a vampire, since both vampires and erotic love flourish at night. To my shame, I almost hoped the blowout, when it came, might happen over dinner. Aside from Frank, with whom I must monitor my conversation in public, I shared the table with a boring widow on the make, a young woman whose I.Q. seemed to be double her age, and a pair of aging lovebirds completely wrapped up in one another. To be fair, Brad did join in the conversation to point out that there wasn't any more wine. Instead of asking why-the-fornicate didn't he order the next bottle, Frank gave the wine waiter a sign. I turned my head and looked him full in the face. He looked back. Words could not have added so much as a footnote to that silent communication.

Since more wine was on the way I broke my usual pattern and ordered dessert, a crème caramel, followed by a bit of Stilton, the cheese I would take to that hypothetical desert island. (Why do phone-in shows always want to know about desert-island books, never food or drink?) Elinor, too, loves Stilton, our mutual admiration of that splendid cheese an early bond. Frank went for chocolate cheesecake and passed on the cheese. As neither of us drinks coffee at night, we excused ourselves as a pair and, before Elsie had a chance to bring up the subject of the show, walked briskly from the dining room.

With a sure homing instinct we rode the elevator to our deck and headed down the corridor toward the cabin, only to discover John, our bumbling butler, readying it for the night. This entailed folding down the bedspreads, turning back the covers, and placing a chocolate on each pillow. I have always wondered who eats chocolate immediately before retiring. Aside from its rotting your teeth, who needs a sugar rush when trying to nod off. I will save the chockies to take home to Elinor for her grandchildren. Let them bounce off the walls.

Like most men of my generation, I dislike obsequiousness. In order to avoid an encounter with smarmy John, I gave Frank the nod and we continued on down the corridor and out onto the stern deck. On both the port and starboard sides there was a small sheltered triangle of space, enclosed on one side by the ship's rail, on the other by a flight of stairs leading to the pool deck. A delightful spot, just large enough for two people to lean on the rail and look out to sea, it was further sheltered by the upper deck forming a ceiling.

"Before I light up," said Frank, "I'm going back to the cabin for a slash. If I'm not back in ten minutes, it means the toilet has got me."

"Hang onto the towel rack. It's too wide to go down, even if you pull it off the wall. I'll wait here and make a wish on a falling satellite."

Leaning on the rail, looking into what was essentially a void, I thought of the times, only a handful, when I had seen Elsie Connors since leaving university. We had not been close friends at college, as we moved with a different crowd. I have always harboured an aversion to team sports of any kind and avoided both the games and those who played them. Elsie, on the other hand, hung out with the jocks, attended games, wore the team colours, and fended off advances after the players had downed a few celebratory or defeated beers. I always thought Elsie an airhead, and was consequently surprised to receive an invitation to her wedding.

She had met Dennis Connors through football; he was some sort of back—halfback, quarterback, fullback, outback—don't ask. They dated, courted, became engaged. I can remember Elsie showing off her engagement ring, two shades of gold in which, barely visible in the midst of an elaborate filigree setting, a tiny diamond battled for attention. She made the right decision. Elsie had not been born to chart new paths through unexplored terrain. Nor for her the surgeon's scalpel, the judge's gavel, the engineer's slide rule. Her destiny was to be a wife and mother, and she wasted no time in answering her calling.

The wedding set no precedents: a matron of honour in powder blue, two maids of honour in dusty pink, Elsie herself in white lace and tulle floating down the aisle on the arm of her father's morning coat to meet big, beefy, bluff Dennis, buttoned uncomfortably into a tux. During the reception the groom steered me away from Elsie's watchful eye and up to the bar where we knocked back a few until Elsie arrived in hot pursuit.

The reception was to set a precedent. During the early years of the marriage I received a few invitations to dinner. Prior to sitting down to one of Elsie's substantial, wholesome meals, Dennis would find a pretext to lead me downstairs to his den. From a drawer in the rolltop desk he would produce a bottle of scotch, always the best, to which he would add a little water from the laundry tap. The two of us would drink, I slowly, Dennis more rapidly. By the time I had downed two scotches with water he had polished off almost four. It seemed an odd, joyless way of being convivial, but still preferable to the sherry, Dubonnet, and sweet vermouth offered upstairs.

After Dennis had graduated in size from large to immense, his doctor laid some heavy words upon him about risks to his health. Dennis listened, then climbed onto the wagon. Having shed the liquor habit he no longer had any need for a drinking buddy, or walking alibi. Without the bond of sneaking shots, Dennis and I had few interests in common. Professional football bored me into a near coma, and Dennis boasted that he hadn't read a novel since completing his freshman survey course. I also suspect Elsie looked on me as a subversive influence, one who might push Dennis off the wagon. Invitations petered out, to my relief. Those were the days when I was running around, on the wrong side of the fence, according to my upbringing, and dinner with straight couples playing games was a real drag.

This newfound sobriety left Dennis with large blocks of time on his hands, and he turned his attention to restructuring the family business. He prospered, and bought Elsie a three carat diamond solitaire to replace the original engagement ring. Elsie raised three children, the nuclear family plus one for good measure, and worked tirelessly for local charities. When only middle-aged, Dennis succumbed to prostate cancer and was buried with all the trimmings, including a mixed choir, poetry read to the accompaniment of a harp, and a fulsome eulogy delivered by his sales manager.

Elsie soldiered on, easier when one has been left stocks, bonds, and a large, paid-for house. She launched her children into careers and marriage, and continued to work for charity. I ran into her here and there—an opening at the museum, a benefit for the opera, a Christmas cocktail party—where we caught up in that three-to-five-minute fashion. Then she managed to land herself a strong secondary role in *Hedda Gabler*, where she read her lines as if from a teleprompter. Frank seemed like an unlikely choice for Elsie, far too urbane and worldly for her limited sphere of good works and homemade jam. Apparently she had never pondered why he might still be single. Like the rest of us, Elsie was growing older; she would not be the first to seek a companion for what are laughingly called the golden years. I applauded her initiative, at the same time wondering how much of Elsie I was prepared to put up with for the rest of the cruise.

Frank came to stand beside me. Before leaning his forearms on the rail he lit a cigarette. "Elsie must surely know that you are keeping company with Elinor, so I must be the main event. Poor Elsie. For someone who deals in platitudes as freely as she does, I'm surprised she hasn't learned you can't get blood from a stone."

"I certainly don't look forward to dodging her for the next few days," I said.

We were silent for a few moments while Frank smoked. "Are you going to marry Elinor?" he inquired, casually, as if wanting to learn the time.

Surprise made me stand upright. "What makes you ask that?"

Frank laughed quietly. "Curiosity I suppose. There are worse ways to grow old than in the company of someone like her."

"That's just it," I replied. "I don't know whether I want to grow old, really old, with Elinor. She is younger and would probably end up being my nurse. When I get to the point of needing that kind of care I would prefer to be looked after by professionals, people for whom geriatric nursing is a job, not a cause."

"Why don't you let her decide that?" asked Frank as he carefully extinguished his cigarette in a nearby ashtray. Passengers had been strongly urged not to throw their butts off the upper decks, and each of the tables held an oversized glass ashtray, too large to be casually swiped by a passenger wanting a souvenir. "She seems to be very fond of you—which demonstrates a certain lack of judgement on her part."

"Go to Hell. Go directly to Hell. Do not pass Go. *Et cetera.*"

Frank continued. "Maybe you're better off not getting married—from the financial point of view, but these things can always be arranged by a lawyer, or a notary. All I'm saying is that maybe the decision is not completely yours to make. That is unless you are dead set against the idea, and somehow I don't think you are."

Not having a ready answer, I said nothing.

"I know you're not interested in gambling," said Frank, "but I may go and look in on the casino, possibly play a little blackjack. Don't worry. I never lose more than fifty dollars before I quit. You won't have to pay my way back home."

"Glad to hear it. But remember: they don't like it if you count the cards. If I'm not in the Blue Lagoon, I'll probably be back in the cabin. And don't be too late. Remember: nobody is ugly after two A.M."

I preferred to stay where I was, wedged into my secure little corner, enveloped in the warm tropical night. Frank's question about whether I wanted to marry Elinor had caught me off guard. The idea that a longtime widower and a recent widow might remarry did not strain the limits of credulity. I suppose what surprised me most was that the question had come from Frank, not the standard advocate of family values, whatever they are. That he might consider my marrying Elinor as a logical development made me realize I had rejoined a part of the world where appearances led to assumptions. I certainly could not plead ignorance or naïveté; I am neither stupid nor inexperienced, but I had lived for so many years as an independent agent that the idea of a legally sanctioned permanent relationship seemed as remote as the moon.

True, I had been married once, forty years ago, caught up in that mating instinct made up of love, desire, and the drive to establish oneself as independent from family. Today's young people appear quite content to remain under the parental roof indefinitely. Sometimes the reason is financial, but often I get the impression that a comfortable inertia prevents them from moving. To live alone means stocking the refrigerator and doing your own laundry. Young people of my generation, however, longed for independence. To use a then-current term, we wanted to untie the apron strings and look out for ourselves.

As soon as I graduated from law school, I married. To have a child was part of the package, and in due course I became the proud if bemused father of a baby girl. She entered my life, remained briefly, and died in the same accident that killed her mother. Had she lived she would now be a grown woman, possibly with children of her own, but I can scarcely remember her now. Grief fades, sorrow diminishes, and memory, at best unreliable, shifts or reorganizes events. Some moments remain bathed in light; others blur and overlap so that remembering becomes almost as much an act of faith as an effort of will.

What I do remember is embarking upon a brand-new phase of my life. Many of my parents' friends were widows, not surprising, as most of them had married men years older than they; but I was the only widower. To have been married and bereaved while still young is not without a certain glamour, and in certain circles I was kept under observation. Once a decent interval had elapsed I was bound to marry again. A lawyer who had married, fathered a child, and lost his family was a bullish stock on the marriage market, way back at a time when marriage really mattered. It seemed only a matter of time.

Instead the closet door swung open on noiseless hinges. Centrally heated, comfortably furnished, book lined, it was a closet I never fully left, which is another way of saying I did not flounce out, slamming the door behind me, announcing to the world at large that I was—what: gay? At the time few homosexual men were gay; rather they were morose, introverted, and dissatisfied with their lot. Not I. Shielded by my widowhood, my three-piece suits, and my natural diffidence, I ventured forth. It was a strange time, light years away from the accepting attitudes of the Nineties. Gay men no longer felt obliged to enter the priesthood or join the Foreign Legion, but they still turned up at public functions with dates. I solved the problem by avoiding public functions. I went to the office, did my work, and shed my suit after six. Chinos and a crew-necked sweater hardly add up to a radical outfit, but without a tie I felt almost reborn.

I had fooled around a bit before my marriage, both with boys and girls. To hit on girls was considered perfectly acceptable, laudable even, so long as one did not tear clothing or leave bruises. To fool around with boys was another story entirely, unquestionably unacceptable, and all the more alluring for being that. The young Frank Wilkinson had been the first boy I messed around with. Hungry as we were for sexual experience of any kind, we still had to pay lip service to the idea that, were the girls more readily available, we wouldn't have to resort to these secondary solutions. All cats are not gray in the dark, but we felt obliged to admit they were.

George Bernard Shaw once observed that marriage is popular because it combines the maximum of temptation with the maximum of opportunity. In my case it turned out to be true. Short marriages are frequently happy marriages; mine lasted under two years. There wasn't time for boredom or bickering, exasperation or emotional entropy. Susan and I were still in love when she died, so the love never ended. I know it is still there, like heirlooms in a vault, seldom visited but cherished nonetheless. And while it is easy to remember the results of an emotion, it is often difficult to recall the emotion itself.

Nevertheless I was still young, and after a decent interval of mourning I began to hear those jungle drums, softly at first, but increasingly steady in volume. One night I answered the call. Then again the next night, and the next. After three years of connubial fidelity I was ready to experiment.

I also had to learn a new set of rules. Raised on the code that a gentleman does not kiss and tell, I was astonished at the candour with which other homosexual men (the word "gay" had not yet become mainstream) discussed their sex lives. At times they sounded almost like engineers, with detailed dimensions, specific positions, performance statistics, and locations. I could never bring myself to share in this confessional mode. Knowledge is supposed to be power, but withholding information can also confer advantage.

Another notion that I had to reconsider was that of sexual fidelity. Such affairs, to use the word of an earlier generation, as I had experienced were all with women. Once an understanding had been reached that we were seeing one another, we both took for granted that we did not sleep around. The turnover may have been high, but for the duration of the relationship fidelity remained the rule.

Not so in the gay world, where fidelity defined itself as not being in bed with two people at the same time. A kind of flamboyant promiscuity was the rule. A promiscuous person has been defined as someone who sleeps with more people than you do. Whatever the measuring rod, the turnover in the gay subculture astonished me, although I turned out to be a quick and eager pupil. From time to time women entered the picture, if only briefly. By then I had learned to be a freewheeling agent, and I resented any attempts to circumscribe my activities. I did not want to account for time spent elsewhere. Engagements planned weeks in advance made me chafe. The affair seldom lasted more than a few weeks, and then it was back to the bars.

It was only after I finally fell in love—truly, madly, deeply —with another man that I realized I had crossed my own Rubicon. There was no turning back now. Although the relationship did not last—intensity ends by consuming itself—I understood that were I ever again to experience that incandescent feeling, it would never again be for a woman.

VII

Considering the quantities of scotch and wine Frank and I had put away the previous night, we ought to have been stretcher cases. I don't know whether to blame the bracing sea air or the sensation of being cut loose from my regular surroundings, but I felt merely slow, not wiped out, as I levered myself upright and went to the bathroom. After ringing for coffee, I crossed to part the curtains and check the weather.

"Is it worth getting out of bed?" asked Frank, sleep and whisky making his voice deep and foggy.

"Most definitely. The sun has burned away yesterday's haze."

"You know what they say," rumbled Frank. "Red sky in the morning, sailor's warning. Red hankie at night, sailor's delight."

"That's not quite the way I remembered it." I crossed to open the door for butler John, considerably less effusive now that I had gone over his head for the pillows and ashtray, mute testimony to his incompetence.

"Are you up to going down for breakfast," I asked as I handed Frank a cup of coffee.

"Thanks, and yes, I would like some breakfast. I feel better than I have any right to, but I still know last night happened." He lit a cigarette. "You don't mind, do you? My smoking so early."

"Not in the least. Remember, I grew up at a time when not to smoke branded me as odd. When I think for a moment of what we city dwellers breathe: diesel fumes, furnace exhaust, all those ventilating systems spewing noxious emissions—I don't worry about a little cigarette smoke."

"I wish there were more at home like you."

"I think perhaps one of us is enough. While you finish your coffee and cigarette why don't I shower."

I came out of the bathroom to find Frank studying the list of daily activities. "I'm worn out just reading about all the things we could be doing. Do you suppose "crafts" could teach me how to construct masks that won't get in the singers' way? I'm supposed to design an *Elektra* next year, and the director wants to do it as an authentic Greek tragedy, masks and all."

"Perhaps you could fashion the masks out of construction paper and pipe cleaners. I shouldn't imagine the "crafts" materials will be too adventurous."

"I suppose. My turn to shower," he said.

We rode the elevator down to the sparsely populated dining room. I suppose for many of the couples on board, those who had not brought their children, the chance to sleep late seemed more tempting than being served breakfast. Always an early riser, I relished the idea of breakfast without effort. This morning I ordered poached eggs on corned-beef hash, as foreign to my normal routine as baked stuffed yak. Frank compromised on ham and eggs.

Our irrepressible waiter wanted to know if we had slept well and whether we were going ashore. He seemed busier than he had been at breakfast yesterday, and I realized our moody busboy was not on the job.

"You seem to be all alone this morning," I observed.

"Gabor is sick."

"I hope it's nothing serious," I said, wondering if staff on ships ever suffered from motion sickness. Yet the ocean glimpsed through portholes seemed as calm as a pond.

"I don't think so. It sounds like bronchitis," he said as he refilled our coffee cups.

A cheery "Good morning!" caused us both to swivel around. Looking like a page from the Sears catalogue, Elsie walked briskly to the table. She wore a white pantsuit, in some sort of shiny, wrinkle-resistant fabric, over a fuchsia blouse, and managed to look what in an earlier time was called "cheap." Whatever happened to "cheap," one of those serviceable oxymorons having little or nothing to do with the amount of money spent. Looking cheap often required a considerable financial outlay. Those little bolero sweaters dotted with sequins, ankle-strap high-heeled sandals, or transparent plastic handbags did not come inexpensively. Unfortunately, cheap has been cheapened. Punk, grunge, counter-culture have wrenched cheap from manicurists, waitresses, and stenographers and thrust it into the limelight. Yet certain fabrics, styles, colours will never escape the imprimatur of cheap. Fuchsia, for example. Along with encouraging acceptable table manners and the correct use of irregular plurals, parents try to wean children away from fuchsia. Only a fuchsia bush can wear fuchsia. On anything else it looks cheap.

"Don't get up," she admonished us as, conditioned by our upbringing, we went through the motions of attempting to rise. I suppose standing when a lady joins the table is sexist, chauvinist, condescending, and all those other undesirable things; but early brainwashing dies hard. Without bothering to consult the menu Elsie ordered All Bran and a fruit plate with cottage cheese. By way of protest I broke the yolk of my second poached egg and let it run into the cholesterol-rich corned beef hash.

"And what do you two have planned for today?" she asked without preamble.

Frank and I exchanged a quick glance which telegraphed "You!" "No, you!"

"Nothing very energetic," I volunteered. "We may amble down the gangplank and shuffle into town. Are you planning to take an island tour?"

"Perhaps. I haven't bought my ticket yet, but it seems there is another minibus on standby. You didn't go to the show last night?"

"No. Frank went to the casino for a bit, and I turned in early. Sea air always knocks me out," I added, glossing over the fact I had drunk far more than I usually do.

"I brought my copy of *Hedda Gabler* along," admitted Elsie with a little laugh. "By the time I get back to Montreal I want to be line-perfect."

"Try to imagine yourself inside that woman's head," said Frank, speaking for the first time. "Then you will find a logic in what she says. One of the problems with untrained actors is that they fall out of character between speeches. You must be Thea Elvsted every second you are on stage, not Mrs. Elvsted one second and Elsie Connors the next."

"I'd never thought of it like that." Elsie almost laughed. "That will be such a help in memorizing all those lines." Her eyes shone with delight.

"I'm surprised the director didn't point that out," said Frank as he placed his knife and fork together.

"He spent so much time trying to get Audrey not to overdo that he didn't have much time for the rest of us." Elsie gave her tightly permed head a little toss.

"I venture to say. All set?" Frank asked me, code for "Let's get out of here."

"All set," I echoed. "Please excuse us, Elsie. We'll see you later."

We returned to the cabin to collect our bits and pieces for going ashore, sunglasses, guidebook, Frank's roll of duct tape, and a tote bag, then rode the elevator to the embarkation deck. Why was I not surprised to see Elsie loitering in the lobby, her white pantsuit an open invitation to spots and stains. On seeing us, she brightened perceptibly.

"Hasn't your tour left yet?" I inquired.

"I decided not to take the tour, bouncing around the island on a small bus. I think I'll just go into Bridgetown and do a bit of shopping. May I share your cab?"

What was there to say but yes. The cruise ships docked at some distance from the town itself, too far to walk, so the taxi ride was unavoidable. Our driver, inevitably, wanted to know where we were from. On learning we hailed from Canada he admitted to having a sister living in Montreal whom he visited annually. As evidence of his familiarity with our city, he recited a random list of landmarks: the Olympic Stadium, the Sun Life building, Place d'Armes, St. Joseph's Oratory, the Forum. This catalogue lasted for most of the drive into Bridgetown and spared the passengers any need to converse.

We disembarked on Broad Street and walked the short distance to Trafalgar Square, dominated by a statue to Lord Nelson.

"We have a monument to Lord Nelson in Montreal," said Elsie. "It does seem rather a waste to come all this distance to see another."

Frank ignored her and spoke to me. "Did you know that the Portuguese named the island Los Barbados, the Bearded Ones, because of the beard-like roots hanging from the fig trees? It says so right here in the guidebook."

"No, I didn't know that factoid," I replied. "Thank you for sharing it with me."

Frank and I broke into laughter; Elsie looked mystified but insisted on taking a photograph of Frank and me standing in front of Lord Nelson. We walked over to admire the Senate and the Assembly, handsome Victorian Gothic buildings, and ended up our walk at St. Michael's Cathedral. According to the guidebook the building has suffered repeated demolition and damage from hurricanes. The superstitious might argue that God is saying something about the Church of England in the Caribbean, but hurricanes are an occupational hazard of life in the tropics. Paradise has its price.

The cathedral sat in the middle of a small cemetery planted with trees and shrubs that hardly looked real, so vivid were the colours. No pastel pinks and lavenders, art deco greens and mauves, but brilliant, aniline hues that vibrated in the intense sunlight. I was glad to go indoors. In the cool semi-dark of the cathedral, Frank and I browsed our way down the side aisles and read some of the memorial tablets. Elsie looked as bored as she felt and spent most of the visit trying to remove a spot from the lapel of her suit with a Kleenex.

After inviting herself along on our excursion, Elsie had turned into ten thousand pounds of dead weight. Not even re-motely interested in sightseeing, she had gone into Bridgetown to shop, only to realize Frank and I were more interested in monuments and buildings than in producing our credit cards. Why she did not leave us to browse so she could shop her way down one side of Broad Street and up the other, I do not know. Plentiful taxis sat parked in the main square; returning to the ship with her purchases presented no problem. As a homosexual man, I have always guarded against female bashing, an easy pit-fall when in the company of bitchy queens. But the ineluctable fact remains that some women are silly and tiresome, and no amount of indulgent thinking can excuse them. Were Elsie really making a play for Frank, she could not have been showing herself in a worse light, with little huffs of impatience, a marked tendency to trail behind, and an evident lack of interest in what we were visiting.

I am certain that Elsie, like many on board the *Blue Horizon*, booked herself onto the cruise fully expecting to have a good time, almost as if Monarch Cruises issued guaranteed amusement vouchers to make them happen. Elsie had attached herself to Frank and me, and waited expectantly for one of us to wave a wand or murmur a spell that would cause the day to shimmer and the outing to sparkle. Uninterested in sight-seeing, unwilling to cut loose and shop, Elsie telegraphed her boredom to operators unwilling to pick up her signals.

As we emerged from the church, almost against my better judgement, I said out loud to no-one in particular, "I saw what looked like quite a good jewellery store on the main drag. I'd like to pick up something for Elinor."

Elsie almost jumped to attention, all traces of ennui and fatigue erased like marks from a blackboard. The prospect of shopping, furthermore for jewellery, had her almost dancing with delight. I had uttered the magic spell. We retraced our steps about a block and entered the handsome shop, one whose advertisements I had noticed in the guidebooks.

"What are you going to buy?" asked Elsie.

"Yes," added Frank, "after you have bought me the gold watch with matching bracelet that is."

"I had thought I might look at a gold chain for Elinor."

A young woman with skin like buckwheat honey inquired if she could help.

"I'd like to look at the anchor chain," I replied, pointing through the glass counter at a row of chains.

"Anchor chain?" she repeated.

"I think he means the Gucci chain," suggested Elsie.

"No, I mean the anchor chain, the second from the left."

"Oh, the Gucci chain," repeated the salesgirl with a smile.

I felt not unlike someone trapped in an echo chamber. "Look, I am referring to the chain which is a miniature copy of the great chains used to raise anchors on ocean liners, in the bad old days. The oversized links fitted onto a huge winch used to raise and lower the anchor. I don't know how or when Gucci got into the act, but the chain remains an anchor chain. End of lecture. How much?"

"There's a darling chain over here," said Elsie, examining the jewellery on display like a child studying penny candy, with little chirps of admiration. I moved over to look at a gold chain with intricately chasened links set with precious stones at two-inch intervals, a ruby, a sapphire, an emerald. "I'm sure Elinor would adore it," she added.

I was equally certain Elinor would not. The necklace was far too busy for her tailored style. Elsie herself loved a bit of glitter; many of her clothes featured sequins, bugle beads, jet appliqués, gold or silver trim.

"I don't think it really is Elinor's style," I said. "I think I'll take the other chain."

Elsie looked crestfallen. What was the point of bringing her along if we weren't going to follow her advice.

"If you like the jewelled chain that much," suggested Frank, "why don't you buy it for yourself as a souvenir of the cruise?"

"You know, I think I just might," exclaimed Elsie, her good humour quite restored. We paid for our respective purchases and the three of us left the shop.

"Now where shall we go?" asked Elsie, her appetite for shopping fully whetted.

"I'm about ready to go back to the ship," said Frank. "I'm having a bit of a sinker, courtesy of last night. We've seen the sights, and there's nothing I want to buy."

"Suits me," I said.

Visibly torn, Elsie did not want to let us out of her sight, nor was she ready to return to the ship and skip the shops. Fortunately for us, the shops won. We waved her off, then ducked into a liquor store where Frank duct-taped a mickey of scotch to each leg. We hailed a cab whose driver did not ask us where we were from.

"My god, she's a boring woman!" exclaimed Frank. "What are we going to do?"

"I don't know, short of being rude. And we are both victims of our upbringing, meaning we cannot be rude to someone like Elsie."

"I wouldn't bet on it. Is she going to spend the rest of the cruise waylaying us?"

"I hate to think so. I had not planned to spend my time on board sneaking about like a stowaway."

"You have to think of something, Geoff. You're older—and you're tall enough to be my father. She's enough to send me straight into the arms of a double martini."

"Gin-and-vermouth-to-mouth resuscitation?"

"You've used that line before."

"Perhaps, but not on you."

The taxi pulled to a stop at the gangplank. An officer in

white checked our tote bag, innocent of contraband. If Frank walked a little more carefully than usual, only his hairdresser would have known for sure.

I was beginning to feel more at home in the Blue Lagoon than in my cabin. We chose to drink in the bar, as we had both wanted a bloody mary and our contraband liquor was scotch. This time the bartender gave our table the evil eye, but he got the order right.

"Geoff, I hope I'm not keeping you from touring the island or going to a beach. You don't have to keep me company."

"Not to worry. I'm on holiday, and a holiday does not include visiting points of no interest because the tour has to last a certain amount of time. Were I to go to a beach I would have to sit in the shade. I burn in minutes. One doesn't come to the Caribbean to see the sights."

I was not simply being agreeable. The Caribbean islands are beautiful to many, but not to me. Tropical vegetation is vaguely alarming. Often it looks scruffy and tired, as though it had endured too many dry seasons and survived one too many hurricanes. So do the buildings, those that the passing visitor gets to see. Island cities look worn, bleached, unpainted, used up. Distance lends charm to poverty, but seen at close range most of the towns look derelict and depleted. Unfortunately, the casual visitor seldom gets to meet the middle class whose houses are secluded from day trippers pouring off the ships. There has to be grace and elegance, beautiful gardens and handsome rooms, where life continues in a tropical approximation of that lived in Canada by the people I know. How many visitors to Montreal get to meet only cab drivers, tour guides, hotel clerks, and those in the service industry. Travel is such hard work, I wonder at the numbers of people prepared to undertake the task.

"I can think of no place I would rather be at the moment," I said as if to underline the thought, "other than in my own apartment watching a travelogue on Barbados on the telly."

"Sounds good to me," said Frank. "We could go out to dinner by ourselves instead of buying wine for all those drearies at our table. And herself would be out with her own friends."

"By 'herself' you mean . . . ?"

"The very same. I feel if I say her name out loud we will be overwhelmed in bad luck, like uttering the name of the Scottish play in a theatre."

"There you are!" called Elsie as she bore down on our table.

"That didn't take you very long," I said, giving Frank a chance to rearrange his expression. "I thought you were going to put the Broad Street retail trade into the black."

"I went into a few shops," admitted Elsie, "but then I ran into a woman I knew from the ship. Her cabin is just down the hall from mine. She says it really pays to wait until we land in St. Thomas. There are wonderful bargains to be had, or so she says. So I decided to wait. I did buy a couple of blouses, though, a white silk with pearl appliqués on the collar. It's dreadfully impractical; I'll have to wash it by hand. But I just couldn't resist."

"I dislike buying clothes," said Frank. "The large is the message, and it's too depressing."

"Will you have a drink, Elsie?" I asked as the waiter had begun to hover.

"Perhaps a mineral water. I must have had too much sun, as I feel a bit flushed." Her fair skin did look pinkish, but Canadians recovering from a long, dark winter can burn quickly under a blazing tropical sun. It is possible that Else's unexpected arrival was good for our health, because by tacit agreement Frank and I decided against ordering a second bloody mary. Since we appeared to be stuck with Elsie, we might as well eat earlier and escape to the cabin. She told us she had enjoyed a very nice light lunch yesterday in the Coral Reef Café, but when we expressed a preference for the dining room, she decided to tag along.

I knew I couldn't very well ask her not to have lunch at her own table, but the subversive thought flashed through my mind. Elsie was one of those people who blocks the view. How much easier it would have been to deal with her had she been rude, or aggressive, or just plain bitchy. Instead she remained pleasant, bland, dull, a walking Hallmark card. She contributed nothing in the way of ideas or humour, stimulation or challenge; but her presence prevented Frank and me from talking with our customary candour. We turned out to be the only ones at our table to show up for lunch. Over the fish we all ordered, Elsie told us in some detail about her work with Meals on Wheels. Even as I admired her evident care and dedication to seeing that the old and immobile are decently fed, I found myself smothering yawns. Frank ate his sole amandine in sullen silence.

Elsie picked at her salmon without much interest, refused coffee, and finally excused herself to take a nap.

"I feel a little out of sorts, but a little sleepy-bye will set me up. The sun in town was terribly strong. Perhaps I'll see you later in the bar."

"Cocktails tonight in the cabin," announced Frank as soon as she was out of earshot.

"We'll drink to the duct tape," I said.

When I awoke from my nap, Frank still slept. I dressed quietly and went out on deck. A hugely overweight young woman in a snugly fitting one-piece bathing suit lay on the recliner she had occupied since this morning, reminding me of a wildlife program I had once watched on sea lions. Her skin glistened with sunblock, but under the sheen she had turned an ominous flamingo pink. As I looked up and down the rows of recliners, I could see an inverse ratio in operation: those most advised to shield their bodies from public scrutiny were the ones on display in abbreviated suits. Of girls who might be called foxy or men qualifying as hunks there was a dearth. No doubt they could be found on cruise ships less dedicated to family values.

For a while I leaned on the rail watching the wake. There was a lot of ocean out there. Perhaps I should have been meditating on my own insignificance in terms of the Grand Design; instead my thoughts turned to what I intended to do with the rest of my life. I had now been retired long enough for the sheen of novelty to have dulled. This is not to say I was bored with my retirement. On the contrary, I found the days flowing past at an astonishing rate. How had I ever found time to go to the office? I loved not having to rush in the morning, to linger over coffee and the newspapers. Three mornings a week I went to my health club for a workout aimed more at keeping me mobile than turning me into a poster boy. Often I met friends for lunch, a pleasant way to visit. Unlike dinner, which can drag on into the late evening, lunch is not open-ended: an hour and a half, perhaps even two before the claims of the afternoon intrude.

What greater pleasure than to rent a movie for home viewing, far from the madding crowd, the talking patrons, the uncomfortable seats above floors sticky with spilled drinks and crunchy with discarded popcorn. How pleasant to press the Pause button in order to answer the phone, take a pee, get a drink. I still buy the books I want to read, meaning they are always at hand. Most evenings I hang out with Elinor, either going to her house for dinner or inviting her to my apartment for one of the dozen or so recipes I can prepare without tears. We have started going to the symphony, the opera, on occasion to the theatre. The last few weeks had been absorbed by *Hedda Gabler*, a charitable project only if one considers stroking Audrey Crawford's ego an act of selfless dedication.

I am old enough to have been raised in the belief that citizens enjoying good fortune owed something to the community. Today people declaim in strident tones about their rights, but with these same rights come responsibilities. Could I in all conscience continue to drift through a succession of days with no higher aim than to keep myself amused? I knew the answer to be a resounding no, at the same time shrinking inwardly at the idea of giving up whole afternoons to meetings. Another inverse ratio is that the more worthwhile the cause, the less efficient the people in charge. I have worked on more than one committee endorsing a platform of making our imperfect world a better place. Meetings turn not into occasions to transact business but opportunities to promote one's image as a committed human being, to air grievances, often at length, to lobby for better habits of mental health and positive thinking, or, on occasion, to volunteer a recipe for bread and butter pickles. At the time I took consolation from the idea that, in order to attend the meeting, I was out of the office. Now were I to volunteer or be solicited into worthy work, I would be doing so on my own time and giving up one of those delightful leisure activities which pass the hours so pleasantly. Had my father been alive, he would have chided me for my selfishness. He would probably have been right, but I am now older than he was when he died. Nostalgia is not history, but the world today is a different place from the one in which I grew up. Whatever the answer I sought, it was not to be found in the turbulent water off the stern of the ship.

When Frank awoke he rang for tea. To our surprise the tray was delivered by Gisela, the young woman who made up the cabins in the morning. In heavily accented English she explained that John was sick. Groping unsuccessfully for the word in English, she fished out "la grippe."

"Flu?" I repeated.

"Yes," she confirmed, and withdrew.

"I guess that is what felled our busboy," suggested Frank. "The waiter said bronchitis, but in the early stages who's to know?"

"Have you had a flu shot?" I asked. "I have one every year."

"I'm not old enough." Frank struggled to keep his face straight. "Flu shots are for the elderly."

"Fuck you too, dearie."

"You have filled my tea with lumps of sugar, and though I asked most distinctly for bread and butter, you have given me cake. I am known for the gentleness of my disposition, and the extraordinary sweetness of my nature, but I warn you, Mr. Chadwick, you may go too far."

"Well get you, Gwendolyn." We both broke into laughter.

"*The Importance of Being Earnest* was one of the first plays I ever designed." said Frank. "It has become part of my collective unconscious. I think I'll take a turn on deck. The ship is about to sail. Want to come?"

"Sailing is no big deal. No raising of anchors, or tugs, or streamers, or photographers. They unhitch the hawsers, winch them up, start the engines, and away we go. It's about as exciting as taking a bus. While you're out I'll change for dinner."

Unwilling to risk running into Elsie, Frank and I had a drink in our cabin. Although I would not have bothered to smuggle liquor on board I still found an almost adolescent delight in pulling a fast one on Monarch Cruises.

"I had one of those random flashbacks on deck," began Frank after lighting a cigarette. "Do you remember Adam Evans?"

"Do I not. Many an evening of wink, wink; nudge, nudge."

"You too, eh? I think almost every curious adolescent boy in Montreal had a go at Adam. Talk about naive enthusiasm. You didn't even have to ask. Is he still with us, or did he succumb, like so many generous people we once knew?"

"Not at all. He married and moved to Toronto. Took over the family business when his father-in-law retired. He has five children and an undetermined number of grandchildren. He has also aged wonderfully. That Raphael cherub look has given way to a kind of Giotto austerity."

Frank poured us both another drink. "There is a moral to be drawn. Not everyone who plays around as a youth comes to a bad end. Did your parents actively discourage sex, even with girls?"

"Not really," I replied. "The subject was never brought up, always skirted. There were never any *dos* and *don'ts*. Instructions or injunctions would have acknowledged that sexuality existed. Like most enterprising children I learned about sex in the gutter, and then from compliant friends."

"By far the best way. You didn't have to worry about going

insane, or hair and warts on your palms. If my mother only knew what I did with her hot water bottle and cold cream."

"He's engaged; he's lovely; he uses Ponds?"

"Not quite. Shall we have another small one before we go down to dinner?"

"Why not?"

By the time we made our way down to the dining room Susan, Darlene, and Brad were already seated; but Elsie had not yet come in. The wine waiter, hoping for a repeat of last night, hurried over to take our order, in this instance two scotches, water on the side.

"Did you have a pleasant day in Barbados?" I asked to cover the fact that neither Frank nor I was buying wine for the table.

"We went shopping," volunteered Darlene, "but I found the prices high. We were told there were terrific bargains to be had in the Caribbean, but most of the stores we visited were a real rip-off."

"Most people on vacation shop for luxury items," said Frank. "Naturally they will find prices high. How much perfume or jewellery, how many watches or evening blouses do you buy in any six-month period at home?"

The calm voice of common sense brought silence. "How was your day, Susan?" I asked.

She shrugged golden shoulders, exposed by a sleeveless dress.

"I went on an island tour with my aunt and uncle. There isn't very much to see. I wanted to go shopping, but they want to wait for St. Thomas." Nobody at the table could be in any doubt that Susan believed herself hard done by. How someone so young and beautiful could radiate such negativity escaped me.

"I wonder what happened to Elsie," said Darlene. "She's usually the first down here."

Our drinks arrived and I signed the bill. "I have no idea. The three of us had lunch today. She was feeling a bit out of sorts but claimed all she needed was a nap."

"Maybe she decided to eat in the cafeteria," suggested Brad, stretching himself in a muscle shirt that showed off a once good body going to seed.

"Somehow I doubt that," said Frank. "Why stand in line with a tray when you can be properly served at a table?"

There was one advantage to having our busboy laid off; the waiter had extra work, meaning he was not at liberty to cross-examine us about our day ashore. We ate the unremarkable food served with great flourish and made talk so small it could have been pushed through a sieve. Susan continued to impress me as petulant and none too bright. The heavily made up Darlene still turned the full blaze of her attention onto Brad who, my gut instinct told me, had already begun to lose interest. Some women never learn that a little reserve is a powerful weapon in the war.

The most remarkable feature of the meal was the absence of Elsie. For the first time since finding her on board I was almost sorry she was not present. Elsie would have helped to carry Susan, Darlene, and Brad through soup, entree, main course, salad, and dessert. Our table mates made uphill work; but to be fair—a vastly overrated virtue—I could well imagine the other three found Frank and me off-putting. We were older and sure of ourselves. We had no interest in sports and little in shopping. We had never been to Disney World, and we did not surf the Net. We were not on a first name basis with characters in TV sitcoms, but we had both been to the National Gallery in

Washington. We decided against being campy, and the subjects we enjoyed discussing would have branded us as nerds, snots, dorks, and worse. Elsie was proficient at chatter without content, and for the first time she was missed.

Frank had more of a sweet tooth than I. While he tucked into a pastry topped with glazed strawberries I indulged myself with the excellent Stilton. We did not tarry once we had finished. In that patently insincere fashion, to which we had both been raised, we said we hoped we would see everyone later, and fled. As we rode the elevator to the upper deck, I asked Frank whether we should perhaps check on Elsie. It struck me as odd that she would skip dinner, with "the two most attractive men in Montreal," as we had been billed.

"If anyone is going to telephone her cabin, I would prefer it be you," said Frank. "She knows about you and Elinor. I don't want to appear too solicitous, for obvious reasons."

"Understandably. But if I'm going to make a solicitous inquiry I could use a little of our contraband scotch, as a digestif."

Suitably fortified, I asked the switchboard to connect me with Mrs. Connors' cabin. The phone rang three times before Elsie picked it up. "Hello?" she said in a voice thick with sleep.

"Elsie, it's Geoffry. You weren't at dinner, and we wondered if you were all right."

"Dinner? Did I miss dinner? What time is it?"

"Twenty minutes to ten. Are you not feeling well?"

"Not really. If I didn't know better I'd say I had the flu."

"I understand a few people on board have come down with it. Is there anything you want or need? Aspirin? Tylenol? 222s?"

"No, I have all that. If I want anything I'll ring for the cabin steward."

"He'll bring you a tray, if you are hungry."

"I don't feel the least like eating, only like going back to sleep."

"Then I won't drag this out. If there is anything we can do, anything at all, just give us a call. If we are not in the cabin, then leave a message with the switchboard. I'll check. We both hope you'll be feeling better tomorrow."

"Thanks for calling, Geoffry. Goodnight."

I hung up. "I guess you could figure out from the conversation that Elsie has the flu."

Frank moved to stand in front of the window, his back to me as he looked into a void. We did not speak. Had God looked into my soul at that moment He would not have been pleased. Much as I would not have wished illness on Elsie, or anyone else for that matter, the problem of how to deal with her had been solved. A dire solution, granted, but she would not be waiting to waylay us tomorrow morning as we set out to explore Martinique. We could drink in the bar without her smothering, tea-cosy presence, her awful niceness. In spite of the full realization that her vacation was being spoiled by sickness, I experienced an intense, almost feral feeling of relief. I could only hope the Deity had his eye on the sparrow and not on Frank and me.

"Evil creature!" exclaimed Frank without turning around.

"Why do you say that?" I asked, fully aware what the answer would be.

"Because I know without having to be told that you are thinking what I am thinking. This calls for a penitential drink, in the bar, on me."

"I will flagellate myself with the swizzle stick," I said. "Lead on!"

VIII

No quality is more difficult to define than charm, but you know when it is there. More than perhaps any other Caribbean island, Martinique has charm to spare. Possibly it springs from the feeling that Fort-de-France, with its rusting iron balustrades and faded pastel facades, is less a Caribbean port city than a slightly raffish suburb of Paris, one that is not on the standard tourist itinerary. The island itself, although small, rises abruptly in almost theatrical fashion to volcanic mountain peaks, lush and vaguely forbidding. Someone once told me at a cocktail party that Martinique harbours the fer-de-lance, a snake whose venom is so lethal the only cure is to amputate the afflicted limb to prevent poison from spreading throughout the body. Far away, in that northern living room, I felt a little *frisson*; however, as Frank and I had decided to limit ourselves to exploring the town on foot, I believed we were in no real danger.

The day promised much. I opened the curtains to a travel-poster view of the harbour and, to the right, the weather-beaten ochre fort which gives the small city its name. Coffee arrived on a tray carried by Gisela, who looked short on sleep. She explained that many of the service staff had come down with flu, leaving the healthy ones to work double shifts. After she left, Frank propped himself up in bed. I could not help admiring his well-developed torso, a result of genes, not exercise. Perhaps my slight envy could be traced back to those advertisements I used to read as a child about Charles Atlas and dynamic tension. According to a cartoon strip incorporated into the layout, the young Charles, at the time a 97-pound weakling, was lying on a beach with his girlfriend, minding his own business, when an older, heavier bully kicked sand into his face and decamped with the girl. The angry and humiliated Charles then practiced dynamic tension, isometric exercises by any other name, until he had filled out to the point where he was able to fell the sand-kicking bully with a single punch accompanied by a "Take that!" in the speech balloon. Whether or not he reclaimed the girl was never made clear, but she was evidently not the kind of woman to stand by her man. My own problem with the Charles Atlas fantasy was that most of the people I wanted to bring down with a single punch were not older teenaged bullies but fully grown adults, foremost among whom was my algebra teacher. Algebra has nothing to do with real life, as any thirteen-year-old is eager to point out. But children of my generation did not punch out adults, regardless of how much metaphorical sand was kicked in our faces. Now I go to my health club and pump iron, not so I can knock down bullies but mainly to keep breathing. And since I never spend time on the beach, the chances of anyone kicking sand in my face are slight, those of trying to steal my girl nonexistent.

As I had been asleep last night when Frank came into the cabin, I asked him how he had fared at the casino.

"Thirty dollars to the good, to be spent on contraband booze. What did you do while I was gambling recklessly?"

"I watched the closed-circuit movie until I fell asleep. Before that I read a not very illuminating guidebook on the islands. I learned that Martinique is part of France, so that the monetary unit is the franc; but, not surprisingly, shops will accept U.S. dollars. The languages are Creole and French, the religion Roman Catholic, and the major products are sugar cane, cocoa, bananas, coffee, rum, and sugar. Should I strike up a conversation on shore, I will be in a position to ask informed, intelligent questions, like, 'How many francs were you paid for your last load of bananas?'"

"How to be the life of the party, or the guided tour. Do you suppose we ought to check in on Elsie?"

"I thought I would call after breakfast. She may still be asleep."

Once again Frank and I were the only ones at our table to show up for breakfast, so our chatty waiter was able to tell us that a quarter of the crew had succumbed to flu; furthermore, the ship's doctor was one of the most seriously ill, with a soaring fever and all the classic symptoms of aches and chills. As I ate my cheese and ham omelette I could only hope my flu shot had kicked in. A ship offers a perfect environment for spreading illness, what with many people in close contact and an air conditioning system that instantly chills any passenger coming inside from the hot, moist, tropical air. I did not want to consider the ventilation system and its potential for recycling virus and what my mother would have called "germs."

Short of abandoning ship, there was little we could do other than hope the infection would pass us by. After eating we returned to the cabin, where I telephoned Elsie. A wan voice came onto the line sounding as if it came from another continent. She was running a temperature and wanted nothing more than to be left alone. The cabin steward had brought her bottled water, and as soon as she felt up to eating something she would take aspirin to help lower her temperature. No, there wasn't anything she needed. After promising to call back later in the day I relayed her condition to Frank. Since there was nothing for us to do at the moment, we prepared to go ashore.

Downtown Fort-de-France lay close to the pier, and soon we entered what looked like the main avenue, where an open air market was in progress. Local women spoke among themselves in a language I could not understand, but to my surprise I asked a question in French and received an intelligible reply. Merchandise was suitably miscellaneous. Not interested in lengths of fabric, fresh vegetables, straw boaters made of stamped plastic, or unmatched plates and cups, I purchased a small oil lamp made from a tin can. All it lacked was a wick. Skilfully shaped and soldered by a local tinsmith, it spoke of a community where electrical power is expensive and limited to the more thickly settled areas. Caribbean islands do not blaze with light after sundown.

When the woman in the market asked five dollars for the lamp, she may well have expected me to bargain. It is hardly necessary to point out that bargaining is as foreign to my nature as robbing banks, and without a murmur I took a five dollar bill from my pocket.

"You could have had it for less," whispered Frank as we moved away. "Come to think of it, I could get you a very good deal on the Brooklyn Bridge."

"Thanks, but I bought the Olympic Stadium before I left Montreal."

"Why did you buy a lamp, an oil lamp at that? Are you expecting a power failure when you get home? I keep a flashlight handy, myself."

"My dear Frank, you may go to Hell. Go directly to Hell. Do not pass Go, and so forth."

While we were both laughing Frank, bent down to pick a coin from the cracked sidewalk. "You may not have collected two hundred dollars, but you now have five centimes. This coin will bring you luck."

The tiny brass disc, smaller than a dime, came with impeccable French credentials: the words "*République Française*" flanking a heroic female profile on one side, while on the other "*Liberté, Égalité, Fraternité*" unfurled themselves above "5 Centimes." I felt that between my locally fashioned lamp and the coin, fallen from the purse or pocket of an inhabitant, I had two souvenirs of unimpeachable authenticity. Now to collect some impressions.

Somehow Fort-de-France managed to carry off its air of jaunty seediness with panache. I found the people to be the most handsome I had yet seen. The younger ones dressed with style. Young men had swagger, young women a luminous beauty. And I had reached the comfortable age when I could look with admiration, nothing more. Frank and I set off to visit the Romanesque cathedral, after which we looked in on the archaeological museum, a kind of national attic. Next we stopped to admire the Bibliothèque Schoelcher, with its ornate iron-and-tile facade, named in honour of the French abolitionist. A short walk brought us back to the market where I had bought my lamp.

As we were not yet ready to return to the ship, we headed off down the wide street which had the look of a principal thoroughfare. Both Frank and I watched our footing carefully as we negotiated the heaving sidewalk. We crossed a side street and saw to our right a walled enclosure whose main gate was casually locked with a heart-shaped padlock hanging from a length of rusted chain. The place looked like a cemetery, but unlike any other I had ever seen. Following the wall to the left we discovered a small doorway which, with only slight hesitation, we used to enter the walled space.

"I don't think we're in Kansas anymore," was all I could think of saying. I have not thought a great deal about cemeteries, but I tend to visualize them as green spaces, more than gardens, less than parks, with grass and flowers surrounding the graves. What I saw was row upon row of white-tiled mausoleums laid out in avenues. Had the Seven Dwarfs built a town to their scale, it might well have resembled this unusual place. I thought it strange and wonderful, a celebration of death. In front of several of the low, rectangular buildings, vases of plastic flowers had been placed, or low pots of ceramic blooms, like those found in cemeteries in France. We stood in a walled village, no two dwellings alike. Some had windows through which one could glimpse a concrete sarcophagus; others were set off by low wrought-iron fences; still others held shrines. The overall effect was surprisingly cheerful, as though the people buried there had not really left but only moved onto a different level of existence.

As we strolled toward the far end of the deserted main avenue, Frank put his hand on my shoulder. I was intensely aware of the gesture, not that I minded, but neither Frank nor I are touchy-feely. For just that reason the physical contact had a resonance. It was not the casual back-slapping, ass-grabbing horseplay of the locker room. Nor was it a sexual touch, but still a communication that went beyond words, a kind of affirmation. It was also no more than a friend putting his hand on my shoulder. "I don't think I'd mind spending eternity in a place like this," he said with a smile. "We northerners make death into something so solemn—limestone, granite, marble, basalt. This is the spot where the body is buried. Here it feels as though the dead are merely resting."

"Waiting for the Resurrection?"

"Perhaps. Now that's a production I'd like to costume!" He lifted his hand from my shoulder; I felt equally conscious of the broken contact.

"I don't think it matters much," I said. "Once I have fallen off the twig I don't much care what happens. Graves are for the living."

"So is life—to coin a phrase." Frank gave a suggestive wink.

"The depth of your perceptions continues to astonish me."

"I would say something very rude, were it not for the sanctity of the place." He glanced down the avenue. "Uh-oh! Here comes Middle America."

A couple had rounded the corner from one of the side avenues. I recognized them from the ship.

"Bad news," muttered Frank. "I've seen them in action at the casino."

The unexpected meeting compelled us into speech. After the orthodox greetings, spoken words invading the still, warm air, Frank and I stood with the slight awkwardness which springs from an urge to move away coupled with an equally strong urge not to appear rude. The woman insisted on learning where we were from, expressed amazement at our being Canadian, then volunteered Idaho as her domicile.

"What is Canada really like?" she asked, her remark prompted not by the desire for a response but a wish to show she came in peace.

"Canada is knowing where your wallet is," I replied.

She laughed, a high-pitched laugh through shiny squirrel facelift cheeks, before looking around like someone in a silent movie. "Doesn't this place give you the creeps?" she asked.

"Not in the least," I replied, at the same time wondering why a woman with saddlebag thighs would wear madras Bermuda shorts. "I feel wonderfully at ease here. Death is a benign presence, embraced rather than rejected."

"I suppose," she said, looking dubiously around through sunglasses with rhinestones on the temples.

The husband, bald, paunchy, and surprisingly handsome, spoke. "We were thinking of hailing a cab for a tour of the island. Would you folks care to join us? Fifty-fifty shouldn't set us back too much."

"That sounds delightful," replied Frank without skipping a beat, "but we're meeting friends for a drink on the ship before lunch." He stole a tactful glance at his watch, then at me. "Perhaps we should think about getting back."

"Enjoy your tour," I added, "and stay out of the woods. Some of the fauna is unfriendly."

We moved away. "Nicely done," I whispered once we were out of earshot.

"Time off for good behaviour. Do you want to stroll through the botanical gardens? Explore the old fort?"

"We have wonderful botanical gardens in Montreal. And I once visited the fort in Puerto Rico. Forts are like football fields; you've seen one, you've seen 'em all."

"Come to think of it," he said, "a bloody mary and a little lunch doesn't sound half bad."

"I have my lamp, my coin. We've seen the major sights, I'm awash in sensations, and I'm more than ready for that drink."

We did not tarry in returning to the ship.

The Blue Lagoon sat empty except for one party at the far side of the room in the nonsmoking section. Frank and I ordered our usual bloody marys. Frank lit a cigarette; I reached for a handful of salted peanuts. There had been no message from Elsie, and I did not want to wake her with an importunate call.

"If I say out loud that this is very pleasant," Frank inhaled deeply, "will God punish me by sending a hurricane?"

"I seriously doubt it. I don't think God is nearly so mean-spirited as He is often made out to be. Careless perhaps, but not malevolent."

"I'm sure He welcomes your endorsement. Did you acquire your theology from the Internet?"

"No, fortune cookies. I am privy to the accumulated wisdom of the mysterious East."

"Like I was saying," continued Frank, "today is the first day I feel as if I were on holiday. Are you sorry we didn't tour the island with the couple we met at the cemetery?"

"My heart leaps down at the very idea. We would have been at their mercy for the entire outing. I fear we would have learned more about Idaho than either of us wants to know."

Frank reached for a handful of peanuts. "Have you noticed how as you age you fine-tune your antenna—antennae? My take on that woman is that she would have told you all about her family, and especially about the prettier younger sister who was their parents' favourite. He would have steered me aside for some serious jock talk, business, sports, politics. I'll bet you a zircon against a diamond that he is a Republican, somewhere to the right of Genghis Kahn, and that a couple of times a month he takes his secretary to a motel where they do a number of things he'd never dare suggest to his wife."

I laughed into my ice cubes. "But you have to admit we are

meeting new people and enlarging our horizons. Pity we have only a couple more days. Tomorrow, Antigua, Friday, St. Thomas, Saturday, home. The cruise should be longer—but never look a gift horse in the ticket, or is it a gift cruise in the mouth?"

"Sounds dirty. Let's change the subject. In Antigua do I have to fumble in French, or can I trot out my refried Spanish?"

"English will do, I think, especially if backed up by the American dollar. But don't count on it. I haven't read up on Antigua yet in my guidebook."

"I had sort of planned to take a cruise this past winter," began Frank. From the change in his tone I knew he had switched gears. "There was a man—" He twisted one corner of his mouth to suggest things had not worked out. "I actually believed I had latched on to something permanent. As you can imagine, my kind of life—always on the move—makes establishing something lasting very difficult. While I was younger I enjoyed the high rate of turnover, but it began to pall during the middle years. Then I met this man in San Francisco, Clifford—he insisted on being called Cliff—married, with three children in high school and college. The arrangement suited us both. I was never around long enough to be importunate, and I knew where he was when I was out of town." Frank paused to butt out.

"We had an agreement: once the children were launched, he was going to ask his wife for a divorce. It was going to be a tough call, but he had every intention of providing for her." Frank lit a fresh cigarette. "Am I boring you with my soap opera saga: *The Old and the Feckless?*"

"Not in the least."

"Well, to continue: the youngest graduated this past fall, right into a sweetheart job. And guess what? His wife mixes up a pitcher of martinis, asks him to sit down, and announces she is leaving him. It seems she has found another man, bags of money, so she doesn't want alimony, only an amiable separation so they can be parents to the children."

"Sounds too much like a fake happy ending. I fear the worst."

"And rightly so. No sooner had his wife moved out than Cliff went off like a champagne cork. Exploded out of the closet and tried making up for all those wasted years: bars, baths, parks, tearooms—you name it."

"How did you find out?" I asked.

"I had my doubts, so I hired a detective. The poor guy was out of breath just trying to keep up. Aside from a considerable blow to my ego, that kind of behaviour puts everyone at risk. I had no idea whether or not Cliff was playing it safe. I doubt it. In some ways he was pretty naive. You can't catch up in your fifties for what you should have done in your twenties, but he gave it the old college try. Plus he had not, like so many of us, seen friends die before we fully realized the gravity of the plague. We have reached the point where fidelity is no longer a romantic ideal but a survival strategy."

"I take it you gave him the heave."

"Did I not. He was so besotted with his newfound freedom he hardly noticed. What I found myself missing is not the man himself—how could I have shown such poor judgement? – but the relationship, the anchor, the promise of stability. We are both losers. I'm just too old to begin again, and he will probably kill himself by picking up a virus during an unguarded moment. What a waste."

During the pause that followed, I signalled for two more drinks.

Frank butted the cigarette he had neglected to smoke. "My

problem, if such it could be called, is that I am not a chicken queen. I'm not interested in people half my age or younger, with their invincible egos, their limited experience, their easy certainties, their unswerving belief that there is a solution to every problem, a pill or a shot to cure every illness, and their unshakable conviction that things have to get better. Just try as a gay man over sixty to meet someone reasonable your own age: impossible!"

"I have to confess I haven't tried recently. But sometimes I glance at the personal ads: 'Men seeking men.' Forty seems to be the cutoff point—and the forty-year-olds are seeking eighteen-year-olds who, it goes without saying, like long walks, classical music, good books, who don't do drugs and are not into the bar scene. Not very promising for the over-sixty set."

Frank gave a short laugh. "You've got it. Even were I not travelling a good deal of the time, San Francisco—the entire state of California—is hooked on youth. Unfortunately I lack your renewable resources of heterosexuality. I fear I shall remain gay."

"Better gay than grumpy! But to a more serious topic. Are we going to the Captain's cocktail party this afternoon?"

"I didn't know he was having one. Are we invited?"

"The invitation was left in the cabin last night while we were at dinner. I left it out for you to see, but forgot to mention it. Anyway, five to seven, in the Golden Grotto; that's the nightclub. That's also where mass is said in the early morning and the crafts classes are held. Dress semi-formal, which on this ship means wearing shoes."

Frank gave a shrug. "I don't see why not. Let's grab all the freebies we can. Have you any idea why we are so honoured?"

"My guess is that whoever donated the cruise tickets for the raffle wants the winners to get the V.I.P. treatment: the good cabin, the fruit basket, the personalized stationery, and a couple of free drinks."

"I am quite underwhelmed. Shall we have some lunch? I confess I feel a bit bushwhacked and I would like a sleep before the Captain's *son et lumières*."

I signalled for the check.

Anyone in retirement who does not nap in the afternoon is squandering one of the main prerogatives of that enviable state. How many afternoons in my office did I feel myself on the verge of nodding off. On occasion I would ask my secretary to hold calls, allowing me to doze at my desk, my head resting on folded arms. Twenty minutes, and I awoke feeling as though I could move mountains, not that I wanted to. Weekends were invented for napping, and I often fibbed my way out of afternoon engagements in order to indulge my not-so-secret vice. Here on the *Blue Horizon*, adrift on the glassy sea, I felt it would be almost immoral not to sleep the afternoon away.

I awoke before Frank. His breathing sounded so deep and regular I went into the bathroom and used the extension to call Elsie's cabin. Although awake, she sounded as though she had just floated up from a coma, her voice faint and breathy.

"I hate to hound you, Elsie, but you are on my mind. Is there anything, anything at all I can do?"

"Not at the moment thanks, Geoffry."

I felt certain that one day God would get me for the involuntary rush of relief that surged through me. "Are you running a temperature?" I tried to sound solicitous.

"Yes, but aspirin has brought it down a bit. I just feel so

weak and washed out. All I want to do is sleep."

"That's by far the best thing for you at the moment." I tried to sound at once businesslike and caring. "Now if you want me for anything, anything at all, just leave a message."

"You're a lamb, Geoffry, but I don't need anything at the moment."

"I'll check in tomorrow unless I hear from you."

I hung up, then rang for tea.

Much as we may try, we never fully shake off the early conditioning that masquerades as upbringing. Without ever hearing anything specific said on the subject, I still managed to absorb the attitude that illness was bad manners. My parents, both of whom enjoyed excellent health, felt almost apologetic about catching cold or suffering from gastroenteritis, dismissed as the collywobbles. A headache would always pass, a cut or a bruise was nothing, and a fall on an icy sidewalk was dismissed as stupid clumsiness. Women were predictably struck down by the curse, but this evidently taboo malaise remained shrouded in secrecy. Major surgery and childbirth passed muster as acceptable afflictions; but anything that obliged children to be kept in quarantine—measles, chicken pox, scarlet fever—was seen as a huge inconvenience to be blamed on someone or something else: careless schools, feckless parents, or those old standbys, dirty towels and toilet seats.

Fortunately, I moved beyond the strictures of childhood, yet I have never felt comfortable around the sick. Early attitudes aside, I am not by nature a caregiver. I lack those vast resources of unemployed kindness that find fulfillment in plumping up pillows and serving meals on a tray. Other people's aches and pains leave me incurious as to their cause. When learning of a recent death I do not press for details of the final moments. "Cancer" tells me all I want to know, more than willing as I am to forego details of what kind, the rigours of treatment, and the final exit.

On occasion I have reflected on whether I am not a caring person. Did I fail to inherit a compassion gene, the one that sets alarm bells ringing at the faintest hint of illness? All I can offer by way of defence is that whenever I am sick, for whatever reason, I want to be left alone. Spare me the pillow plumpers, the poached eggs, garnished with parsley and a slice of orange, on a tray. Bar the door against those bearing candy, cookies, thrillers whose spines have begun to crack, and pots of yellow mums. Bright, brittle, bedside chatter does not cheer me up, and I do not wish to be told to my gaunt, unshaven face that I am looking marvellous. Perhaps it is not the ill who should be chided but those who attempt to carry the lamp. One Florence Nightingale is enough.

When the tea arrived I decided to wake Frank, as he wanted to be on time for the captain's cocktail party. We could certainly afford all the drinks we wanted, but Frank considered it almost a duty to drink the captain's liquor. At first he resisted my gentle shaking, pulling the covers over his head and turning toward the wall.

"Are you prepared to pass on the free drinks?" I asked in a low but penetrating voice. By way of reply he grunted, rolled over, sat up. I handed him a cup of tea, which prevented him from lying down again.

"Whew, did I ever sleep. I think I had dreams. Perhaps I'll take a shower to wake myself up. I want to be alert for the social event of the cruise."

Resplendent in white uniform, the imperiously handsome captain greeted us with a handshake as we entered the Golden Grotto, a bit tawdry and strident in the uncompromising light of a tropical afternoon. Gold was the order of the day, from the epaulettes, bars, and buttons on the captain's uniform to the golden chandeliers and mirrored glass behind the bar. Lesser amounts of gold twinkled from the uniforms of the junior officers flanking the captain, all but eclipsed by his condescending grandeur. He reminded me of all the headwaiters in the world. A refreshingly tacky note was provided by the activities hostess, a raddled blond who had been around the track. Flinging one arm around my shoulders, the other over Frank's, she corkscrewed her body sideways and smiled the *Blue Horizon* smile while the ship's photographer snapped a picture. As quickly as we had been embraced we were shunted to one side to make room for the next guests, while we blinked our eyes to dissolve the purple dots from the flash.

Waiters stood about holding trays of champagne flutes.

"Screw this," whispered Frank. "I want a real drink."

On the far side of the room I spotted our perky waitress from the Blue Lagoon, the one with the ponytail. Intercepting her with a smile, I asked if it was possible to order something besides champagne.

"Certainly, if you would prefer something else," she replied. Most of the guests had bought into the universal myth that champagne is the dream drink. After requesting two double Black Labels on the rocks, Frank and I looked about for a place to sit.

We found a banquette for two with a view of the dance floor. A small orchestra played dance music from long ago, foxtrots and sambas, waltzes and tangos. I felt as if I were in a time warp, the bandbox-fresh but still gaudy decor, the nightclub ambiance, the music to which I had danced at college. In summer blazers and ties Frank and I had hit the middle level of dress, which ranged from shorts and thong sandals to business suits.

People stood around or sat in pairs and small groups. Nobody mingled. The hostess was far too busy hustling business for the photographer to make introductions. Rather than bringing passengers together, the atmosphere of fake friendliness kept people apart. Couples who would have fallen easily into conversation on deck stood holding their champagne flutes like shields, stricken with shyness.

One couple danced, a white-haired man in a pearl-gray suit and a woman who must have been his second, trophy wife. She wore a strapless lace cocktail dress with a stripe of white skin over each shoulder where the straps of her sundress or bathing suit had blocked tanning. The couple had obviously studied ballroom dancing, as they spun around the floor with silent concentration demonstrating all the steps worked out in dance class. Her *pièce de résistance* was to circle slowly under his outstretched arm, at the same time extending her unengaged arm in a kind of ersatz arabesque. Their dancing was free of joy, or humour, or sexual tension; but they refused to quit, changing steps with the music, she turning under his arm while extending her own with all the spontaneity of a church procession. It was enough to make Frank and me order another drink.

"I hope you can stand the excitement." Frank reached for the ashtray.

"Barely. The scotch helps. Better than Prozac, or so I've been told."

"What's your take on the captain? Think he might come across?"

"Possibly, but not on board his ship. Celibacy is strength. The minute you start sleeping with underlings—and that includes the passengers—you lose face. And our captain is far too grand to fool around. Also I hate to think of him having a bit of slap and tickle while the ship ran aground on a reef or a sandbar. With gold braid comes responsibility."

"Not the way I use it." Frank laughed. "I once did a production of *The Daughter of the Regiment*, and the gold braid cost more than the orchestra. I exaggerate, but it was a beautiful production, every way but musically. Still, you can't have everything."

"I suppose not. Lo, our ponytailed angel of mercy draws nigh. Shall we throw caution to the winds and order another?"

"Why not. We owe it to the captain."

By the time the orchestra filed out and the hostess began circulating to ask people whether they had enjoyed themselves, Frank and I were both drunk. Yet ours was not the tense, strung out, jagged euphoria that comes after too many drinks swallowed too quickly after a hard day at the office, but a kind of amber glow in which the steep, the rough, the irritating turned obligingly into their opposites. We had nowhere to go, nothing to do, nobody to see; not a single outside pressure threatened the bubble of slightly fatuous good humour in which we were enclosed. Once the receiving line had thinned out the captain worked his way efficiently through the room, pausing at our table only long enough to murmur "Good evening" and stare disapprovingly at our drinks. Frank and I dodged the hostess, busy chatting up the guests while the photographer clicked industriously away.

"Too soon to go down to dinner," said Frank, "let's have one more pop in the cabin."

"Are you sure you wouldn't like a healthful turn around the deck—to work up an appetite?"

"Not on your life. The road to happiness on this bloody boat lies through hyperactivity. It is my sacred duty to be sedentary."

As the Golden Grotto was located on the same deck as the Blue Lagoon, we had only to walk down one flight of stairs to our cabin.

"Shall I ring for ice?" I asked.

"Not unless you want some. With this flu on board, and overworked staff, I don't want to ask for anything I don't really need."

"You're right. I don't need ice. A little water will clear us of this deed."

"That sounds surprisingly like a quote. I did a production of 'the Scottish opera' a couple of years ago, all breastplates and bearskins. God, it was dreary, but the critics loved it." Frank poured as he talked. "Cheers!"

"Cheers! Frank, my boy, Mother always said it's rude to make personal remarks, but you're a bit flushed. Are you feeling okay?"

"Am I not! And who wouldn't be flushed after the tumblers of scotch I just put away. I feel great. If the truth were told I feel as randy as the troops. You wouldn't let me take a run at the captain, so maybe you'll just have to pay the ultimate price yourself."

Frank was drunk, but then so was I, with the result that I started to laugh. "La, sir, thou art a rogue. Only a rakehell would hit on a sweet kid like I."

"Get thee, Loreli Pinchwife." Putting down his tumbler,

Frank plucked mine from my hand and set it down beside him. Then, grabbing me by the shoulders, he kissed me.

If it is possible to describe a kiss as forceful and refined, that was the one. Caught by surprise, I did not resist. Nor, it must be admitted, did I want to. Ever since Rudolph Valentino had his masterful way with Agnes Ayres in *The Sheik*, the idea of being set upon by someone hugely attractive has become part of North American sexual mythology. I am the first to admit that I found Frank hugely attractive, but that did not mean I had to have sex with him. I find my Italian greengrocer very toothsome, but I do not pinch his tomatoes. I thoroughly enjoyed being kissed by Frank, especially as he did not perform a tonsillectomy with his tongue, but warning bells went off in my head.

"Enough! I am not your casual plaything. Besides, I have to call Elsie." Ducking nimbly around Frank I picked up the telephone. After four rings I figured she must be asleep; there seemed no point in waking her. I checked with the switchboard to make doubly sure she hadn't left any messages.

While I was telephoning, Frank lit a cigarette. "Now that you have stopped playing angel of mercy, can we resume our discussion?"

"No, we can not. Much as I love being a sex object—a geriatric sex object—I think that under the circs discretion is the better part of valour."

"You don't need valour to get it on. And I have no objection to being discreet." He laughed. "Sure you don't want to shag?"

"No, I prefer broadloom."

"Ouch! That's dreadful. People have been made to walk the plank for less. Tell you what. I'll back off until after dinner. Think about my offer. I'm not asking you to take me on as a retirement project, or to pay my debts. I am not looking for a longtime companion but a roll in the feathers. You're very hunky—for a man of your age." Frank couldn't keep his mouth from twitching. "And to paraphrase G.B.S.—sharing a cabin provides maximum temptation with maximum opportunity. Just think it over."

Saved by the bell. From the loudspeaker in the passageway outside our cabin door I heard the chimes announcing the second sitting for dinner. Finishing off the rest of my drink I opened the cabin door and stepped into the passageway. Frank butted his cigarette and followed.

IX

Around the dining room, ordinarily filled for the second sitting, I could see gaps at some of the tables, suggesting that the resident flu virus had taken its toll. To the casual observer it appeared to be business as usual, only our usually garrulous waiter had no time to chat. He had been assigned an extra table to serve, meaning his greeting was blessedly perfunctory. Frank and I arrived to find Susan already seated. We exchanged minimal politenesses and were handed our menus when Brad arrived with the news that Darlene had been felled by flu and was asleep in the cabin. I murmured a few predictable platitudes of commiseration, which Frank seconded.

Brad appeared to be taking the crimp in travel plans very much in his stride, turning the full force of his attention onto Susan and pretending interest in her day ashore. Had I bothered to give the matter any thought I could have predicted she would have hated Martinique, an island as remote from her Barbie-doll world view as it was possible to get. Susan thought the island dirty. She didn't understand Creole or French, and had difficulty with the English as spoken onshore. Her aunt and uncle had insisted on touring for the day, with the result that all she had to show for her outing was a gold bracelet.

Frank wasted no time in summoning the wine waiter and ordering scotch I did not really want. Otherwise he remained silent, having nothing in particular to say to the dissatisfied

Susan or the predictable Brad, whose main interests were professional sports, computer games, and, I surmised, chicks. Ignoring Frank and me completely, it having become evident that we did not intend to provide wine with meals, he proceeded to come on to Susan, who was obviously quite happy to receive male attention, even if the swain was already spoken for. Before our orders had been taken, Susan had agreed to accompany Brad to the evening's show, a cabaret of sorts. I wondered how the stricken Darlene would have felt had she known how expediently Brad was filling the gap.

As further proof of his dishonourable intentions, he ordered a bottle of wine. To his evident relief both Frank and I declined a glass, leaving him to ply Susan with the cheapest white on the list.

We were an odd group, Frank and I both preoccupied, Brad telling Susan how great she looked in pink, and two empty chairs tacitly reminding us of illness on board. What would happen to these sick passengers when the boat docked in San Juan was anybody's guess. I hoped Elsie would be well enough to travel, so I could get her back to Montreal. Perhaps I had better find out whether we were booked on the same flight home.

Tonight's menu featured lamb chops cooked with risk-free rosemary. By now the unaccustomed amounts of food had begun to tell. Three large meals a day, two more than I eat at home, had filled me to the point where a few bites quelled such small appetite as I had. I made rather a show of eating, hoping Frank would do likewise and sober up. I didn't think the idea of our shipboard romance was the greatest and hoped the notion would simply blow over.

Susan was telling Brad about her tour of the island with the aunt and uncle in tow. The taxi had no, like, springs, and because of all that scenery there was little time to go, like, shopping. She could barely utter two sentences without using "like" to get the motor turning over. I found myself anticipating every "like," then almost wincing at the word.

Frank never said much at meals. Realizing that his interests lay light years away from those of his table mates, he kept a low profile, speaking when spoken to and volunteering little. Tonight he remained mute, but I wrote it off to his being slightly drunk. I felt relieved we had only a couple more days on board, as the high life had begun to wear me down. I was drinking more and enjoying it less, while the food, good without being outstanding, arrived in such quantities as to verge on excess. I have never advocated the loincloth and begging bowl, and a cruise is supposed to be a holiday; but more than enough is too much.

Having refused coffee, Frank and I excused ourselves, leaving Susan and Brad to finish the wine. By now he had his arm over the back of her chair, his hand only millimetres from her bare, golden arm.

"How about a turn around the deck?" I suggested.

"Suits me," replied Frank. We rode the elevator to the upper deck and pushed our way outside. Surprisingly few passengers were to be found on deck, no doubt a result of the idea that we were not aboard a ship but a floating hotel where evenings were to be given over to shows, dancing, gambling, and movies. The tropical night came straight from a 1940s Technicolor musical, its soft warm breeze and full moon dappling the water with jittery bars of light. In the distance we could make out the lights from another cruise ship plying the same islands as our own. The fact that we were on a kind of holiday bus route in no way mitigated the beauty of the evening, so romantic as to be downright corny.

After a few turns around the upper promenade, Frank started down the stairs leading to the stern deck where the small area, sheltered by the upper level and the staircase, protected two people from the wind. Naturally, we gravitated toward the moonlit side, one of those vistas that, not unlike a Key West sunset, is probably bad for the viewer, a case of Nature imitating paintings on velvet. As I looked around the rear deck I saw, almost with dismay, that the area stood empty except for Frank and me. I knew what was going to happen and realized I intended doing nothing to prevent it. When, tucked snugly into our corner, Frank reached for me I returned the gesture in kind. When he kissed me, a deep masculine kiss tasting of scotch and tobacco, I returned the kiss eagerly, like a reformed alcoholic falling off the wagon or a cokehead with two neat rows and a twenty dollar bill. To hold a bulky male body close, feel the masculine configuration, inhale the pungent odours, and experience the rasp of stubble made me realize how much a part of me had been on hold since Patrick died. In that schlocky, make-believe setting Frank kissed me in a way I shall probably never forget. After all, I don't have that much time left to remember.

We held one another close, my better judgment having been bound, gagged, and relegated to the distant part of my consciousness. We were about to kiss a second time when Frank pulled away.

"Uh-oh! I think I'd better get back to the cabin." Without pausing to explain he almost bolted across the deck and through the door leading into the ship. I hesitated for a moment, suddenly aware that what I was about to do wasn't very ethical. Not to put too fine a point on things, I intended to cheat on Elinor, the woman with whom I was currently involved and the one who had made it possible for Frank and me to come on this cruise. I did not like what I was going to do, return to the cabin and go to bed with Frank. No matter what did or did not happen—allowances being made for age and alcohol—the intention was clear in my mind. I fully intended to have a fling, in all likelihood the last fling I would ever have. Although I am not the first to have observed that the things in life which we regret are those we did not do, I would be obliged to deal with my conscience in due course. In the meantime, it would have to fend for itself.

I walked slowly across the deck and into the ship. At the door of our cabin I inserted the coded plastic card into the lock and went inside. The cabin stood empty, but I noticed the bathroom door was shut. Without giving the matter much thought I crossed to sit in one of the armchairs. I heard the violent flush of our commode, but still Frank did not emerge. After a few moments I thought perhaps I had better knock and make sure he was all right, when the door swung open and Frank came slowly into the room.

"Guess what, Chadwick. I've got it."

Events of the past few minutes had blunted all but my most basic responses. "Got what?"

"The flu. I've been feeling odd since lunch, but I thought it was too much sun. I'm afraid I have to go to bed—I just lost everything. Damn, I hope I haven't given it to you."

"Time will tell," I said. "Fate and my flu shot will decide. I'll turn down the bed while you undress. Don't bother; I'll hang up your clothes."

Frank stripped to his shorts and shirt, then half sat, half collapsed into bed. I pulled up the covers as he lay, eyes shut, breathing heavily.

"I'm afraid we'll have to postpone the magic moment," he said.

"It had occurred to me. Perhaps I had better take your temperature. If it is way up you might take aspirin. The ship's doctor is out of commission, so it looks like we are on our own."

"Do you have a thermometer?"

"Of course. Travel brings out my latent hypochondria."

Frank lay with his eyes shut, the digital thermometer under his tongue. I am not a doctor, but I have read that fever is the body's way of burning off infection. To lower the temperature with analgesics is not always recommended. But here we were, in the middle of the Caribbean, on a ship whose doctor lay bedridden. Doing something, anything, seemed better than passive acceptance. No Navajo I.

The thermometer registered 103 degrees Fahrenheit. I gave Frank two aspirins and helped him to sit up so he could drink. At once he lay back and closed his eyes. I knew that all he wanted to do was sleep, so I hung the "Do Not Disturb" sign outside the door and turned off all but one light. There being nothing more for me to do, I said I would look in shortly and went out, closing the door behind me.

For a few moments I stood irresolutely outside the door. Within a matter of minutes my plans for the evening, for tomorrow, for the rest of the cruise had drastically changed. The cabin had turned into a sickroom; watching the closed-circuit movie offered few blandishments with Frank, feverish and comatose. I certainly did not want to intrude any more than necessary. To be ill is unpleasant at best, but how much more disagreeable on a ship thousands of miles from home. Perhaps I should check on Frank in a bit to learn if his temperature had gone up. To do so would mean waking him, and what I would do were his fever to have increased was anybody's guess.

For want of anywhere better to go, I rode the elevator down to the purser's deck where I inquired what provisions had been made for the sick passengers. The meticulously groomed young woman on duty behind the desk had been well schooled in the art of saying nothing. Yes, there was a problem with illness on board, but steps were being taken. No, the doctor was not available for consultation, but another doctor was coming aboard tomorrow when the ship docked in Antigua. The captain had provided a list of procedures to follow for those who believed they had the flu. As she burbled on I scanned the list: bed rest, plenty of fluids, Aspirin to lower temperature, and so forth. Nothing we didn't already know from our elementary school Red Cross rules. When I asked about arrangements for sick passengers when we returned to San Juan, I was assured in a voice sounding post-coital with sincerity that passengers would be taken care of and helped either to the hospital or onto their flights.

By now it had become abundantly clear that nobody on the ship had any idea of how to deal with endemic illness on board.

"May I speak to the purser?"

"He's not available at the moment, sir."

"Does he have the flu?"

Her momentary hesitation before replying gave me the answer. "I'm not at liberty to say."

"Why not? If the purser is not available and he is not sick then who's minding the store?"

The young woman smiled a smile that even by *Blue Horizon* standards looked strained. "Perhaps if you could come back tomorrow. The office is closed for the day."

On the point of suggesting she might think of applying for

a job on the *Empress of Ireland*, I reconsidered. The woman had no real authority; and tomorrow, after the day trippers had gone ashore, I would return when the office was open, make myself very large, and insist on seeing the person in charge.

I inquired whether there were any messages for me from Mrs. Elsie Connors, cabin 401 on the Rio Deck. Elsie had not tried to reach me, but a telegram had just arrived, so recently in fact there hadn't been time to deliver it to my cabin. I tore open the envelope and read: JANE HAS A SON STOP EVERYONE WELL STOP WISH I WERE THERE STOP LOOK FORWARD TO SATURDAY STOP LOVE ELINOR

I am bored by coincidence. People who tell long-winded stories about amazing coincidences that have reshaped their lives are almost as boring as those who relate their dreams. Yet to have been chaperoned by the flu and prevented from pulling a fast one on Elinor, only to receive her telegram, gave me the uncomfortable feeling that someone out there was watching. I do not suspect God; He has better things to do then keep track of sexual misdemeanours. From one point of view there hadn't been any hanky-panky, nor would there be before the ship docked. From the opposite viewpoint I had kissed Frank as ardently as he had kissed me, and were he not ill we would both be in his bed at this very moment.

I reentered the elevator and got off by mistake on a lower deck from mine. I pushed my way outside onto the lifeboat deck which I had not visited since the lifeboat drill. A handful of people leaned on the rail looking at the moonlit night. Had they been stricken with moon madness like Frank and me? I sat on a bench, feeling not unlike a stowaway. Where was I to go? I did not want any more to drink, so the bars were out. The show was by now well underway, nor did I wish to be stunned by sound. Watching other people gamble is about as much fun as mowing the lawn, and the library had been colonized by passengers playing bridge. Overcome by lassitude I remained where I sat. The bench was not in the least comfortable, but I couldn't be bothered to move.

Another coincidence I would happily have overlooked was that Frank had been the first boy I ever kissed, and he might well turn out to be the last. In spite of myself I almost laughed out loud. How sweet sixteen could I possibly get: "the first boy I ever kissed"? It was one of those feminine clichés like "the love of my life," or "the father of my children." Naturally I speak of a time when boys could not admit to kissing other boys. We had to talk about girls' tits and how all we wanted from life was to get laid. Some of us even carried a condom, purchased from a distant drug store where the buyer was unknown, to carry in the snap-clasp change compartments of our bulky wallets, proof that we were, like the Boy Scouts, always prepared. To admit to a tender feeling, even for a girl, was seen as a sign of weakness. Timid, insecure, fearful of our sexuality, unsure of ourselves, we pranced and preened and pretended to be irresistible. We did not talk about the first boy we ever kissed.

An icy wind from the west stung our faces as we stood on the crest of the slope in our local park.

"Race you to the bottom!"

"Last one down is a rotten egg!"

Poling my way to a start, I attempted to keep my skis parallel, knees bent, poles tucked under my arms as I had seen older, more experienced skiers do. So did Frank, who somehow managed to cut across my path at the foot of the short hill, causing us to collide and crash, with no damage, as neither of us had been going fast.

How intensely I disliked skiing—all sports, were the truth to be told. Having realized my reluctance to play on a team, my father, anxious that his only son be an accomplished athlete, bought me a tennis racquet and skis. The racquet had been strung with nylon rather than gut, the latest thing at the time and the envy of my peers. Unfortunately, the nylon strings demonstrated tremendous driving power, so on those few occasions I connected with the elusive ball it went sailing out of the court and, oftener than not, over the enclosing wire mesh into the bushes. I spent as much time looking for balls in the rough as any golfer.

Winter torment turned out to be a pair of skis, with cable harness and, wonder of wonders, steel edges. The fine print said that with my boots clamped firmly to the ski, the steel edges cutting neatly through the packed surface of the slope, I would skim down the hill, swerving gracefully to the left or the right, neatly avoiding all obstacles, and coming to a tightly executed stop in a cloud of powdered snow. To me the stupidity of climbing a hill, only to speed to the bottom on a pair of boards, exceeded even that of hitting a ball over a net. At least tennis had rules.

Frank felt the same way as I about sports, only with his more compact and muscular build he was naturally a better athlete. Small matter. With extreme reluctance the two of us headed out on that Boxing Day, shamed into trying out the latest word in ski equipment our fathers, no doubt in collusion, had placed under the respective Christmas trees. I don't know about Frank, but in my case the gratitude was by rote. All of which explains how the two of us ended up in a tangle of arms, skis, and poles at the foot of that hill.

"I'm cold," I said as I stood and dusted myself off. On Christmas Day the temperature had plunged; my face tingled and the breath smoked from my mouth. My hat, a baseball cap with ear flaps that tied under the chin, failed to protect my face, and wind caused my eyes to water. I was not having fun.

"So am I," agreed Frank. "Let's go home. Aunt Eileen said we could come over."

"Let's go back to my house," I suggested. "My parents have gone to the country for a Boxing Day party, and my sister is visiting a friend in Ottawa."

The idea of a house empty of grownups and importunate sisters was a draw. We could sneak some sherry, more tempting than Aunt Eileen's wholesome cocoa or ginger ale. In deference to our new skis, we switched the position of the cables encircling the grooved heels of our boots, from the downhill to the cross-country settings and skied along streets lightly dusted with snow whipped up by the wind.

Letting ourselves into the basement, we took off our boots and outer clothing, mindful of my mother's injunctions, and climbed to the ground floor where I immediately poured some sherry into a kitchen tumbler so as to escape detection. Sherry gets you there in a hurry, and after only a couple of sips we felt the effect, as though we were no longer firmly attached to our present surroundings. By now we had gone upstairs to my bedroom, considerably tidier than those of my other school friends. Instead of photos of athletes covering the walls, my room displayed a set of Air France travel posters, *faux-naif* gouaches of prominent French landmarks. Books in neat rows filled shelves on top of which sat my collection of shells and beach stones. Although in no way effeminate, the room did not reek of testosterone.

"I'm going to take a shower," I announced, and proceeded to undress. Although accustomed to changing in front of other boys as a result of that twice-weekly humiliation known as gym class, I felt suddenly shy with only Frank in the room. I drank more sherry and went into the bathroom wearing only my jockey shorts. The hot water caressed my thin body, erasing all sensation of cold. About to turn off the taps and dry myself I heard Frank say, "Leave the water running. I'm coming in."

Opening the curtain at the end of the tub away from the shower head, I stepped out and Frank got in. Many was the time I had seen him nude in the shower room, but always surrounded by twenty or so classmates in various stages of undress. Here, in the bathroom I shared with my sister, he seemed less nude than naked, his skin milky white and alarmingly tactile.

I towelled myself dry. "Is there any more sherry?"

"No," replied Frank from behind the curtain. "I finished it off."

"Piggy-wiggy," I said with a laugh as I fastened the towel around my waist.

"Up yours!" retorted Frank, not ordinarily given to rude outbursts, but liberated by the sherry.

I returned to the bedroom where Frank, still drying himself, followed. One of the reasons Frank had become my friend was that he did not push or shove or punch people. He disliked roughhouse and body contact sports. How surprised I was when he flicked his towel at me, neatly connecting with my ribcage.

"Ouch!" I yelped as I freed the towel from around my waist and snapped it sharply to catch him on the right buttock. In retaliation he grabbed my towel to yank it out of my hand, leaving me weaponless. Not wanting to be flicked again I made a dive for him, wrapping my arms around his so they were pinned to his sides. Shorter than I but stockier, he pushed me toward the bed where we both toppled onto the spread. For a few moments we wrestled, laughing as we struggled.

Suddenly we were no longer laughing. Struggles ceased as we clung to one another, stunned and speechless at the shock of desire. It was all over in seconds and we lay side by side, panting from surprise as much as release. Wordlessly I went back to the bathroom to shower again, leaving the water running for Frank. Hastily we dried ourselves and dressed. I smoothed out the bed and led the way down to the kitchen, where I made coffee. I didn't ordinarily drink coffee in the afternoon, but this was no ordinary occasion. Besides, if we drank more sherry my parents would notice the drop in the level.

Frank sat at the kitchen table, his hands crossed solemnly in front of him. "I think we're probably oversexed."

"I think you're right," I agreed. "I mean it's not as if we wouldn't prefer a woman—if we only had the chance."

"But we never get the chance. If I go out on a date my parents are waiting up when I get home."

"That's just it. How can we bring girls home when our parents are always around. You don't have a sister, but mine is a real pain in the neck. I can't get rid of her. Cream and sugar?"

"Yes, please."

All trace of our former jollity had vanished. We realized we had crossed some sort of Rubicon; sex that involved another person. We also understood that what we had done lay beyond the pale. It was what sissies, pansies, nancy boys, fags, and homos did. We could not bear to think of ourselves as homos, so we were obliged to invoke the desperation clause.

"Have you ever done it with a girl?" asked Frank, knowing

full well what the answer would be.

"Not yet. But I sure want to. I'd like to do it with a Jewish girl. Jewish girls have nice tits."

"But they don't put out. You have to marry them to get them to put out, and they don't want to marry guys who aren't Jewish."

"I suppose so. But it's really hard when you're oversexed."

"It sure is." We drank our coffee in silence.

The telephone rang. I answered to hear my mother's apologetic voice explaining that the party was dragging on, meaning she and my father would be late getting home. Could I scrounge something from the refrigerator for my supper? There was cold turkey and stuffing, and some of last night's mashed potato I could reheat in a double boiler.

"That's okay, Mother," I said. "I'll be fine. Don't worry. Enjoy your party." I hung up. "My parents will be late getting home. Can you stay for a bit?"

"I'll call home and say I'm here."

As he hung up the receiver, after promising to be home in an hour, or so, we fell silent; the silence hummed with possibilities.

Torn between fear of rejection and the wish not to let the precious hour slip away, I summoned up all my courage. "Would you like to go upstairs for a bit?"

"Sure, if you would."

We wasted no time. When the clock told us Frank had to dress and leave, the bed looked like a bomb site, as we had tried out a number of quite grownup activities. We did not kiss, tacitly drawing the line at the one sexual activity restricted to men and women. Frank scrambled back into his clothes. I let him out the basement door, and he trudged off, carrying his skis as it was already dark. "So long. See you." I called.

"Sure thing," he replied and disappeared around the corner.

So began an odd, intense period of my life. Frank and I became what would now be called lovers, although we would have been shocked and astonished to consider ourselves in that light. We were merely finding an outlet for the sexual energy that social attitudes, parental disapproval, and professional virgins refused to accommodate. We became sly, alert to those rare times when one of our houses stood empty, communicating in code lest we seem overly eager for what was no more than a makeshift measure. We took to going to each other's houses to study for our impending matriculation exams. Luckily we were both good students as those afternoons in an empty house saw little studying while we went at one another with silent ferocity, too inexperienced to realize that our so-called makeshift solution was what we yearned for. On occasion we double dated, to our parents' mutual delight, only to return our dates safely to their wide-awake mothers before sneaking into the basement for sex in the furnace room while the household slept upstairs. While performing various acts that in those less enlightened days could have sent us to prison, we never kissed, at least not then. To kiss on the lips was the last taboo, an act to be performed only with our dates on the doorstep while their anxious mothers hovered inside.

All the time we understood that what we were doing was forbidden: against the law, against nature, against the social codes, and most definitely infra dig. So we covered our tracks. Oddly enough, we continued to be good friends. We went to movies, helped one another study in the school library, did chores for each other's parents. Mrs. Wilkinson thought the young Geoffry Chadwick a perfect gentleman, and my own mother rejoiced in my having a really nice friend like Frank, a young man who was interested in something else besides sports and parties. I realize now with 20/20 hindsight that I was probably as close to being happy as I have ever been. Granted, it was an illicit happiness, but what North American does not feel deep down that risk enhances pleasure. Is it sexual desire that sends adults into motel rooms, or the urge to give the finger to the status quo?

Every garden hides a serpent. In the case of Frank and me it turned out not to be our indiscretion but the company for which Frank's father worked. The promotion, for which he had lobbied, entailed moving to Toronto. When the news broke, the senior Wilkinsons had decided to postpone telling Frank, on the point of writing important exams. They feared, and for once they were right, that he would be upset.

Alone in my room one afternoon, having written my final exam in the morning, I was thinking about asking my father to let me visit Ottawa, to see the Houses of Parliament. I wanted Frank to come with me, and Father could probably persuade Mr. Wilkinson to let Frank tag along. What I envisaged was a dirty weekend, even though I would have been the last person in the world to describe it as anything but an educational outing with a good friend. We could stay in a cheap hotel, a whole weekend together to see the sights of our national capital. Downstairs I heard Mother say, "Frank dear, what a pleasant surprise. Yes, Geoffry is here. He's upstairs in his room."

Looking over the railing to the ground floor I saw Frank take the stairs two at a time. He motioned me into my room and shut the door. I could tell he was utterly distraught.

"My father is waiting outside. We're driving to Toronto this afternoon, for good. They didn't tell me earlier because of my exams. Mother is staying to deal with the house and pack, and

Father and I will be staying with my aunt. Shit!"

As Frank did not use profanity I knew he was beside himself.

"Is this a permanent move?" I asked dumbly, unable or unwilling to grasp that Frank would no longer be two blocks away.

"Yes. Will you come to visit?"

"Of course I will—and I'll write."

"I can't stay. Father wants to get there before dark. I just learned. Shit, I don't want to go to Toronto. I feel like I'm being kidnapped."

I could see tears threatening. Without thinking I put my arms around him. Fortunately he had shut the bedroom door.

It was then that we kissed for the first time, a deep, lingering, passionate kiss that said in seconds what it would have taken hours to relate. I had never kissed like that before, not on porches, in cars, in the movies. I wanted to kiss him again, and again. But he pulled away and was gone, back down the stairs, uttering polite exit remarks to my mother, into the waiting car, and out of my life.

I fled the house to walk for hours through the city, consumed by an overwhelming restlessness that physical fatigue could not begin to assuage. I did not realize, or refused to admit, that I loved Frank. Love remained an emotion limited to something between men and women. Whatever men did when alone together, love had no place. Yet I could not explain away the tight feeling in my throat nor the curious sensation that I had a large hole where my stomach should have been.

Frank and I wrote to each other, dull, lifeless letters about college and the weather. We feared putting down in words what we truly felt, blue pencilling any emotion so the paragraphs came out flat and pedestrian. Once in a while we spoke on the phone, at a time when long-distance calls remained an extra-vagance restricted to adults who paid their own phone bills. When we finally met again, after we had both graduated from university, we discovered we had each moved in a different direction. What remained was an enormous affection for a person whose language you no longer spoke. Although we knew, without having to be told, that we were both gay, the languages of law and theatre were foreign. We did not camp; we were both respected professionals; we remained friends, no more, no less.

But whenever we met, a presence shimmered between us, the ghost of a remembered emotion. We no longer loved one another, but once, without the experience to name what we had known, we shared that elusive feeling. The man I kissed earlier this evening was no longer the youth I had kissed just before he drove out of my life. But those few seconds had certainly muddied the waters.

My bum ached. I rose from the uncomfortable bench and went to stand at the rail. What I saw was the monthly full moon reflected in lukewarm salt water. Spare me the magic.

Maybe a drink in the bar wasn't such a bad idea after all.

I located a house phone and dialled Elsie's cabin. After three rings she picked up the receiver.

"Elsie, it's me. Correction: It is I, G.C. Just checking in. Hope I didn't wake you."

"No, you didn't. As a matter of fact I just had tea, dry toast, and a little soup, hardly a feast, but I got it down."

"That's good news. The bad news is that Frank has been laid low."

"Oh, dear, no! Poor Frank. It certainly ruins a cruise. How

are you feeling, Geoffry?"

"So far, so good. I had a flu shot. What I wanted to know, Elsie, is what flight you are taking to Montreal on Saturday."

"I don't have my ticket handy, but I'm reasonably sure it's around noon—the flight to Atlanta. Then I switch planes for the trip to Montreal. I think the plane leaves Atlanta around five."

"It sounds as though we are on the same flights. Perhaps you could locate your tickets and jot down the precise information. Fingers crossed, if I don't get sick myself I can see you through the ordeal. Even if you are feeling a bit better you still won't be fully recovered by Saturday."

"That's very sweet of you, Geoffry. But what about Frank?"

"I don't know. He just became ill. I only hope he'll be able to get home. Anything you need the cabin steward can't provide?"

"Not at the moment, thanks."

"I'll check in tomorrow. Goodnight, Elsie." I fought down the impulse to add, "Try and get some rest." Just about every bad movie I have ever endured has a scene where somebody says, in an unctuous, syrupy voice, to someone else on the verge of hysteria, "Try and get some rest." What had Elsie been doing for the past twenty-four hours but sacking out.

Time to check in on the other patient. I let myself into the cabin to find Frank sleeping heavily. He didn't appear to have moved. So deep was his breathing that I could have spoken to Elsie on our cabin phone without disturbing him. Waking Frank to check his temperature seemed like an exercise in futility, so I put a bottle of water, a tumbler, and the aspirin on the night table where he could reach them without getting up.

About to leave the cabin I paused for a moment to study the sleeping figure. Unconscious, he looked younger, not that

I have ever considered youth a plus. I have always preferred faces that look lived in. Lines, pouches, wrinkles are a lot sexier than smooth, untroubled faces, innocent of experience. I am the first to admit thinking in stereotype: the more battered the face the greater amount of experience it registers. That the interesting furrows are more likely to be a product of genes than tempestuous love affairs in no way diminishes their attraction. Whenever I go to a good guy/bad guy movie I generally find the good guy so improbably clean-cut and wholesome that I end up thinking impure thoughts about the villain. Why is sexual energy always equated with evil?

Frank did not look like a villain, but he had lost the beauty that had been such a burden in his youth. He had frequently been accused of being "too good looking for his own good," a typically tight-assed Canadian observation from my adolescence. As a teenager I was to learn that beauty, talent, intelligence were all seen as highly suspect qualities. Beauty led to vanity, a swelled head, and, in the case of young men, a preoccupation with appearance that was sexually suspect. Intelligence turned a young man into a smarty pants, or someone who was "too big for his britches." The preoccupation appeared to be with trousers, as really intelligent young women were adroit enough not to let their intelligence show. Talent, most particularly that for performing, led to accusations of being a showoff. Whatever the cause, to draw attention to oneself invoked censure. I wonder if moving from an outhouse culture to one of indoor plumbing did not help to loosen our nation's collective ass. The True North strong and a little more free.

Frank had been impossibly good-looking, talented, and a straight-A student. With age he had outgrown the curse of beauty; smoking, drinking, and who knows what else had imposed a patina of experience bordering on the jaded. I found the look irresistible. Steady on, Nurse Chadwick, one is supposed to care for the patient, not bump one's uglies on the feverish body. Yes, sir, Dr. Hippocrates.

Not being ready for sleep I shrugged one of those "What-the-hell" shrugs and went upstairs to the Blue Lagoon. From force of habit I crossed to the table in the smoking section where Frank and I usually sat. The bar held just enough people to give it ambience. Most of the patrons sat in the non-smoking section, evidently preferring their modest vices unsullied by secondhand smoke.

The noticeable exception was two couples seated at an adjacent table, three with cigarettes in hand. Unlike the others in the bar, they made rather a show of enjoying themselves. They were, to borrow a term from the British sitcoms I watch on PBS, "a bit flash," but considering the drab competition, my observation was not criticism. Silent as I was, I could not help hearing bits of conversation delivered, I half expected, as if meant to be overheard.

"Our lady-what-does, the one who makes up the cabin, is efficient," said the older of the two men, "but she isn't in tune with her hair. She looks like a bad bust of Beethoven."

"Perhaps she doesn't comb after every meal," said one of the women. "At least she hasn't succumbed to whatever it is that is knocking everybody out." The speaker looked a few years older than the other woman; I could only surmise she was with the older man. If one could find a common denominator linking the four together, it lay in the quantity of gold jewellery they all flaunted. Both men wore heavy gold chains, identification bracelets with links the size of pennies, and massive signet rings. Ditto for the women, only they were hung with more of everything, all gold, and at the very least fourteen carat. I could only surmise they had been on a shopping spree, as few travellers would pack that much jewellery for a trip.

"You really should have come to the Captain's cocktail party," continued the older man. "It was like the best of all Tupperware parties. Photographs with our gracious and lovely hostess, the ginger ale of champagnes served in flutes, and all the cheese straws you could eat."

The four of them laughed, a bit archly. As I was listening with only one ear, as my mother used to say, it took me a moment to realize the next remark had been addressed to me.

"If your friend is not going to join you, will you have a drink with us?" Again the speaker was the older of the two men.

"Sorry," I replied, "I didn't realize you were talking to me."

"Won't you join us?" he repeated. "You know the rules for Monarch Cruises: everyone has to have a wonderful time. Being alone is considered subversive."

I laughed and carried my drink over to their table, where a place was made for me between the younger man and woman.

"I'm Huntley." The older man shook my hand. "This is Georgette—and Charlotte—and Greg."

"How do you do. I'm Geoffry, Geoffry Chadwick." I could see at once that Huntley was in charge. I could guess he was old enough to collect social security, but between the bronzing and the blow-drying, the highlighted hair and the expensive resort clothes, he belied his age. Deep pouches under his eyes and liver spots beneath the tan told their own story.

Georgette, a handsome, angular woman with short hair beautifully cut, wore a pantsuit that showed off her boyish figure. On the arm not weighed down by bracelets she wore a man's gold Rolex. The second woman, Charlotte, looked as though

she had stepped from a 1940s film noir. Her long blond pageboy, tailored suit, and black pumps all managed to suggest the
bad girl who turns out in the last reel to have a heart of gold.
Small and compact, Greg had conventionally clean-cut good
looks with plenty of black chest hair on display, as the top
three buttons of his shirt were undone. He wore white trousers
and white deck shoes without socks.

"Shall we pull up a chair for your—friend?" inquired Huntley.

"No, he won't be joining us. And he's not my friend, but
just a friend." Without having to be told I realized that Huntley and Greg were together, probably as were Charlotte and
Georgette.

"Oh, dear, I hope I haven't spoken out of turn."

"Not in the least," I replied. "I'm old enough to know that
two and two do not always add up to four."

Everyone at the table seemed to find my observation hugely
amusing. Then again they were drinking brandy with a beer
chaser, a combination that can add mirth to any situation.

"Then we don't need to draw up a sociogram," chuckled
Huntley. "As a matter of fact we do add up to four, but not in
the *Blue Horizon* way, even though 'way' rhymes with 'gay.'"

"Better gay than grumpy," I repeated for the second time
today. "I presume the four of you decided to travel as a group so
that Middle America could draw its own conclusions."

"Correct," said Georgette. "But we had no idea how conservative the ship would be—to the right of Rameses II."

"When they have ring-around-the-collar it's red," volunteered Charlotte.

Greg had not spoken. I suspected that whatever his at-
tractions, they did not extend to conversation.

"I know," I said. "Several times I've caught people giving

Frank and me the laser look. What are two men of their age up to, travelling together. Frank has come down with flu, so I guess that makes me a grass widow."

Again my remark set them off into peals of laughter, so much so I began to suspect they were sorely in need of outside stimulation. Travelling in a group can be isolating, particularly for four gay passengers on an aggressively straight ship.

"We're all drinking brandy because it helps to kill the germs." Huntley took a hefty swallow as if to underline his point. "Will you have one?"

No thanks. I'll stick to scotch. It's full of vitamin C."

Huntley signalled for another round. I didn't want another drink, but I lacked the willpower to refuse. "What made you all choose the *Blue Horizon?*" I asked.

"Schedule, mainly," replied Georgette. "This seemed to be the only week we could all manage to get away. Added to which it wasn't the height of the tourist season."

"Does that mean the natives are not allowed to shoot at us?" I asked, to be met with another round of laughter.

"Everyone needs to get away from Chicago," added Charlotte, a remark that surprised me, as her voice suggested Great Britain.

"And we had a very nice letter of introduction to a jeweller in Barbados," said Huntley, "as you may have noticed."

"What will you do at customs?" I asked.

"Brazen it out. Wear everything as though we never took it off. Look the customs inspector in the eye. Always look a person in the eye when you are lying."

Our drinks arrived and Huntley insisted on paying for mine. In the flurry of activity involved in clearing away glasses and setting down fresh drinks, I grew aware of Greg's knee pressed against mine under the table. As there was little room to manoeuvre, I moved my leg as far as I could to the left, but the knee followed. I cannot say I found the sensation unpleasant, but putting the make on someone else's boyfriend was not on the agenda. The thought occurred to me that perhaps Greg had sniffed or puffed or otherwise ingested a controlled substance, as he was not in the least subtle. It must have been perfectly obvious to the other three what he was up to. I resolved to finish my drink, then excuse myself.

Suddenly the affable mood around the table changed. Huntley leaned back in his chair, crossed his hands on his chest, and suggested that after this round we all head off to the casino.

"Count me out," said Greg, speaking for the first time. "I'm sick of blackjack."

"Now, now," Huntley's tone was cajoling, "how else are we going to pay our bar bill? Are you coming, Jette?"

"Sure thing," replied Georgette. "Charl?"

"I may look in later," replied Charlotte. "I don't want to spend the rest of the evening gambling."

"Are you just going to sit there and get pissed again?"

"Jette, stop being such a bloody cow!"

The two women locked glances, leading me to suspect there was more at stake than cards. Huntley turned his attention back to Greg. "Come along, kiddo, if only for a bit. You did so well last night. Seventy dollars, wasn't it? We won't stay long."

The knee continued to press mine. I know that out there in gayland there are young men who prefer older men. *De gustibus non disputandum est.*

"I'm not gambling tonight," announced Greg. "Stop organizing me. I'm staying here with Charl—and Geoff." For the first time he looked directly at me. It would not have required huge amounts of I.Q. to realize something was going on, and I was about to be embroiled in whatever it turned out to be. I felt not unlike the innocent bystander who is shot in the leg, the same leg that was trying unsuccessfully to break contact with Greg's importunate knee. Huntley continued to smile, but the expression looked painted on.

I decided to act. Finishing my drink in two quick swallows I stood. "I really should get back to the cabin and check on the patient. He may need something, and even the effort of ringing for the steward can be a millstone when you feel rotten. Thanks for the drink, Huntley. Good luck at the tables. May you end up rich beyond the dreams of avarice."

Since Dr. Johnson could not be improved upon for an exit line, I left the bar. Down in the cabin Frank still slept. I poured myself a glass of water and sat on the edge of my bed. I had aged. Twenty years ago I would have been delighted in being taken up by a gay group, enjoying the repartee, the tensions, the secret signals, the feeling of belonging to an arcane society. Most probably Greg and I would have sneaked back to his cabin or, better still, tipped a steward to let us use one of the empty ones. Above all, I would have thought of myself as having a wonderful time.

Yet in spite of wanting to avoid complicating the situation or being the cause of a lovers' quarrel, could I honestly, now, in the solitude of my cabin, resist a little jolt of pleasure at the idea that Greg had come on to me? Drunk as he probably was, obvious as he had been, there remained enough of my former vanity to be just a little pleased that an attractive young stud had made a play. I did not intend to follow it up, but it was still good to know I wasn't too old to cut the mustard.

Life seemed complicated enough without another

shipboard romance. One was enough. I desperately wanted Frank to get better, but I did not want to resolve the dilemma of whether or not to sleep with him. I didn't know what I wanted. Hadn't this cruise been a shitty idea!

I took two of the aspirin I had set out for Frank and went to bed.

X

During the night I became vaguely aware that Frank was moving about the cabin. I figured he had to go to the bathroom, and I also assumed that if there was anything he needed he would have the wit to wake me. I kept quiet, and soon I heard him lower himself into bed with a grunt and go back to sleep. When I telephoned for coffee in the morning I also requested a pot of tea and some dry toast. Unappetizing as they sound, I have been told that tea and toast sit lightly on an uneasy stomach.

Frank still slept. No point in waking him, so I opened the curtains just enough to let me see that we had docked in Antigua under a hot, hazy sky. The coffee arrived with a clatter in the nervous hands of an unfamiliar steward who had the craven look of a newly released hostage. Although I indicated the sleeping man, the steward, miming silence, managed to slam the cabin door. How fortunate for the world he had not chosen to become a brain surgeon.

The noise caused Frank to stir. "Are we there yet? Christ, I feel awful, but I have to go pee-pee."

"I ordered you some tea and dry toast."

"You're all heart." Frank levered himself upright. "Sorry, that was a cheap shot, but my buoyant good humour seems to have deserted me."

"Not to worry. Go pee, then I'll take your temperature."

Frank managed a wan smile. "Aren't you sorry you didn't

pack your crisp white uniform along with the size-12 white shoes? And the cap you clamp on with two bobby pins?" He shuffled into the bathroom, and I opened the curtains wide. All I could see was the corrugated metal roof of a low building beside a stretch of pier. From the bathroom I heard the sound of the shower, a good sign. Shortly Frank emerged with wet hair and wearing a towel inside the neck of his robe, like a prizefighter.

"Sit down and have your tea, but first open up." I slid the thermometer under his tongue, then removed it to read that his temperature had gone down one degree. I handed him a cup of tea. "I shouldn't imagine you will be going ashore in Santa Maria de la Antigua, as Columbus named it when he first saw the island."

"Wasn't he the busy explorer. 'In fourteen hundred ninety-two/ Columbus sailed the ocean blue.' I remember that from school. It's about all I remember from school."

"Do you want aspirin? If so, you'd better eat something."

"Maybe later." He put down his cup, which I refilled. "Geoffry, I'm so sorry about all this. What a pisser it must be for you."

"Don't even think that. I am fully prepared to believe you did not get sick on purpose. At the very least I appear to be holding up—touch wood!" I wondered whether stroking what was probably plasticized wood veneer worked the spell. "And Elsie is somewhat better. She's chowin' down on toast. What concerns me is what we do on Saturday, when we dock in Puerto Rico."

"I'll get you to send a wire to San Francisco. Someone will meet me at the airport."

"But what about this end? We will be on different flights, and I'll have to keep an eye on Elsie."

"Not to worry. I'll manage. This isn't the first time I've been sick on the road." Frank reached over and squeezed my hand. "You've been swell. I can't thank you enough."

"What have I done? Given you some aspirin and taken your temp. Not even a cold compress. But I have an idea, a far better one than dealing with the purser and his minions." I glanced at my watch. "Elinor will not be happy, but what the hell!"

I picked up the telephone and dialled the operator. "I wish to make a ship to shore call to Montreal, Canada. Please charge it to my cabin." I gave the operator Elinor's phone number. I dislike imposing on people, but this was an emergency. After a brief delay Elinor's voice came onto the line. I wasted no time in niceties.

"Elinor, my love, I apologize for the hour, but I'm on the spot."

"You must be or you wouldn't have telephoned. What's the problem?" Her voice hummed with brisk reassurance.

As succinctly as I could I explained how Frank and Elsie had come down with flu. I dreaded the crush of getting off the ship with two sick passengers and facing the gauntlet of getting them to the airport with their luggage. Would she get in touch with Hartland Crawford; he obviously knew someone with clout in Monarch Cruises or we wouldn't have been given the tickets. Tell him to lean hard. I want a limousine to meet the ship, and a nurse. Money no object. I'll owe everyone for the rest of my life, but there you are.

"How are you bearing up, Geoffry?"

"So far, so good. I had a flu shot. If I go down we are in deep faeces."

"I'll get onto it right away. And I'll plan to be at home this evening, if you want to call me again. Or I can send you a wire. Why not both? This is not a social call and I know it is costing the earth. Hang tough, kid. I'll be at the airport to meet you in Montreal."

"Ciao, babe—and thanks."

I hung up. Frank began to laugh. "Jesus, Geoffry, you are something else. I am lost in admiration."

"Hartland has angles. And he owes me a few, not least for suffering through the dress rehearsal of goddamned *Hedda Gabler* while he hid out at the office. Eat your toast."

"Yes, sir, Nurse Chadwick."

"I'm going to clean up. If you think you can handle any more food I'll order it."

"This will be more than enough. All I want is to get back to bed. Who would have thought? Geoffry Chadwick, formerly boy curmudgeon, now angel of mercy."

I tried not to smile. "Don't push your luck, Wilkinson. I still have two more days to ruin your life."

"I am in your complete power. Pity I'm feeling so punk. I'd love to be your sex slave—but some other time."

When I came out of the bathroom Frank had gone back to sleep. I headed down to the dining room where I enjoyed the luxury of a solitary breakfast.

St. John's, the capital of Antigua, doesn't have a lot going for it. Not wanting to tie up the day with an island tour, including the obligatory visit to Nelson's Dockyard, I wandered off the ship by myself. My destination was the Cathedral of St. John, dominating the small city from its strategic position on a hill. The gangplank emptied passengers directly into a shopping mall bearing the historically charged name of Heritage Quay. Those with a yen to shop could do so no more than a few hundred yards from the ship.

Resisting the lure of merchandise I could buy in Canada with Canadian dollars, I walked the short distance into the town itself. As Bette Davis once said, in that peerless piece of camp, *Beyond the Forest*, "What a dump!" Shabby, unpainted, charmless, the town boasted the added hazard of ditches serving as gutters, meaning pedestrians were obliged to cross a trench to get from street to sidewalk. It made Fort-de-France look like the Emerald City. Taking the cathedral as landmark, the way people in Toronto use the CN Tower, I made my way up the hill and into the grounds of the church.

Inside, the cathedral felt deliciously cool after the humid warmth of drab streets. Wooden pews, a pine ceiling, and beautifully turned railings had darkened with age, making the interior a haven from the hard morning light reflected by the still sea. All doors stood open, creating a welcome series of cross drafts, while I read the marble tablets and bronze plaques mounted on the walls in memory of prominent citizens. A handsome woman, whose voice suggested she had gone to school in England, explained that the church, rebuilt after a severe earthquake in 1843, had suffered more than its share of natural disasters, the most recent being a hurricane. Beside one of the open doors beneath a sign which read "Donations for Restoration" sat a young woman to whom I gave a ten-dollar bill. By way of thanks she tendered a brochure on the history and specifications of the building.

Brochures remind me of homework. One has the nagging feeling the pamphlet ought to be read, its miscellaneous bits of information on the cornerstone, the foundation, the square feet of pitch pine incorporated into the structure, the consecration, and the inadequate endowment all absorbed as part of one's store of general information. Perhaps I would read the pamphlet back on the ship, in the cabin, while waiting my turn in the bathroom.

I tucked the pamphlet into my tote bag and moved toward the main entrance. Part of the front steps still lay in shadow from the twin Baroque towers, and I sat for a moment looking down over the town to the docks where three giant white cruise ships were moored for the day. How much more romantic it would have sounded to say they lay at anchor instead of being attached by pastel nylon hawsers to what looked like enormous cast iron mushrooms. Distance lends enchantment. It was almost possible to see the vessels as ships, with prows and sterns and portholes, not as floating resorts.

I felt no urgency about returning to the ship. The cabin as sickroom held few blandishments. Later on I would check in on Frank, take his temperature, and, if necessary, contact the doctor due on board. My own experience with flu is that the patient can do little but wait it out.

I felt relieved I had called Elinor, as I knew from past experience that disembarking is chaotic, at best: all those passengers trying to locate luggage, find a porter, board the right bus. With two sick friends it could be pretty hairy. Hartland would come up with a solution, I had no doubt. He thrived on challenge. As I sat on the steps of the cathedral, sliding on my dark glasses so I could look with comfort over a picture-postcard Caribbean vista, I was swept with a sudden longing for Montreal, for Canada, for the comforting routine into which I had fallen since retirement. Fed up with trying to have fun, I found myself in some very profound way bored out of my mind. I had

sailed on a ship designed for passengers with limited imagi-
nations, and perhaps it was this universal willingness to accept
the frankly second-rate as excellent that seemed so depressing.
Not to mention two sick passengers for whom I felt responsible
and a crew keeling over like toy soldiers. For luck I rubbed the
arm into which a nurse had plunged the needle filled with flu
vaccine. As Elinor had said, "Hang tough, kid."

I was probably one of the last children to be born into that
attenuated tradition beginning roughly with the *Romance of the
Rose* and ending with *Tristan and Isolde*. My mother, who
resisted information the way a duck's feathers repel water, held
an almost superstitious belief in love as a kind of universal
panacea. By love I refer to romantic love, the kind that drove
two incompatible people into a marriage that began to fray
almost before the children arrived. This love had strict rules,
one of which being that it lasted forever. Always a tentative,
timid woman, my mother lived her married life in a constant
state of apprehension around my father, as if he were a large,
boisterous dog, born to herd sheep and discourage wolves, who
at any moment might put muddy paws onto the settee or clear
bibelots off the *étagère* with one wag of his powerful tail. His
good-natured energy appeared to diminish her own; they never
fought, as whenever Father was at his most robust, Mother lay
practically supine. Yet she never ceased to love him, or to
believe she loved him, which often amounts to the same thing.

For his part, Father treated her with the exaggerated chivalry so often demonstrated by men of his generation toward
the fair sex. By today's standards the attitude seems almost un-
bearably condescending, as it circumscribes women and treats
them as creatures of limited intellect. In many cases, he was
right. Women like my mother were raised to be dim. Their

intellectual feet were bound from childhood and they remained in a constant state of bafflement, like Adam and Eve in the Garden before things acquired names.

My father would not have had her any other way. An intelligent man himself, in that forthright, factual way that dismisses imagination as insubstantial fancy, he mistrusted intelligence in women. Stupidity remained closely allied to purity, another of the rules which stated the woman one loved must be innocent. Father had read enough history to realize all the great courtesans were women of intellect. But fascinating though they might be, courtesans remained ill equipped to run a semi-detached house in Westmount and raise two children with all the traditional middle-class values.

A courtesan did not merit a pedestal, and the woman one loved must inhabit at the very least a plinth. I am reminded of the line about sex on the television. It can't hurt unless you fall off the set. By the same token, when one is stuck on a pedestal it is difficult to fool around. I have no idea whether my father strayed. I tend to doubt it, although the rules allowed men the occasional indiscretion provided they were discreet, a *cinq à sept*, more likely a one to three masquerading as lunch. Mother had a few admirers she called her beaux, single gentlemen much interested in opera and antiques, who were always available at a moment's notice to round out a bridge table or fill a gap at a dinner party.

After Father died, Mother relaxed into alcohol and reminiscence. Now that she no longer had to deal with the first draft of her husband she was free to blue pencil the past. In due course any rough passages were edited away, and she fell in love a second time, this time with a memory. I could see she was not only a lot more happy in this revised version of her life, but also a good deal less demanding. As a result I have never tampered with her scenario.

By nature a tractable and obedient child, I never found it necessary to challenge my parents. When I rebelled, as what child does not, I did not wear a sandwich board. Most parents want to believe the best about their offspring, if only because it takes so much more time and energy to criticize and demand explanations. Although I myself had many hard questions, I soon discovered the answers proferred by the sages did not bear scrutiny. Take sex, for instance. Whenever adults of my parents' generation talked about the troublesome topic with the young, the conversations brimmed with metaphor but remained short on technical details. So I learned by doing—often the best way. The same has been said about computers.

More perplexing were the attitudes I absorbed about women. So many of the girls I knew at school, whom I was raised to regard as vessels of purity, enjoyed listening to what were then considered dirty jokes, and frequently told them—to boys. More than one vision in white organdy or dusty pink tulle turned out to have a body under the frock or gown, moreover a body as eager for experience as my own. Nor was I vain or naive enough to consider myself irresistible to the opposite sex. Nothing I had absorbed from my elders suggested that women enjoyed sex. In all the talk of being in love and sowing the seed and the male prerogative was there ever a hint that women enjoyed a bonk for its own sake.

Another attitude I found incomprehensible was that grown women, many of whom had jobs and families, were seen as helpless and incompetent the second they entered our front door. They could not be expected to hang up a coat, light a cigarette, pour a drink, or have an idea. No woman could be expected to find her way home unaided, unless she had come in her own car. I spent my teens operating a limousine service with the family Buick, chauffeuring dinner guests home because taxis were seen as extravagant and some of the drivers were foreign.

When I finally met an independent girl who could open a car door and light a cigarette, who argued with my father and suggested his ideas were out of date, who got herself outfitted with a diaphragm and admitted to enjoying sex as much as I did, I married her. We enjoyed a brief period of intense happiness, and then she died in an accident along with our infant daughter. She was the only woman I ever truly loved, yet lest I sound like someone carrying an immense torch, I did love a number of others, only they happened to be male.

Sometimes during the frankly permissive Sixties and early Seventies, when people played with sex the way they now fool around with computers, I wondered if I would have turned out differently had I been born a decade or so later. Had the women I met during adolescence not been trapped in the attitudes and prejudices of an earlier time, had we all been able to admit that nice girls enjoyed sex, might I have gone straight? Who knows, or cares? Sometimes girls who were seen as "nice" girls slipped. Well and good, but if they ended up pregnant all hell broke loose. We lived in fear of pregnancy the way the young today live in fear of a life-threatening disease. Either way love is a trap. I look with sad bemusement on the ready access to condoms today, devices promoted as a way to save your life. In my youth we used them too, but to prevent initiating a life for which we were not prepared to take responsibility. When you got it on with another guy you did not risk pregnancy. Nowadays two men contemplating an interlude are strongly urged to use a condom. Civilization as I knew it totters.

When I met Elinor, it did not take me long to realize she was a woman who put to flight all the female stereotypes on which I had been raised. Starting out as a nice girl, with all the attendant restrictions, she married, divorced, and raised two children as a single parent. Somewhere along the way she stopped being a nice girl and turned into an adult woman. She does not believe that if a man gives her a decent fuck she has to kick off her shoes and follow him into the desert. (That scene from the end of *Morocco* had Mother nearly prostrate for days. Now there was love!) Elinor has developed smarts; she knows enough to come in out of the rain, but she does not teeter on the edge of paranoia. Not every man at rest in a public park is waiting to expose himself, and not every canvasser who calls to solicit for charity is trying to defraud. She does not call the police if she sees the police. She understands that some women are born to lead disorganized lives and seek out emotional chaos the way some men become mercenaries. Aggression takes many guises. She is kind without being cloying and de-monstrates humour more than wit. Humour wears better on a daily basis.

I am a fortunate man to have a human being like Elinor in my life. In my own, highly idiosyncratic way I love her, but I wish I could love her the way a heterosexual man loves a woman. Never have I responded to her embrace the way I did last night when Frank kissed me on deck. No matter how many people you can fool some of the time, you cannot fool yourself. On the other hand too much truth is not always desirable. All too often candour leaves a disagreeable odour, like certain cleaning solvents best used in small quantities. How I longed for this cruise to end. A shift in geography would bring a stop to uncertainty; home would supply the anchor I sorely missed. I felt adrift, in the Caribbean, in my head, in my life.

My bum, sore from sitting on a stone step, told me it was time to move. Stiffly, I stood, glanced at my watch, and decided it was time to return to the ship. A pair of workmen was engaged in relaying the paving stones of the walk leading from the main gate to the cathedral. In the heat of the morning they had removed their shirts, and their lean, well-muscled bodies shone like highly polished mahogany. Young enough to be my grandsons, their tactile male beauty gleamed with invitation; however, my life was complicated enough at the moment without undertaking a brace of stonemasons. Once through the cathedral gate I found the cracked sidewalks and deep gutters of the angled streets claimed all my attention as I made my way back to the *Blue Horizon*, my home away from home.

To get to the ship, it proved impossible not to pass through the Heritage Mall, and I thought it might be advisable to stock up on aspirin. My meagre medical chest had not been designed to combat an epidemic. Had I wanted to outfit myself with a trousseau—silver, crystal, china, linens—the mall offered the ultimate in one-stop shopping. Aspirin, however, turned out to be a different story. After walking the length and breadth of the area, I found a drugstore disguised as a perfume boutique. At the rear crouched a few shelves holding toothpaste, shaving creams, antacids, and a few standard analgesics, including aspirin.

On my way back to the gangplank I ran into Susan from our table, who was being escorted by Brad. The fact that he did not have his hand down the front of her dress might be explained by the presence of an older couple whom I presumed to be her aunt and uncle. Courtesy demanded that I stop and say good morning. Brad greeted me in the hectoring, good-buddy fashion that made him sound like a sportscaster. Susan made introductions. "Geoffry, this is my aunt and uncle. Geoffry's one of the men at our table." She offered no names, so I shook hands, said how-do-you-do, and asked if they were enjoying the cruise.

"Oh, yes, very much, thank you," replied the aunt, a woman with the soft, unfocussed look of someone who lives on the edge of other people's lives. "We sort of wanted to visit Nelson's Dockyard, but Susan persuaded us to go shopping."

"If you want to visit the Dockyard," I suggested, "why not hire a cab to drive you there and back. That way you won't have to take the whole island tour."

"Not a bad idea," said the uncle, American gothic slightly softened by resort wear in pastel tones. "We might do that, Marge."

"But we have to be back in time for the dinner. Tonight is the Captain's dinner," she added by way of explanation, "and we don't want to miss that." The aunt raised her voice at the end of every phrase, a vocal tic that used to indicate a question but now suggests generalized non-aggression.

"Why don't you go visit the Dockyard?" suggested Brad. "I'll look after Susan."

"But what about my emerald?" demanded Susan.

"Your emerald?" I asked, my curiosity piqued.

"Uncle Wayne promised to buy me an emerald. Who cares about the Dockyard anyway?"

Whether or not Susan acquired an emerald was of no concern to me, but suddenly I wanted to shaft this boring, acquisitive, Barbie-doll bimbo, who was so obviously taking her kindly, dim relatives for a ride.

"Antigua is not the place to buy gemstones," I began. "I have it on good authority there are better bargains to be had in St. Thomas, where we dock tomorrow. For what it's worth, I would be hesitant to buy something as costly as an emerald from just anyone. If you find, once you get home, that the stone is substandard, what recourse do you have? I would be more inclined to go to a wholesale jeweller in my own city, or country; someone who will stand behind his merchandise. I am sure there are plenty of honest jewellers in the islands, but still . . ." I trailed off. The damage had been done.

"Geoffry here's got a point," said Uncle Wayne, no doubt less enthusiastic about the purchase than Aunt Marge. "Let's wait until we get home."

"But you promised!" insisted Susan. Stamping a foot in a pink canvas tennis shoe has little impact; otherwise she would have tried.

"Perhaps Uncle Wayne is right," said the aunt, a woman easily swayed, "and it would be nice to visit the Dockyard."

"I must get back to the ship. My travelling companion has flu." I smiled and bowed. Susan gave me a look of such distilled dislike I could have laughed out loud. It was the first time I had seen that beautiful blank face register genuine feeling, and who does not experience a pleasurable *frisson* after disturbing a little shit.

XI

"Look at you, all tarted up. What the young today might call a geezer hunk."

"I didn't know you were awake. I've been creeping about as though I came in to rob the cabin."

"Open the curtains, will you. I've forgotten what daylight looks like."

I pulled aside the curtain to flood the room with late-afternoon light. "Are you feeling better?"

"It's hard to tell. I think I may live, but I'm not sure I want to."

"Perhaps I'd better take your temperature." I slid the thermometer under his tongue. "The geezer hunk, as you so charmingly put it, is off to the Captain's dinner. This is the night that all the men who rented tuxedos, with matching bow tie and cummerbund, get to wear them, while the women get the opportunity to flaunt their tans, their new jewellery, and the chic little outfits they bought in 'better dresses'." I checked the thermometer to learn Frank's temperature had gone down half a degree or so, hardly a major improvement, but still better than up. "You seem to be on the mend." I put my hand on his forehead, then under his chin. "You don't feel as warm."

Before I had a chance to remove my hand Frank covered it with his. "You make one hell of a nurse. Would you consider taking me on as a full-time patient now that you are retired?

Think about it: your own room and bath, full access to the bar, travel, house seats for all my productions—all in exchange for various light, and pleasurable, duties. You'd be a fool to refuse."

"Will you need references? Clean, honest, hardworking. Goes to church on his Sunday off and doesn't have women in his room."

Frank laughed weakly, a good sign. "No references necessary. Are you going to have a drink before you leave to set hearts aflutter?"

"Sure, if it won't bother you."

"I'd enjoy the company, even though I never thought the day would come when I would watch you drink alone and not join in. My liver must be having a little holiday."

I poured myself a shot of contraband scotch and added a little water from the bottle on the night table. "Dinner will be about as much fun as a kidney transplant. Three of our table companions are sick, and Brad is hitting on Susan, who is mad at me because I persuaded her aunt and uncle not to buy Miss Wisconsin an emerald."

"How so?"

I told Frank about our meeting on the pier and my raising the spectre of doubt. We were both laughing when the telephone rang. I answered to find Elinor on the line. "Geoffry?"

"A.k.a. Nurse Chadwick. What's up?"

"Hartland got in touch with his friend who's on the board of directors for the cruise line. There will be a limousine at the pier, and a nurse to help you through the airport. Can you think of anything else you may need?"

"Not at the moment. I must say I feel a lot more confident about our arrival knowing we will have a car. I suppose I could have arranged things from this end, but I believe there is less chance of a foul-up if one of the head honchos is on the job. Thanks ever so. Frank, too, is sending thanks, from his bed of pain."

"How is he doing?"

"His temperature is down a bit. But these infections really whack you. It will be a while before he feels one hundred per cent."

"I guess. Give him my love. Well, kiddo, I won't drag this out. Day after tomorrow you will be home and we'll catch up then. Best to Elsie, and to you—*ça va sans dire*."

"Okay, Elinor, kissy-kissy. See you soon." I hung up. "The gist of that wasn't too hard to follow. We have our car and nurse. How will you manage when you arrive in San Francisco?"

"While you were out this morning I sent a wire. I'll be met at the airport. I don't look forward to the trip, but it will pass."

"Shall I have another drink, or would you prefer to be quiet?"

"All this talk has worn me out. I'll sleep for a bit, then order something to eat from room service. You go flaunt your finery in the bar."

"I'll check in after dinner."

"That would be good. Have fun."

"I'll try, but I'm not holding my breath."

By the time I let myself out of the cabin Frank had already closed his eyes.

Because of the Captain's dinner, the ship hummed with excitement. Added to the faint but palpable vibration of engines revving up for departure, the electricity in the air generated a kind of benevolent tension, as though the entire week had merely been preparation for this moment. Doors opened and closed up and down the corridor as families began heading down to the dining room for the first sitting. Every last woman was turned out for the occasion in the kind of sensible styles one might reasonably expect from those travelling with children. The emphasis appeared to be on wrinkle-resistant fabrics in pastel shades and not too much exposed skin. Children wore the freshly scrubbed look of celebrants at a birthday party. Their fathers ran the sartorial gamut from tuxedos through business suits past blazers to one disgruntled parent who had fastened the top button of his floral Hawaiian shirt and added a tie. They hurried down the staircase or stood impatiently waiting for the elevator, all gripped with a sense of occasion.

I climbed to the top deck and walked into the Blue Lagoon, only to find it packed with people celebrating the last big night on board. My favourite table by the window had been appropriated by the large female who had spent the cruise parboiling herself on deck. In a black skirt and voluminous white lamé top, she looked like a fudge sundae. Her companion, a woman in her late forties, wore black evening pyjamas trimmed in feathers. They made an odd couple, but no more so than the rest of those in the bar, most of whom were dressed as if to attend a Christmas cocktail party. The fact that it was late spring in the Caribbean had not dampened the urge to wear chiffon, lace, lamé, velvet, jersey, sequins, bead trim, matching gold kid evening bag and shoes, along with the occasional little piece of fur. In my navy-blue tropical blazer and pale-gray slacks I felt as though I should be serving drinks, not ordering them.

Faute de mieux, I took a seat at the bar and, in a gesture of defiance against a hostile universe, ordered a dry martini. As a compromise with fate, I ordered it on the rocks. I knew even before I took that first astringent, delicious sip that I would be sorry in the morning. But tonight's need sent tomorrow's remorse scurrying for cover.

I knew I should make the drink last as long as possible, but that first, cold, bitter, aromatic swallow cried out for another. About to lift the glass, I felt a hand on my shoulder and heard a voice saying, "Drinking alone is too impossibly dreary. Do come and join us."

At first the voice seemed to issue disembodied from a cloud of expensive cologne, but I turned to see Huntley smiling and gesturing toward a table in the far corner. "There's a vacant chair at the adjoining table," he continued. "Bring your drink."

Pausing only to pay my bar bill, I picked up my glass and followed. Georgette and Charlotte smiled and nodded; Greg managed a "Hi, there." Both men wore dinner jackets in the shade once called midnight blue. Huntley wore a black-velvet butterfly bow, Greg a kind of ribbon that crossed at the throat. Georgette, too, wore a tux; her bow tie looked as if she had tied it herself, and Charlotte wore a long black sheath. Were it not for the quantities of gold jewellery, the group looked as though they had just come from a wake, although their minimalist chic was more to my liking than the baubles, bangles, and beads surrounding us.

"And how did you spend your day?" inquired Charlotte, seated at my right.

"I walked into town, visited the cathedral, kept an eye on the patient. Completely uneventful."

"We hired a car to take us to a beach. The ship packed a lunch. We drank too much wine and got too much sun. Drove past Nelson's Dockyard but didn't stop. All eighteenth-century dockyards look alike."

"I must say you're looking very 'tanned and fit and rested,' as they say in the papers."

"God, I'll be glad to get home!" exclaimed Georgette, inhaling deeply. "Will you look at these people—a fire sale at J.C. Penney."

"Oh, they aren't that bad," said Huntley with a little laugh. "Just because they don't have any taste."

It was on the tip of my tongue to say that good taste has been called the consolation prize for lack of talent, but I had no axe to grind with these people. It was evident that the quartet had grown weary of one another's company and longed for a new face and point of view.

"What do you do, Geoffry?" inquired Charlotte. "I know it's none of my business, but on this ship what you do is what you are."

"I'm retired now. I was a lawyer, the kind who stays out of the courtroom. I have never enjoyed the limelight."

"Do you miss not working?" asked Huntley.

"Not really. I found the idea of retirement more alarming than retirement itself. I wondered if my inner resources would have to be constantly replenished by single-malt scotch, but so far I've managed to keep busy and avoid A.A. I've never been much for hobbies—tying trout flies, or collecting snuff boxes, or learning to play the recorder; but life has a way of filling in the blanks. Sometimes I wonder how I found time to work."

"I'd love to retire," admitted Huntley, "but business is good at the moment. I'm an interior designer." He smiled. "Texture is back, in case you didn't know. Time to trash all those smooth surfaces: the lacquer furniture, the polished floors, the faux-marbleized walls. Things must look rough, hammered, crumbling. Fieldstone fireplaces, hand-hewn beams, abrasive upholstery fabrics. I detest them all, but who am I to buck a trend." He paused to drink. "I wish I could be as confident as you about filling in time. The prospect of idleness terrifies me."

"Believe me," I said, "it doesn't hurt a bit. It's the Peter principle in reverse: Leisure expands to fill the time available for its enjoyment."

"I'm sure you're right." Huntley nodded. "And sooner or later I'll have to step down. I'm grooming Greg to take over the business. I've made him my heir."

Now the focus of attention, Greg shifted in his chair, luckily across the table from mine so I did not have to deal with his knee. So far he had ignored me, outside of his initial greeting. He wore dark glasses, pointless now that the sun had set. I have always found wearing dark glasses indoors a foolish affectation, like carrying a plastic bottle of water on the bus. So far he had given little evidence he could speak an entire sentence, let alone run a business. Did being Huntley's heir mean the relationship had been formalized by a will? The present relationship seemed tenuous at best, not to say frayed. It was one thing to bring along a squeeze for a week of sun and sex, another to make a long-term commitment like a will, if indeed a will there was.

Over the years I had met many couples like Huntley and Greg. The older man, usually affluent and affable, wants to be liked, and fears ending up alone. All too often this man ends up with a much younger man, with whom he has little in common outside of being gay. As a result the pair find themselves forced into a series of weary compromises, the younger man for financial security, the older one bargaining for companionship. What I would find alarming is having to contend with some-one like Greg on a daily basis. He might well be a ten in the kip, but I would give him a three in most other departments. If he was willing to put the make on an old fart like me then he would hit on anyone, not a sane or safe way to behave these days. During my fauve period I turned dozens of tricks like Greg, twinkies, men you wanted to have sex with without the boring preliminaries of conversation. They were fun for about an hour, sometimes a whole night. A few even lasted an entire weekend, followed by a promise to call. Some did, but not many. A few turned into relationships lasting weeks, sometimes months. But once the sexual novelty had worn off we were thrown back on whatever else we had in common. Ay, there's the rub. So long. See you around. Good luck. Take care. Call me.

Of the present quartet I felt sure I would have enjoyed Huntley had I taken him on *mano a mano*. He did not interest me sexually in the least, but he had lived his life in a field I found interesting. I am sure he had tales to tell. Yet he had burdened himself with two women and a male bimbo, and I knew we could never have any kind of real meeting with the others present. Yet I probably had more in common with this group than with anyone else on the ship except Frank. What the hell. I offered to buy the next round, and was accepted on condition I join them for a drink after dinner.

By the time the gong for second sitting had sounded through the public address system, we were all, to borrow an expression of my father's, feeling no pain. After the third martini—it's reassuring to have a partner in crime—Charlotte became quite chatty, loquacious almost, and told me about her job as a fundraiser for various cultural organizations. She did not call herself a fundraiser, but an arts consultant, although beating the bushes for donations was how she earned the rent. Almost immediately she assured me that she did not raise money for the kind

of group that encouraged macramé wall hangings or poetry
written in lowercase letters. Symphony orchestras, opera com-
panies, art galleries were her principal clients. I listened and
learned. Nobody young gives money for the arts. All those
fresh-killed fortunes from computer technology and currency
speculation sat untapped, earning compound interest. Old
money, meaning that which had been in the family for at least
one generation, still underwrote Beethoven, Bellini, and
Boucher. Furthermore, old money had lost its cachet, having
been replaced by fame, or notoriety, as the currency of choice.
Better to be famous than rich as fame had become a highly
marketable commodity. "Poor little famous girl."

Huntley interrupted to suggest another quick round before
heading down to dinner, but I begged off. Three martinis were
already two too many, and the night was young. Charlotte and
Georgette had just lit fresh cigarettes, but I excused myself.
The dining room staff, decimated by illness, had enough problems without diners arriving half an hour late and expecting
service as usual.

A long line waited for the elevators, so I took the stairs, one
hand resting on the handrail. One of the sure signs of older
middle age is to realize a handrail is no longer merely decora-
tive. In the Sweaty Palms couples danced to a Latin American
beat I could not place, neither rhumba, samba, nor mambo.
Time, even that with a bongo beat, marches on. On entering
the dining salon I was immediately struck by the level of noise,
all those pre-dinner cocktails. Then I wondered if I had chosen
the wrong table as the one where I usually ate was almost full.
On moving closer I realized that both Elsie and Darlene had
risen from their sickbeds to attend the Captain's dinner. Not
the best idea in the world, I would have thought, and I could

only hope they were no longer infectious.

"Well, well, Elsie, Darlene, I see you are able to sit up and take nourishment? Susan, Brad." Susan looked at me as though I were the Antichrist; Brad nodded.

"I suppose I shouldn't really be here," confided Elsie in her most disarming voice, "but I just hated the idea of missing the big dinner on board."

"Are you well enough to be up?" I inquired, trying to keep my voice steady. Having just drunk three martinis, perhaps the most behaviour-altering substance permitted by law, I found my behaviour altered. Anger surged through me as I realized that Elsie was putting her recovery in jeopardy for the sake of a damn dinner. "What happens if you have a relapse?"

She gave a nervous little laugh. "I always have your strong right arm to depend on."

"Not if I get sick you don't!" There must have been an edge in my voice, because the table fell silent. "How are you feeling, Darlene?" I asked to mellow the mood.

"As well as can be expected," she replied, speaking not to me but to Brad and Susan, "all things considered."

I wondered if her intuition had been picking up signals, or perhaps that omniscient little bird had somehow managed to tell Darlene that Brad had not been letting the grass grow while she lay ill in the cabin. Poor Darlene, she looked dreadful. The pleated white dress with its sweetheart neckline might have suited her fifteen years ago, and a faded tan made her look sallow under masses of hair tumbling out of control. With heavy makeup hastily applied she was no match for Susan, serene in her blank golden beauty buttressed by youth. Sex is not an equal-opportunity situation.

Brad had evidently rented a tux with powder-blue bow tie

and cummerbund. He managed to look like the headwaiter in a third-rate gay restaurant (there are no first-rate gay restaurants), but I decided to keep the observation to myself. Elsie had somehow found the energy and dedication to visit the ship's hairdresser; her crowning glory looked suspiciously like epoxy, but her eyes under the eyeliner were puffy and tired.

As tomorrow would be the day that tips were handed out, our waiter nearly bent double to be accommodating, handing out the oversized menus with a deferential flourish. Almost immediately Brad produced a pen and asked us all to sign his menu. At the same time Elsie waved a camera and asked me to take a picture of the table. I readily complied, as taking the photo meant I didn't have to be in it. My triumph was temporary, as Elsie handed the camera to the waiter and asked him to take us all. Tonight's dinner was table d'hôte with no choice, unless one made a special request. Food is food, and I decided not to argue with the tournedos. Furthermore, in a flush of martinis and relief that the day after tomorrow I would be home, I managed to snag the wine waiter as he went swanning by and ordered two bottles of red for the table. Those who preferred white were out of luck: he who pays the waiter calls the colour. Elsie made rather an issue of saying she really shouldn't; this was the first time she had left the cabin since she fell ill. (She appeared to have overlooked the trip to the hairdresser.) She didn't want to take the chance. The second dinner was over, she was going to retire. It really was very naughty of her to be here in the first place.

Silently, I agreed.

While Elsie was going on at length about the obvious, I happened to glance at Darlene, only to be struck by the realization that she was more than likely drunk. I could well imagine her knocking back a couple of drinks in the cabin while she trowelled on makeup, drinks which, considering her weakened condition, would have hit hard. Like most who have the flu, she had probably eaten very little during the last twenty-four hours, so one drink would wallop her like three. She did not speak but sat slumped, as though the sheer effort of not keeling over sideways demanded all her concentration. I wondered idly whether a time would come, sometime during the next millennium, when the practice of sitting down before the evening meal and drinking quantities of alcohol would be seen as a quaint and ancient practice, like spinning thread on a wheel or winnowing wheat by hand.

The wine waiter arrived, and we went through the equally quaint custom of pouring, tasting, nodding approval, and finally serving. "Cheers," I said raising my glass, "to a safe journey home."

Brad and Elsie repeated "Cheers;" Susan said nothing; Darlene made a guttural noise in the back of her throat before drinking the entire glass of Médoc in two swallows. Before the wine waiter had a chance to serve his other tables, she demanded a refill. By now I was convinced she was away and gone. A slab of terrine provided an interruption and we all fell to. Considering the menu, the chef must have believed the quickest way to a man's heart attack is through his stomach. I felt better with something inside me to soak up the gin, and for just a moment I permitted myself the luxury of enjoying the moment, of believing perhaps things would work themselves out and that I could cope with shepherding Elsie and Frank to and through the airport.

My mini-euphoria was not to last. Susan, whose idea of good food did not extend to *terrine de canard*, smiled at Brad and asked if he would like hers. He grinned at her hungrily and she lifted her slice of pâté onto his plate. This transaction did not pass unnoticed by Darlene, who took umbrage. Pushing herself unsteadily to her feet, she moved to stand behind Brad's chair.

"I saw him first, you interfering little bitch!" she announced in a voice that carried farther than I am sure she intended. Before Brad could get to his feet with a "There, there, dear," Darlene swung a punch, a real street-smart, closed-fist punch which landed squarely on Susan's left cheek. With a muffled shriek, Susan slid onto the floor.

"For Christ's sake, Darlene . . ." Brad jumped up to help the stricken Susan back onto her chair. Before he could round on the outraged Darlene she had collapsed into her own chair and burst into tears. Unfortunately hers were not the delicate, pear shaped, crystal tears that trickle softly down the cheek and into a man's heart, but large, wet, splashy drops that smudged her eyeliner and poured down the side of her nose.

By now the adjoining tables had abandoned all pretence of not looking and stared with avid amazement at the bonus entertainment. All masculine solicitude, Brad ignored Darlene and dabbed at Susan's more user-friendly tears with his dinner napkin while urging her to drink some wine. According to the way I had been raised I should have been mortified; I was in the middle of a scene in a public restaurant. At the same time the subversive Geoffry Chadwick rejoiced at a little unscripted drama livening up dinner with these otherwise dowdy people. However, some action needed to be taken about the sobbing Darlene, who, drunk and feverish, needed to be steered back to her cabin.

"Perhaps Darlene would like to go back to her stateroom." I spoke directly to Brad.

"Nothing preventing her." He shrugged.

"I think she should be escorted."

"So escort her."

I turned to Elsie, who during the past few moments had worn the studiously neutral expression of someone trying not to break wind at a concert of chamber music. "Can you take Darlene up to her cabin?"

"Oh, I don't think I'm well enough."

"Then what the hell are you doing here?" Without waiting for an answer I stood and moved around the table to stand behind the weeping Darlene. Placing my hands on her shoulders in a calming gesture I asked if I could see her back to her stateroom. She did not reply but stood, shakily. I offered her my arm and the two of us edged our way through the dining room, past half-averted but curious faces, waiters bearing trays, and a simmering headwaiter who looked at us as though we had arrived on purpose to disrupt his carefully orchestrated dinner.

Darlene did not speak, and I saw no need. We entered the elevator and she pushed a button, several below the one I was accustomed to pushing. Her cabin lay no more than a few doors from the elevator foyer. While she was fishing about for the card to open her door, I spoke for the first time.

"Dump him, Darlene. He's a prick. I do not confess to be Ann Landers, or Dr. Ruth, or Dear Abby; but whatever it is you are looking for, you won't find it with him."

By now she had stopped weeping. She turned her ravaged face to me and half smiled. "I figured that out already. I think I still love him, but he's a shit. There's no future, and I'm going to clear out." She placed a conciliatory hand on my arm. "I just had to belt that dame. Sorry I dragged you into it."

"Don't be. She had it coming. Will you be well enough to

get home on Saturday?"

"I guess I'll have to be. I'll lie low tomorrow. Thanks, Geoffry, for bailing me out."

She flung her arms around my neck and kissed me soundly on the cheek, in the process managing to wipe some of her foundation onto my jacket. I waited until she had shut the cabin door before returning to the dining room. As I crossed to my table, I could see Brad helping himself to the wine I had bought with the arm that wasn't around Susan's shoulders. Elsie was nowhere to be seen.

I sat at my place and folded my hands on the table in front of me. "Brad, you are an ill-mannered lout, but I will give you a word of good advice. If you go back to your cabin tonight, make sure Darlene is asleep before you nod off. Otherwise she may decide to play a nasty trick when you are least expecting it. Furthermore, if you are going to fuck Susan that is your business, but please do not do so at the dinner table."

His reaction could not have been more predictable. Unwrapping himself from Susan he pushed back his chair so hard it tipped over as he jumped to his feet. "You bastard! I ought to beat the crap out of you!"

"Beating up a senior citizen in front of a room full of witnesses is a bad idea, one which even someone with your limited intelligence should be able to grasp. Now sit down and finish your dinner. I have said what I have to say, and I will not speak again."

By now it had percolated through to Susan that she may have been insulted. "How dare you speak to me like that, you —you interfering old fool!" Without waiting for an answer, she flung her napkin onto the table and bolted from the dining room. She had obviously watched her share of Bette Davis movies on television. Pausing only to call me a son-of-a-bitch, rather a tame epithet considering the things I have been called over the years, Brad followed, to the amusement of the adjoining tables. Ignoring them all I poured myself another glass of my wine and prepared to enjoy the meal in welcome solitude. So pleased was I with the turn of events that I applauded with all the other diners when the lights went out and a brace of waiters carried in a giant Baked Alaska flambé. After that, however, I broke ranks and asked for Stilton. The waiter readily complied. After all, serving one undemanding passenger is a lot easier than waiting on six.

Frank lay in bed laughing as I told him about dining in solitary splendour. His temperature had gone down slightly. While I was out of the cabin he had managed to take a shower and give himself a shave. He still looked under the weather, but clean.

"Chadwick, you are something else. For the first time since I came down with the vapours I feel I've really missed out. How I would have loved to be there."

"I would have liked that. But, who knows, your presence might have changed the dynamics of the situation. With you there I might have behaved. That silly cow, Elsie, blithely assuming that I will drag her old bones back to Montreal regardless. Just pull a fadeout and the nearest available man will bail you out. It was women like Elsie that made me jump the fence," I burst out laughing, "for which I ought to be eternally grateful."

Frank joined me in a laugh. "Can you believe this? I don't have a drink. I don't feel like a cigarette. I still have a fever and I'm laughing. It must be the wonderful nursing care I'm getting."

"*Sans doute*. Are you up to eating something, or someone?

Shall I summon the cabin boy?"

"What a dirty old thing you are. Maybe an egg-salad sandwich, and some tea."

I rang for whomever was on duty, as our butler had been laid low. The call was answered by the efficient young woman who made up the cabins. Not surprisingly she looked tired, but she had not fallen sick. I placed the order and asked if she would let herself in and leave the tray on the table. No great hurry. For that she looked grateful, and I made a mental note to tip her well for her extra care.

"Off you go to meet your friends," said Frank. "I'll be A-okay. Just watch out for the trick. Remember, I saw you first."

I smiled. "I guess you did—a long time ago. Did you know you were my first?"

"I suspected. And you were mine."

"Don't tell me! You can remember as if it were yesterday."

Frank folded back his sheet. "Almost. I can remember how frightened I was, frightened and fascinated. I couldn't believe you could be interested in me. Geoffry Chadwick: big wheel on student council, top student, chick magnet. Christ, when I was kidnapped to Toronto, I thought my life was over."

"I was pretty miserable too. But I guess we survived. One does. If people really died of unhappiness, the world would not be so overpopulated. Well, if you're all right for the moment I'll go and fling myself into the mad whirl. I'll look in later."

"Please do. You know something, Geoff? For someone who's really awful you're not too bad."

"Like Avis, we are more trying." I smiled and let myself out of the cabin. Unsure of where to go, I walked down the passageway and onto the stern deck. I continued to be surprised at how few passengers came outside after dark. Banks of lights beat back the gloom, and the soft tropical air had lost the steamy feel that comes with the sun. For most people the lure of live entertainment, movies, gambling, or just having a few drinks pulled more strongly than the unsophisticated pleasure of being outdoors. Lest I sound like a refugee from Greenpeace, I hasten to add that were the show first-rate, I would be watching. The current film depended less on its actors than on the special-effects studio. The preview had featured any number of automobiles crashing into one another and exploding noisily into bursts of orange flame. I had already drunk more than I normally did at home, and the only attraction the casino might offer was to watch someone who knew how to count cards take out the house at blackjack.

One of the unpleasant side effects of drinking a lot is that concentration goes. I was in no condition to read anything but magazines or pulp fiction. Between the bridge players in the library and Frank filling up the cabin, there was nowhere on board, short of occasional chairs in public areas, to sit down with a book. Uncertain of where to go, I headed for the small triangular area shielded by the steps leading to the upper deck, the spot where Frank and I had made contact, so to speak. I was beginning to think of the area as my own private place and was not in the least pleased to see another couple had colonized the space. Locked in an embrace, they were so involved in French kissing, soul kissing, or eating face, depending on one's formative decade, that they did not see me as I stopped, turned, and retreated into shadow on the other side of the stairs.

Apparently startled by the sound of another passenger coming down the steps, they drew apart, and in the soft clarity of moonlight, the two anonymous figures resolved themselves into Greg and Charlotte. Astonished, I moved silently across the deck to the far side. I don't think they saw me, not that it would have mattered. But something was obviously going on of which I wanted no part. It would appear that both Greg and Charlotte were gay only up to a point, and quite possibly gay only through expediency. Sex is a commodity, like wheat or pork futures. Huntley and Georgette appeared to have the money. Greg and Charlotte had been brought along, like golf clubs and paperback novels, to make the trip more pleasant. Had resentment caused them to drift together? Was it something as simple as desire? Had there perhaps been a shared wish to stick it to the ones who paid the bills and called the shots?

Whatever the reason, I found various pieces of the puzzle fitting into place. So much for my still-potent personal magnetism. What better way for Greg to throw a smokescreen over his affair with Charlotte than to make an obvious and public play for me, or whoever else happened along. I could almost have laughed, even though the laugh was squarely on Geoffry Chadwick.

By now the deck stood empty, and I wandered over to the stern rail from where I could see the lower decks and the turbulence of the wake disappearing into the blackness.

"If you're looking out for icebergs," said a voice at my elbow, "I suggest you try the other end."

I turned to see Huntley, by himself, at the rail.

"If we are done in by a berg that has made its way north from the Weddell Sea or south from Baffin Bay, it will be women and children last, especially after a week of tots and their permissive parents."

Huntley laughed out loud. "A man after my own heart. 'Damn the icebergs! Full speed ahead!'"

"Haven't we switched our frame of reference?"

"Perhaps. How's your friend doing?"

"As well as can be expected. His temperature is slightly down, but he won't be well enough to travel on Saturday. Also my other patient, the one from Montreal, turned up for dinner tonight. She had no business leaving her cabin. I hope she doesn't have a relapse. I hope I don't get sick myself." I paused. "Sorry, I seem to be venting."

"Where better than out of doors, like smoking." Huntley paused to light up. "I may do a bit of venting myself: coming on this cruise has turned out to be one of my less successful ideas."

"How so?" I knew I had been cued to inquire, and I was curious about the answer.

"Trying to keep peace between two battling dykes—excuse me—two gracious and lovely Sapphic ladies—has worn me down. Not to mention my own uneasy relationship with Greg. Am I shocking you?"

"Hardly. I've been on both sides of the fence, although at the moment I seem to be straddling it, with a fencepost up my wazoo. But enough about me. What made you decide to come on this ship, with this particular group?"

"As Charlotte explained, there was a problem of schedule, and we thought by travelling together we would make our own fun. Also persuade those less astute that we were just plain folks. The girls have been at each other's throats since we walked up the gangplank. The only time they behave is when you are around, for which you are in my debt. The few drinks I have enjoyed on board are those I've knocked back with you."

"Happy to be of service," I said, "but didn't you have an inkling of what you were letting yourself in for?"

"I suppose, but I chose to ignore the warning signs. I hoped the balmy tropical breezes would banish care, as promised in the brochures. But the girls have been less of a problem than Greg."

"Huntley, I know it's none of my business, but I'm full of gin. Also you are at liberty to tell me to eff-off, but why does a man of your taste and cultivation put up with a twerp like him?" For a moment I was tempted to tell him about the tryst I had just witnessed, but I wanted to hear what he had to say.

Huntley shrugged an uncomfortable shrug. "I'm not telling you to eff-off because I've asked myself the same question, many times. I guess the bottom line is that I'm afraid of being alone."

"That sounds very like a line from a *télé-roman*, soap opera to you. There are worse things in life than solitude, like having to deal with someone who doesn't share your background, your values, your accumulated experience . . ."

". . . and someone who tries to put the make on a guest I invite for a drink?"

"You noticed?"

"How could I not? If you had moved any farther away from him you would have ended up on the floor. Tonight I seated you across the table, so you could cross your legs. I'll give you credit, Geoffry, you don't trespass on somebody else's turf—unlike many I have known."

"I didn't come on the cruise to make out. I have a relationship going in Montreal, and one is enough."

"So the man you are travelling with really isn't your lover."

"He was once, when we were teenagers, but not any more."

We stood for a while, watching the propellers churn the ocean into luminous foam.

Huntley broke the silence. "I'm glad I ran into you just now. Believe it or not, talking to you has tidied up my thinking. You are right. Greg has to go. He's a bimbo. The cruise has made that inescapable fact abundantly clear."

"You will meet someone else."

"Only another Greg clone. Another nitwit who works out and offers his youth, a flat abdomen, and a heavy dose of pop culture as his share of the relationship." Huntley paused to light another cigarette. "I hope you will take what I am going to say in context, but the person I fantasize about meeting is someone like you. I know it sounds as though I'm coming on strong, but what I mean is—somebody my own age, a man who's been around the track. Someone who could be, in the truest sense of the word, a companion. I could do without sex. I've had my share. I'd gladly trade all the abs in the world for one comfortable warm body with whom I could talk over the day, in words of more than two syllables. Or—in the words of the song —'Somebody like you.'"

Huntley put an arm around my shoulders and gave me a squeeze. "Whoever you are seeing up there in frozen Montreal sure is lucky." He dropped his arm. "And now I'll go and join my party in the casino. By Saturday it will all be over. Who would have thought a tropical holiday could turn out to be an endurance test." He walked over to the door. "Perhaps I'll see you later, if we don't hit that iceberg."

"Women, children, and ex-lovers last!"

He waved, and I turned back to the rail.

Most of the comic strips I devoured as a child would now be held up to censure because of a politically correct mindset that takes offense at separating coloured from white when doing the family wash. The *Katzenjammer Kids* made fun of European immigrants, just as *L'il Abner* lampooned the rural South. Whatever Batman and Robin may have done in private, one suspects that today's issue would be Robin's right to the Gotham City pension paid to his partner Batman, were the latter to be terminated by one of his colourful enemies. As a magician Mandrake would probably be a member of ACTRA, his friend Lothar by now a Black Panther. Would the Lone Ranger be welcome on a reservation when he and his longtime companion Tonto decide to retire?

Even as a child, I was struck by the lack of humour in the funny papers. Those comic strips that were faintly amusing scored points off the unsophisticated: immigrants, rural types, the disenfranchised. Urban strips drew on stereotype: the henpecked husband, Jiggs; the termagant wife, Maggie; short men, Mutt and The Little King; fatties, Wimpy and Smilin' Jack's Mexican friend whose shirt buttons popped off to be eaten by chickens. Blonde airheads were a staple, like Daisy Mae and Blondie, while marriage became a battleground where incompetent husbands like Jiggs and Dagwood spent their time shirking responsibility.

Several of the strips made no attempt at comedy but drew their inspiration from soap operas. That was the time when ongoing radio serials really were sponsored by laundry products, Rinso, Oxydol, Lux. Strips like *Jane Arden* or *Terry and the Pirates* read almost like radio scripts, as did the best, or the worst of the genre, *Mary Worth*.

A silver-haired widow comfortably into her sixties, Mary Worth seemed an unlikely heroine for a so-called comic strip, which turned out to be comic only when read by the jaundiced eye of a teenage smartass. A veritable wellspring of kindly intentions, Mary Worth spent her declining years offering sweetly sensible advice to the lovelorn, the unhappy, and the hard done-by. None of these beautiful people—the strip appeared to have been drawn by a fashion illustrator—ever seemed to take Mary's well-meant advice. Instead they went on to screw up their lives week after week, only to return to Mary for more tea and sympathy. The strip ought to have carried a warning that it could rot your teeth. The last I saw of Mary Worth was in a satirical magazine where she was lampooned as Mary Worthless, responsible for ruining the lives of an entire town.

Now silver-haired and comfortably into my sixties, I was turning into the Mary Worth of the *Blue Horizon*. Twice this very evening I had told people I scarcely knew what to do with their lives, without so much as a "by your leave," or "if you don't mind my saying so." With the social worker's easy certainties, in my case provided by martinis, I seemed to be prepared to advise anyone on anything. Just ask Dr. Chadwick.

The only person on board I could not advise was myself. Far from being able to sort out my feelings for Frank and Elinor, I was drifting in a kind of emotional suspended animation as I waited for the cruise to end. Whether or not disembarking would solve anything was anybody's guess. There are times when I have liked myself better than I did at this moment. It is difficult to like or respect a man in his mid sixties who is pissing and moaning over the confused state of his love life like a spotty teenager. Granted, there are those who would argue that a man of my age was fortunate to find himself in this dilemma, that at a time when many of my contemporaries are worrying about the next heart attack or round of chemotherapy, I am engrossed in the concerns of a man forty years younger. Unfortunately I am not one of those people.

I honestly believed that when I buried Patrick I also buried the capacity for a certain kind of love. Until I met, or rediscovered, Patrick I thought that I had put paid to romantic involvements. Perhaps romantic is an inappropriate word, as it comes burdened with two centuries of baggage. I suppose what I mean is a kind of friendship with an added dimension of sexuality and affection. Who today talks of love affairs, as dated as shingled hair and Pink Lady cocktails. But I had a feeling for Patrick that went beyond mere friendship. I would not have committed suicide on his account, but I would certainly have discouraged him from committing suicide over me.

Then I met Elinor and rediscovered a kind of affection that borders on love. I liked her more than any other woman I have known, except possibly my wife; but liking, no matter how strong the affection, is not love. This absence had posed no problem, as Elinor would have been the last woman in the world to draw a line in the sand. What nobody had ever warned me against was the affective dimension in looking after a sick person. Always having done a major fadeout when someone required care, with the exception of my mother, I had never understood the odd, potent mixture of compassion, eroticism, and power that having a sick person under your control can stimulate. During the last two days I had grown more attached to Frank than I cared to admit. Relinquishing that care would be a deprivation. Saying goodbye at the airport? Well, I would face that hurdle only when I had to.

The wake still churned its luminous way into darkness. I wanted no more company and nothing more to drink. Most of all, I wanted to avoid the gallant disappointment most of the passengers must by now be feeling as the night of the Captain's dinner drew to its unsatisfactory close.

About to leave my post by the rail, I turned to find Huntley crossing the deck, followed by Greg.

"You're still here, Geoffry," Huntley observed with a stagey kind of jollity. "Greg and I were just looking for a spot to have a private word."

"I was just about to go inside. The deck is all yours." I walked briskly to the door leading into the passageway and went directly to the cabin. Frank slept heavily. I did not feel in the least sleepy, and in spite of the filtration system, the cabin had the slightly stale odour of too much humanity in too confined a space. I let myself out again and walked slowly back down the passageway to the rear deck. I did not want to intrude on the conversation of Huntley and Greg, but the space was large enough for me not to crowd them. In spite of Huntley's territorial remark, I had every bit as much right to be on deck as he.

I could see two figures standing by the rail on the other side, not far in fact from where I had seen Greg and Charlotte embracing. In the moonlit semi-dark they looked almost like shadow puppets or mimes projecting their movements onto the giant screen of the sky. As I watched from the far side of the deck I could see the movements were growing animated, agitated even. In fact it looked to me as though the Greg puppet had grabbed hold of the Huntley puppet and a scuffle was taking place. For a moment I hesitated, wondering if I should make my presence known, when I heard a low cry and one of the figures crumpled to the deck.

I crossed in long strides to find Greg half lifting, half dragging a stunned Huntley to the rail with what looked to me like every intention of pushing him over. In fact, Huntley lay face down, his abdomen on the rail, torso over the edge, only his legs on the deck side.

"What the hell!" I exclaimed as I lunged to push Greg to one side and grab the collar of Huntley's jacket, heaving him back off the rail to land in an untidy heap on the deck. "That's one way to end a lovers' quarrel, but the wrong way."

"You son-of-a-bitch!" muttered Greg as he came at me.

A number of things flashed through my mind in no particular sequence. Greg was young, well built, angry. He had just tried to push Huntley overboard, and I had seen him. We were alone on deck. This was no time for sweet reason or even the Marquis of Queensberry rules. Completely unskilled in the finer points of hand-to-hand combat, I needed a weapon. The only object at hand was one of the large glass ashtrays, set out on tables for those who smoked on deck. Reaching for the nearest one I swung it with all my strength just as, with hands outstretched, he grabbed for my neck. The full force of the ashtray caught him on the side of the head with a dull thwack, and he sank onto the deck, stunned. The blow hurt him a good deal more than it hurt me and went a long way toward soothing my still-smarting vanity.

Huntley gave a low moan and began to stir. Stepping over the prone body of Greg, I helped Huntley to his feet and guided him to a chair.

"I think I came out on the deck just in time."

"I think you did." Huntley's voice sounded distant.

"Are you all right?"

"I think so. My jaw is sore where he punched me, but it will pass. What about him?"

I could feel the pulse, strong and regular. "Just stunned. I whacked him with an ashtray. I'd better call an officer so they can put him in the brig, or in irons, or hang him from the yardarm, or make him walk the plank—or whatever it is on cruise ships."

Huntley put a hand on my arm. "Just a minute, Geoffry. I'm not sure I want to press charges."

"What do you mean you're not sure. He just tried to push you overboard. It's a long way down, Huntley. The impact of hitting the water would stun you, and by the time we got the ship turned around you'd be lost in the dark. Not a nice thought."

"No, it's not. You're right. But if I accuse him it will mean a trial. Where? In Chicago? In Antigua? Are we in international waters? You will be called as witness. It will be a messy situation. A trial, a scandal, our names in the tabloids. 'Gay lovers' quarrel ends in attempted murder.' Not the best thing in the world for business. And Greg will end up in prison, guest of the government."

His voice now stronger, Huntley stood. "Now, if I don't press charges and instead simply remove him from my will, my business, my life, he will end up with nothing: no job, no money, nowhere to live, no prospects. You and I will not have to go to court. I know that you are a lawyer and that I am violating your code of ethics, but I would prefer not to pursue the issue."

"What can I say? It's your life."

"Here, help me drag him to the foot of the stairs. It will look as though he fell. And let's make ourselves scarce."

We pulled the unconscious body to the foot of the staircase leading to the upper deck, then went quickly up and walked briskly to the prow.

"I take it the two of you had a little talk, and you told him he was history."

"Correct. Perhaps alone on deck at night was neither the ideal time nor place. If he had pushed me over, he stood to inherit everything."

"Only if he got away with it. I have a feeling his attack was not premeditated, but then again who knows. Did you know that he and Charlotte are having a thing? I saw them necking on deck, but I don't think they saw me."

"Well, well, well, so that's who it was. I suspected there was someone else, but not Charl. Live and learn. When she finds out he doesn't have a penny, she'll drop him like a hot poker." Huntley shrugged as though ants marched down his back. "Can I buy you a drink?"

"Not just now, thanks. I've had enough excitement for one evening."

"Geoffry, I really would rather you said nothing about this, unless I specifically ask you to."

"At the risk of using an inappropriate metaphor, I don't want to make waves. What will you do for the rest of the cruise?"

"There's an empty cabin across the hall from mine. I'll move into it. I'll hang out with Georgette. It will pass."

I turned to go, but Huntley put a restraining hand on my arm. "I don't know what to say to the man who saved by life, but thanks."

"Just watch your step. I may not be around next time."

In the cabin Frank still slept heavily, but I did not feel drowsy. It had been a strange evening. I had witnessed an attempted murder and agreed to say nothing about it. Not conversant with American criminal law I did not know whether or not I was committing a felony. The less said about the matter, the better. Also the only way to keep a confidence is to tell no one, not Frank, not Elinor, absolutely no one at all. And that is what I intended to do.

While waiting for sleep to come I watched the closed-circuit movie, the one about the dinosaurs, without sound. I did not miss it. For a couple of decades, the Thirties and Forties, dialogue counted in films. Nowadays most special-effects movies are silent movies with an added, irrelevant soundtrack. I was astonished at how clearly the film silently unfolded its simple message: The worthy do not get eaten.

It would make a good motto for a sampler, if only I knew how to sew.

XII

The main shopping area in Charlotte Amalie, the largest town on St. Thomas, was a hellhole which, I suppose, is another way of saying it reminded me of downtown Montreal during the Christmas rush. Five cruise ships had tied up at the main wharf in St. Thomas, and hundreds of passengers, avid for duty-free bargains, had surged down the gangplanks and into waiting cabs for the short ride into town. Claustrophobia propelled me off the ship. Frank's temperature had gone down slightly, but he was still a degree or so above normal. He planned to shower and dress so he could get out on deck, giving our overworked maid a chance to make up the cabin. I felt restless. Marooned to a concrete pier, shorn of the glamour of being at sea, the *Blue Horizon* was little more than a second-class resort hotel surrounded by four other floating hotels.

I justified my excursion by saying I wanted to pick up something for Mother. For Elinor I had bought the gold chain in Barbados, and Mother was the only other person for whom I needed to shop. What she really would have appreciated was several bottles of duty-free vodka, but customs restrictions cancelled that idea. Outside of cigarettes and vodka, Mother's wants are few. She prefers Canadian cigarettes to American, so I could not even bring her the solitary carton permitted by customs. Perfume, a scarf, maybe some good soap, or perhaps I would see an item in a window that was just the ticket, although for an old lady living in one room in a retirement home, the choice is limited.

The taxi let me out at the edge of the main shopping area, and I could tell at a glance it was mobbed with shoppers, blocking the road to all but pedestrian traffic. Men stood in the centre of the street shilling and shouting and attempting to divert customers off the main drag and into the side streets, where unbelievable bargains awaited the adventurous. I hesitated. If worse came to worst, I could buy Mother something from the gift shop on board. From the deck of the ship I had seen Government House, halfway up the hill that dominates the town. A handsome, white, neoclassical building, it must offer an impressive view of the harbour. I could see long flights of stairs I did not wish to climb in tropical heat, so I hailed a taxi and asked him to take me to Government House.

I had made the right choice. From the front of the building, whose ground floor was open to the public, the view of the harbour was nothing short of spectacular. Beyond the wide curve of water, dotted with an astonishing variety of boats, from the great white ships moored at the pier to tiny, single-sailed dinghies barely visible from the height, stretched the Caribbean, calm and glittering in the white morning light. Had I been a character in a novel, I would have sat gazing at the view and weighing my options. How many heroines in nineteenth-century fiction stood on ramparts, widows' walks, balconies, bluffs, and cliffs while they tried to decide between becoming a governess or marrying a man they did not love. (They could have skipped down the primrose path, but that never presented itself as an option in the novels I was obliged to read.)

A woman came to stand beside me. At one point I might have described her as an older woman, but she was probably just around my age. The passage of time is kinder to men; age does not rob them of sexuality, at least in the eyes of the world. This woman, whom I recognized from the ship as she sat at an adjoining table in the dining room, was extremely pretty, pale eyes, white hair, and a figure which had resisted the tug of gravity and its complementary lateral spread. As a younger woman, she must have been ravishing. She smiled to indicate that she recognized me and to acknowledge I was there.

I smiled back. "It's well worth the cab ride."

"Is it not." She looked about as if fearful of being overheard. "This view is the first thing on this frightful cruise I have genuinely enjoyed."

I heard myself laughing out loud. "Do I hear the voice of a fellow sufferer?"

It was her turn to laugh. "You do. Between the flu and the undisciplined children and the ubiquitous vulgarity, I'm counting the hours until I can board the plane and fly home."

"I know how you feel. My travelling companion has been felled by flu, and I'm so tired of trying to be happy I'm almost ready to jump ship. I'm Geoffry Chadwick by the way."

"Elizabeth Cartwright." We shook hands. "My children thought this cruise would be a good idea, and they got together and bought me a ticket. It was a lovely gesture. My husband died recently, and they thought it would do me good to get away and meet new people."

"If you ask me," I volunteered, "which you didn't, it sounds to me as though the last thing you need, at a time when you are attempting to restructure your life, is to be thrust into a crowd of middle-aged middle-Americans intent on having a good time."

"My goodness, Mr. Chadwick, how well you have expressed it. What I need at this moment is time to myself, to restructure, as you so aptly put it, the rest of my life. My children—all adults I must add—meant well. They believed they were doing me a favour. But there is a fascist quality to kindness. What could I do but bow to their goodwill and come on this dreadful boat."

I smiled. "To explain why I am here is so bizarre I won't even try. Let me just say the ticket was a prize, drawn from a hat."

She smiled. "I feel vastly relieved. At the risk of sounding presumptuous, you do not strike me as the kind of man who would voluntarily choose the *Blue Horizon* for a holiday."

I nodded as a kind of acknowledgement.

"I do not relish the prospect of the next few years," she continued in a voice filled with New England. "My husband and I had a good marriage. Unfortunately this cruise has only served to underline how alone I really am. I don't relish the prospect of growing old by myself, but I will do so in my own way, not playing Scrabble with strangers."

She gave a deprecating shrug. "Isn't it odd how in this kind of situation you can tell things about yourself you would never admit at home. Had we met across a dinner table I would not have been so candid. I hope you will excuse me."

"What's to excuse? You have enough taste to condemn the pretentiousness of the ship, and you would like companionship for the final years. We were obviously both brought up to believe the truth is rude. We must appear to like everything; criticism is bad manners. One of the few advantages to the mature years is being able to jettison the hypocrisy and say what we think."

"How right you are, Mr. Chadwick. You have no idea how cheered I am to find someone who thinks as I do. I think it is less the idea of misery liking company than in realizing you are not completely wrong."

A woman came out of the building whom I recognized as a tablemate of Elizabeth Cartwright. "Time to head off, Liz," she said, sun-cured in a sundress, "we kept the taxi waiting."

Elizabeth Cartwright turned to me. "I must go. I hope you can make the most of your last day."

"Thanks, Mrs. Cartwright, this too will pass."

We shared a conspiratorial smile and she left. As I had not thought of asking my cab to wait I had to make my way down the hill on foot. Avoiding the steps, I followed the road which wound down to the town, and after a short walk found myself once again at the end of the main shopping area. After walking about two hundred yards I found a shop with silk scarves in the window. Mother did not need another scarf, but it wouldn't take up much room in a drawer. Flowers are always safe, and I purchased a handsome floral print. The blossoms were those to be found growing wild in Great Britain, hardly representative of the Caribbean, but preferable to a candy dish fashioned from half a coconut.

I left the shop and was heading back to the taxi stand, when I heard a voice calling, "Geoffry! Wait!"

I looked around. "Elsie! What on earth are you doing off the ship!"

Elsie looked dreadful in a yellow crepe pantsuit with floral embroidery on the jacket. Not only was the outfit about thirty years too young, the insistent yellow made her look sallow. She had been seriously ill, and it showed. The idea of her putting her health in jeopardy to shop for things readily available in Montreal made me furious. "You should be back in your cabin."

"I know. I shouldn't have come. I don't suppose you could help me find a taxi."

Had I not turned up unexpectedly I am sure Elsie would

have managed on her own, but the temptation to collapse onto a convenient arm was too alluring. Silently I took one of the large shopping bags she was carrying and steered her back to the row of cabs. During the short ride to the pier I did not speak, and I ignored her ineffectual attempt to pay the driver. Once we had navigated the gangplank, I handed her the second shopping bag and said I would see her later.

What provoked me most was that I could not tell whether her Camille collapse was pure histrionics or whether she was indeed having what Mother would have called "a turn." If it were no more than an act, I wondered why she had not managed to be more convincing in *Hedda Gabler*; but here she was playing the leading lady in her own drama instead of second fiddle to Audrey Crawford. Much more was at stake.

I rode the elevator to my floor and let myself into the cabin. To my surprise I found it empty. The maid had given the room a good going over, impossible to do with Frank sick and comatose. As the ship was relatively deserted, I decided now would be a good time to avoid lineups at the purser's office. All the passengers would need cash for tipping the staff. I have always worked on the assumption that a tip is given at the discretion of the person being served as reward for a job well done. Not so on the *Blue Horizon*, where a carefully calibrated tipping guide had been included with the day's newsletter.

I suppose the tipping index was a good idea for a shipful of people whose idea of a gratuity is fifty cents left under the saucer after pie and coffee. Probably tips accounted for a good part of staff income, as I strongly suspected Monarch Cruises paid little more than the minimum wage. I would have to tip for both Frank and myself, taking into consideration the extra effort his illness had occasioned the room staff. My first hurdle was to decide whether to leave a token amount for the butler John, knocked out of service by the flu after two days of doing as little as was humanly possible. Then I thought of all those starving brothers and sisters to whom he was probably sending money so they might have a bowl or two of rice. A dose of guilt is a tip's best friend. I tucked a few bills into an envelope on which I wrote his name. I suppose I would have to entrust the envelope to another staff member, likewise feeding a starving family or saving up for a car. Whether or not the envelope would find its way to the rightful recipient or be purloined en route remained a calculated risk. My conscience was clear.

I had just written and sealed the last envelope when Frank let himself into the cabin, fully dressed for the first time since he became sick. "I've been outside for nearly two hours," he began, "and I feel whacked. I think I'll go back to bed. I thought I'd get used to the idea of being up—training for tomorrow, but it's going to be a long day. Anyway, only the good die middle-aged, so I'll survive."

"There's nothing for you to do but lie around until you have to pull yourself together in the morning. The suitcases are to be brought up by this afternoon, and I can pack for both of us. I got an A-minus in suitcase layout at finishing school."

"The Living End Finishing School?"

"For a sick man you're quick with the lip. I just took care of the tips."

"Bless you for that. I have cash in the safe. Take whatever I owe you for my share of anything."

"How do you know I won't take advantage and steal you blind?"

Frank turned back the covers. "Because you're just like me: the only thing we are completely honest about is money."

I laughed out loud. "What a mean thing to say." I folded back the coverlet he was unsuccessfully trying to discard.

Frank sat on the edge of the bed. "You know what the Bible says: 'Thou shalt not steal.' "

"No, I don't know what the Bible says. I grew up reading novels. Tell me, was your father fond of pointing out that money doesn't grow on trees?"

"Was he not. But I had to find out for myself that happiness can't buy money." Frank lay down and pulled up the sheet.

"Would you like me to take your temp?"

"Not at the moment, thanks. Father also used to say money talks. Wrong again. Money whispers. When it talks it says goodbye."

"That sounds like a *perçu*. I can't go you one better, so I will say *au revoir*. Time for a bloody mary and a bite of lunch. Would you like me to order you something from room service before I go?"

"No thanks. I had a snack on deck. A good sign. I really wanted to eat something. Right now I'd like to sleep."

"Good idea. I'll be back after lunch."

Once again I had the table to myself. So fed up was I with Elsie and her cavalier attitude toward her health I did not want to exchange one word more than necessary. Furthermore, I did not relish the prospect of having her on my hands for most of tomorrow. Brad and Susan did not show up. Either they had gone ashore for the day or had chosen to eat lunch in the cafeteria. I did not expect to see Brad again in the dining room. If he failed to appear for dinner he would not have to tip the waiter. Since he never came to breakfast he could pocket the money. Susan would leave the tipping to her uncle. About Elsie I couldn't tell; she was not stingy, just not very bright. I intended to tip the waiter for both Frank and myself, since he had been obliged to serve as his own busboy. I felt sorry for all those sick staff members who would lose out on gratuities because of the flu, money they had no chance of regaining. But I was a passenger, not the Red Cross, and by taking care of my people generously I was paying my dues.

Six o'clock found me on deck watching the *Blue Horizon* edge slowly away from the pier to begin the last lap of our journey back to Puerto Rico. Although I felt huge relief that this unfortunate week was drawing to a close, I felt deep regret that tomorrow I would say goodbye to Frank. I detest goodbyes. Parting is not a sweet sorrow, nor all we know of heaven. I have reached the dreary age when every farewell could well be the last, one of those bleak universal truths that cannot be made palatable with a greeting card bromide.

Even were I to remove Elinor from the equation—a hypothesis I truly did not want—there remained little chance that Frank and I could build any sort of relationship. Geography would see to that. San Francisco is a long way from Montreal, and I had long ago lost the taste for long-distance affairs. At some point in a life almost everyone falls in love with someone who lives in another city, a different province, a foreign country. Young love thrives on obstacles. Think of Hero and Leander, Héloise and Abélard, Romeo and Juliet. The list is endless, lovers who fell in love in spite of, possibly because of, insurmountable difficulties. Romantic love is not a comfortable emotion, but the young disdain comfort. The straight, narrow, well-tended path leads to indifference, not passion.

In most uneventful lives the main hindrance to love lies not in family feuds, civil wars, or religious anathema, but distance, miles or kilometres, depending on your age. As a younger man I had several long-distance love affairs: New York, Chicago, Vancouver, London, Paris. Absent lovers are fine for a while. Meetings—brief, passionate, intense—are punctuated by long intervals of absence during which no demands are made. I didn't even mind being faithful to a distant lover, wearing my constancy like medals or a coronet. Outside of long-distance calls on a more or less regular basis, I could do pretty much as I pleased, until my next meeting with the *inamorato*.

The inescapable fact remains that presence makes the heart grow fonder. I outgrew these absentee relationships as I left my thirties. Frank and I were way too old to begin one of those commuting affairs. Susceptible as I am to jet lag, by the time I became adjusted to San Francisco rhythm, I would be thinking of returning home. Visiting at any age is difficult; one feels the obligation to make every moment count. The temptation is to overdo, alcoholic lunches followed by boozy dinners. Several months' worth of sightseeing, shopping, and art galleries must be squeezed into a short number of hungover days. (Of course the hangover hots can easily be mistaken for love, but only a tight-assed Italian poet would turn simple lust into a punishable sin.) Most difficult is the interruption of routine, essential to those accustomed to the comforting patterns of work.

Were I to visit Frank I would not need to be entertained. He would be free to concentrate on his next production, leaving me to my own devices. But I would not be at home, following my own inclinations, but a guest under someone else's roof. Visiting creates an artificial situation, the urge to fit in and be accommodating often at odds with the equally strong desire to please oneself. How would Frank adapt to visiting me in Montreal, if and when. After the first night of drinking and sex, what then? At our age we need continuity, pattern, routine— the reassurance of the familiar. Long-distance affairs are disruptive, and sooner or later this disorder must cause friction. Were we in our twenties we would welcome the flights, the inconvenience, the *mise en scène* of a long-distance affair. But not in our sixties.

Elinor offered me order; Frank obstacles. I knew which one I would choose. And the infinite regret I could not keep at bay sprang not only from saying goodbye to Frank but also at my own inflexibility. Late middle age had claimed me as a victim, and I dislike victims. It must logically follow that I did not like myself very much at the moment, and the truth is that I did not.

With all the years of supposed experience under my belt, I should have been able to provide answers. I wish I knew, but I am too old. Only the young know everything.

I went down to the cabin to finish packing and drink the last of our contraband scotch. Had the cruise been longer and Frank well, I would have asked Elizabeth Cartwright to join us for a drink. I suspected she would turn out to be an interesting woman, given half a chance, but the last night of an unfortunate cruise was no time to initiate friendships.

An envelope had been slid under the door, addressed simply to Geoffry Chadwick. Inside, a note from Huntley explained that Greg was suffering from concussion resulting from a fall on deck. The ship's doctor was keeping him under observation until the ship docked. Would I care to join Georgette, Charlotte, and himself for a drink before dinner?

As I did not want to shadowbox and self-consciously skirt

the issue of Greg, I decided to give it a pass. I wanted no more of Huntley. Granted, I had probably saved his life, but that did not mean I must have him for a friend. Had he shown better judgement about Greg, the whole unpleasant situation would never have taken place, and I would not now be burdened with one more confidence not to betray. There are times when ignorance is bliss.

Frank slept. Just as well, as he would need all his energy to get from Puerto Rico to San Francisco, a long journey in the best of health. I drank and moved silently about the cabin. To pack for Frank was easy, as most of his wardrobe hadn't been worn. I would have been quite happy to throw most of my clothes overboard with the suitcase, but I reconsidered.

I waited in the cabin until the chimes sounded for dinner and felt no little relief to be the sole passenger at our table.

After a restive night—I always sleep badly whenever I know I have to get up early—I washed and dressed, then left the cabin for a bite of early and solitary breakfast so Frank could get himself organized. We waited in our cabin until the very last minute. Our orders were to vacate the premises at 8:30 A.M. and proceed to the Blue Lagoon, where we would be instructed to abandon ship according to our cabin numbers.

Frank still ran a temperature, although it hovered below one hundred degrees Fahrenheit. He managed to shower, shave, and dress while I was in the dining room. I presume my tip had been considered satisfactory, as the waiter did everything short of asking for my hand in marriage. In my present frame of mind, I would probably have accepted.

Frank looked pale and gaunt, but I had to admit the pallor

suited him, especially in profile, a profile that would have looked at home on a coin or medallion. Some people, like Elsie, merely look sick when they are ill; others manage to seem interesting. Frank certainly looked no worse than I did, a restless night and freewheeling anxiety having taken their toll. The nurse, whom I fervently hoped would be waiting at the gangplank, would be hard put to tell which one of us was the patient.

Our hand luggage and topcoats lay on the bed nearest the door. I took one last look around. "Now, off we go, to rub elbows with people from whom we would never buy a used car nor permit our daughters to marry."

Frank managed to laugh. "In some ways, Chadwick, you are a dreadful snob. But I don't mind in the least. Snobs are romantics; they can remember or recreate an earlier, better time when imaginary values enhanced a make-believe world. To be a true snob requires imagination, and people with imagination are more interesting to be around."

"I think you may have paid me a compliment, but it came off the bottom of the deck."

"You know something, Geoff? I was wrong when I told you it is impossible to meet anyone congenial at our age. I did, not that it does me much good. I just wanted you to know." He made a wry face. "Maybe it's just as well I got sick. What would have happened if we really got serious?"

"I don't have an answer. At least we would be somewhere. Right now we are less than lovers, more than friends."

"Much more." In a husky baritone Frank began to sing. "'A fine romance, my friend, this is. / A fine romance . . .' Christ! I need a cigarette." He lit up.

"That's a good sign. You're on the mend. This whole situation is too fucking Jamesian for words."

"Isn't it though. Stardust without the star. God, don't the clichés come tumbling out." He brandished his cigarette in a gesture reminiscent of Bette Davis. "Ships that pass in the night."

"Ships that pass in the night do not ordinarily collide," I observed. "But we'll always have Ulan Bator."

A voice crackling over the intercom announced it was time to assemble in the Blue Lagoon. "Time to round up the usual suspects," said Frank. He stood, carefully extinguishing his cigarette, then embraced me. We held one another close, really touching for the first time since our encounter on deck. For a moment he pressed his cheek against mine.

"Time to go," he said.

The debarkation shed defined chaos. Every passenger had been instructed to head for the letter suspended from the ceiling corresponding to the first letter of the last name. As luck, or determination, would have it our nurse waited at the foot of the gangplank with a wheelchair. A crisp, efficient Puerto Rican, she had also managed to lasso a porter to deal with our luggage. Fortunately Chadwick and Connors were located under the giant C. We collected Elsie, her bags, my bags, and headed for the W.

Had many of the passengers truly understood what going ashore would be like, they would probably have stayed home. The enormous shed was so jammed we could hardly move through the shouting, jostling, sweating, angry, and borderline hysterical crowd. Not a few of the passengers, ill with flu, had to be helped along by travelling companions or compassionate strangers. I supported Elsie, already beginning to wilt, while the nurse pushed Frank along the way opened up by our tough and determined porter. Pausing at the W to collect Frank's cases, we made our way to the entrance. Hot and damp though the air might be, it still felt cool and fresh after the claustrophobic clamour of the shed.

A short walk brought us to the limousine, which the driver had obviously not wanted to leave unattended. The minute our car came into sight, Elsie seemed to experience a renewal of energy. She took charge of seeing Frank comfortably seated in the car, tutting and clucking in a theatrical display of concern to the point that had I been the nurse I would have wanted to slap her.

I was helping the driver to stow the luggage in the trunk when I became aware of two baskets woven of palm fronds, one tucked inside the other.

"Elsie, are these yours?"

"Yes."

"They will not survive the trip in the luggage compartment."

"I'm going to carry them with me."

"But you already have hand luggage, plus a topcoat."

"That's true." She smiled a Gee-aren't-kids-great smile. "I thought that if you wouldn't mind carrying my small bag . . ."

"I do mind, Elsie. I have my own case, a coat, and you to look after. I am not taking on a couple of goddamned baskets!"

In the back seat Frank began to laugh quietly, and the nurse struggled unsuccessfully with a smile.

"Well!" exclaimed Elsie, giving her head a vigorous toss. "I only thought . . ."

"You didn't think. Are you going to fly to Atlanta, then on to Montreal with your coat in the overhead rack, your bag under the seat, and two baskets in your lap, all of which you will have to carry on and off the plane?"

"What am I supposed to do with them?"

"Give them to the nurse. Now, let's get this show on the road."

The small airport had not been designed to accommodate hordes of weekly trippers. Other ships besides the *Blue Horizon* had disgorged their passengers, who jammed the small check-in lobby with lines reaching to the main entrance. The holiday had ended; everyone looked wilted in spite of the early hour. I wondered how many of the homeward-bound passengers truly believed they had enjoyed a wonderful time as opposed to the nagging feeling they must believe their vacation a success. To have spent that much money and not to have been overwhelmed with delight is not the North American way.

Accommodation was made for Frank, as a passenger in a wheelchair compels deference, like someone on crutches. He could have walked into the airport, but once upright he would have forfeited the advantage of being seen as ill. This was no time for moral fibre, for proving oneself a real man oblivious to pain or infirmity. The nurse and wheelchair smoothed our path, and I was so fed up with Elsie and her ill-advised shopping expedition that it never even occurred to me to let her use the chair. Fortunately our driver knew all the porters, meaning we did not have to wait for someone to handle our luggage.

Elsie experienced another resurgence of energy as we entered the terminus and demanded to know if Frank wanted anything for the flight: candy bars, magazines, souvenirs? She would gladly have accompanied him right to the departure gate, but I found her a vacant seat and ordered her to stay put with our luggage until Frank, whose flight took off before ours, was safely checked in. Whoever had ordered the limousine must have clout, as the nurse was given clearance to take Frank through security and see him onto the plane.

I accompanied him as far as I could. "I hope you're going to be all right." It was a lame observation, but the best I could do.

"I will. When the stewardesses see me helped on by a nurse they'll get the message. Maybe they can arrange somewhere for me to lie down between flights, and I'll get assistance boarding. I'll manage."

"Fingers crossed."

"Thanks for everything, Geoff. Words fail."

"But not for long. I'll call when I get home this evening, if the hour is not too uncivilized. And remember—you're not well enough to join the Mile High Club."

Frank smiled. "Go to Hell! Go directly to Hell! Do not pass Go, and the rest."

We shook hands, an oddly formal gesture. I thanked the nurse and tipped her, then stood watching until they had passed through security check. Frank turned to give me one last wave, and I had the oddest sensation, as though there was a great, yawning void where my stomach should be. It would have been comforting to weep, but hadn't I been told as a child that big boys don't cry.

Instead I waved back, describing a crescent with my right hand. The gesture meant more, much more, than acknowledging the departure of a friend. I was waving goodbye to my former life and saying so-long to emotional options, to the possibility of being ambushed by unexpected feelings, to forks in the road. The way ahead lay clear and straight, the potholes and deviations easily negotiated as long as health endured. I could not in all honesty say whether I was glad or sorry, but when I returned to Elsie and the luggage I did so as a considerably older man.

Now that she no longer had Frank to fuss over, she decided to wilt. I checked us both in, steered her through security, and settled her limply in the departure lounge with a magazine and a plastic bottle of water. For a woman who has taken vows of chatter the same way some orders take vows of silence, her disinclination to talk suited me fine. A silent Elsie could be more easily endured between Puerto Rico and Atlanta, then Atlanta to Montreal, than a voluble one.

High in the clouds, a sleeping Elsie in the window seat, I was flooded with a kind of weary relief. Time and distance had resolved a situation I was way too old to have allowed to happen. Being old enough to know better does not necessarily mean one does know better. I had certainly failed the test. But it was done. I couldn't say I would do better next time because there wasn't going to be any next time. The best thing I could do was to carry on as though nothing had happened. After all, nothing had.

Having endured the fuss and bother of changing planes in Atlanta, I experienced such a depletion of energy that as soon as the captain turned off the Fasten Seatbelt lights, I pushed back my seat and slept. It turned out to be Elsie who nudged me awake with the news that we were beginning our descent into Montreal. By now night had fallen. Darkness is not a metaphor; it merely prevents passengers from seeing where they are. I hoped the pilot had located the right airport, as I was so anxious to shed this entire experience I could almost taste it. And after a reassuring voice on the public address system told us to fasten our seatbelts prior to landing at Dorval

Airport, I felt so relieved I was able to ask Elsie in a pleasant tone how she had survived the flight.

"Fine," she replied.

Anything more would have been surperfluous.

XIII

Were I shaping this narrative as a story, I would have come down with the flu shortly after arriving home. As I lay feverish, drifting in and out of consciousness, Elinor's cool, comforting hand on my brow, I could have drawn boring, moralistic conclusions about illness and retribution. (Here lies Geoffry Chadwick, after a long and losing battle with an attack of bad taste.) But I did not fall sick; my flu shot kept the infection at bay, and life continued without interruption.

Elinor was waiting at the airport with my car. Anybody watching us would have thought we were an old married couple and not lovers measuring out the relationship in months. Still, I was more happy to see Elinor, conservative in natural fibres, than I was willing to let on in front of Elsie. For customs I wore Elinor's gold chain as if it were my own and declared Mother's scarf, with the result that I was waved through in seconds. Elsie fudged and fussed to the point where she was singled out for special inspection. Once more I rode to her rescue, saying she was just recovering from the flu. The inspectors, with typical Gallic courtesy, gave her luggage a perfunctory glance and told her to proceed. With Elinor's help we got the luggage into the car and Elsie buckled into the front seat.

At once Elinor picked up on my disinclination to talk, and conversation limited itself to getting into the car and out of the airport parking lot. Elinor drove.

"Did the limo meet you at the ship?" she asked as we pulled onto the highway.

"According to Hoyle. The driver snagged us a porter, and the nurse saw Frank onto the plane."

"I hope he got home safely," volunteered Elsie.

"I'll call when I get in," I said. "We're three hours ahead, so it's only early evening in San Francisco."

"I take it I picked the right cruise to stay home from. Excuse the pronoun."

"Preposition!"

Elinor laughed, "I see you haven't lost the edge," as she eased into the flow of traffic. Elinor is an excellent driver; moreover, she enjoys taking the wheel. I don't much like to drive and happily hand her the keys. "Elsie, are you going to be all right on your own? If not, you can use my guest room until you feel better."

"Thanks, Elinor, but I'll be fine. My daughter will come over if I need her, but the worst is past. I would have had a much more difficult time had it not been for Geoffry." She reached back to pat my hand.

"Now, Elsie, I only did what anyone would have done."

"But anyone wasn't there," observed Elinor. "You were. Don't mind him," she confided to Elsie. "He hates to be thanked." They shared a laugh and a moment of female bonding.

"Does the new baby look like a baby?" I asked.

"Exactly like. Round and pink and damp."

"Don't tell me you have a new grandchild!" exclaimed Elsie. "Geoffrey never told me."

What is it about babies that animates women. The heretofore limp and languid Elsie grew vivacious at the notion of Elinor's grandchild, and the ensuing exchange of information—

sex, weight, length of delivery, breast feeding, and name (Charles Alexander) occupied the rest of the drive to Elsie's condo. I carried in her suitcases, submitted to a grateful embrace, and said I would call tomorrow to see how she was doing.

"Now to get you home," said Elinor as I got in beside her. "Would you like me just to drop you off? I'm sure you must be weary."

"I am, but I would like you to stay. I may not tear off your clothes and have my beastly way with you, but it would be *molto* agreeable to be with someone who isn't sick."

"And I would enjoy being around an adult. Granny is awfully tired of tiny tears, tiny shoes, tiny talk. Have you eaten?"

"Only plastic plane food."

"We'll send out for something. My treat." She reached out and put her hand on my arm. "Now that we have shed that nitwit Elsie, may I say how good it is to see you?"

"You may. Likewise I'm sure."

By the time I walked through my own front door I was beginning to wonder whether I really had sailed on the *Blue Horizon* or imagined the whole thing. My own reality crowded out the Caribbean, the bland cabin, the forgettable food, the self-absorbed passengers, and my own lapses in judgement. Once safely behind my own closed door I embraced Elinor, and in her embrace I felt secure.

"Good evening, my name is Geoffry Chadwick. I wanted to know if Frank arrived home safely."

"Hello there. I'm Sally Stevens, a neighbour of Frank's. He got in about an hour and a half ago, and went straight to bed. I was just checking in on him when the phone rang. He told me you might call."

"Is he okay?"

"Tired, but hanging in. If he's not better tomorrow I'll get in touch with his doctor."

"Good. If you'd be kind enough to tell him I called. I'm relieved to know you're on the job."

"No problem. I'll give him your message. When he feels up to it, I'm sure he'll give you a ring."

"Well, I guess that covers it. Goodnight, Sally, and thanks for taking up the slack."

Next item on the agenda was a stiff highball. I felt not so much tired as strung out. Sleep lay miles away. Elinor telephoned for something hot, greasy, and comforting.

"A small token of my esteem and affection," I said as I unhooked the chain from around my neck.

"Oh, Geoffry, an anchor chain! I love it!"

"Here, let me put it on you." Elinor lifted her hair and I fastened the chain around her neck. At once she went to admire herself in the hall mirror.

"You really should have." She played with the links as she studied her reflection. "I've wanted a gold anchor chain for years, but it's not the kind of thing that sensible matrons buy for themselves."

"There you are. Drink?"

"Yes, please. I have much to tell."

"Come and be diverting while I unpack."

The first item on the agenda was the new grandson but, to give Elinor credit, she did not dwell on the subject. Other people's grandchildren are of limited interest to elderly bachelors. The baby was well, also the mother, while the other children seemed to regard the new brother as a kind of inter-active toy. All was as it should be. Pippa passes.

Unpacking took only minutes, and shortly we were settled companionably in our facing wing chairs in the living room, as if the intervening week had telescoped itself into yesterday.

"There is a little problem," began Elinor, putting the last two words into the vocal equivalent of italics. "We all know our Audrey is, as the French would say, *formidable*, but she is on the verge of outdoing even herself. She took quite a bad fall."

"I know. I was there."

"Anyone else would have taken weeks to recuperate. Not our Audrey. She is home, quite recovered from the concussion, operating handily around her taped wrist, and—fasten your seatbelt—she wants to mount the play in mid-June. If we stage it before the St. Jean-Baptiste and Canada Day weekends, we will still be able to draw on most of our captive audience. After Canada Day everyone decamps to the country: the Lauren-tians, the Eastern Townships, Muskoka, Kennebunkport, you name it. She is afraid that if we postpone the production until the fall we will lose momentum."

"So much momentum that maybe the production will have to be scrapped?"

"You are a profoundly wicked man, Geoffry Chadwick, but you have hit the nail squarely on the thumb. To tell you the truth I'm so sick of Hedda bloody Gabler that I'm seriously thinking of moving to Patagonia until the whole thing blows over."

"Patagonia is a long way from the new grandson. What you need is an excuse to get you out of town for most of June."

"Do I not. I could almost face the production in the fall, but at the moment, no. I need a holiday, from Hedda and everything relating to her."

I put down my highball on the coffee table. "Would a wedding trip be an adequate alibi for quitting the production?"

"I suppose. I know you can rent outfits for the groom and his party, but can you rent the groom himself?"

"These days, my dear, you can rent anything, but you can have me for nothing."

Elinor put down her tumbler with a clank. "Geoffry, is that a proposal?"

"I suppose it is."

Elinor burst out laughing. "Elinor Richardson, girl grandmother, has just received a proposal of marriage?"

"She has. But before she decides whether or not to accept, there are caveats." I paused for a swallow of my drink. "To begin with, the gentleman, if so I may presume to style myself, who has just proposed loves the woman in question, but he cannot honestly admit to being in love with her. Should this first caveat present a serious problem there is probably no point in continuing with the others."

"The lady in question—two can play at upward mobility—this lady is well aware that being in love is not part of the equation. She too loves the gentleman in question, but were she in love with him she would decline the proposal. 'In love' is a minefield to be negotiated while one is young. 'In love' leads to misunderstandings, slights, umbrage, taking offense when none is meant, battles that drag on like the Crusades, and steamy reconciliations which can send those in late middle age into physiotherapy. In short, the lady in question neither requires nor expects the prospective groom to be in love with her. Next?"

"The gentleman in question considers it a good idea to

maintain separate establishments until such time as a satis-factory compromise, such as a large condo or townhouse suitable for both parties has been found. Time frame open."

"Agreed. Next?"

"As regards our respective families: we are to wed one another, not our entire clans. I will perform the usual duties—Christmas, birthdays, christenings, graduations—but I will not undertake your parents, children, and grandchildren as a retire-ment project. By the same token I will maintain a decent dis-tance between my own family and the lady in question."

"Excellent suggestion. You will be my iron-clad alibi for re-sisting the gravitational pull of grandmotherhood. Next?"

"The next caveat concerns you far more than me. Elinor, you are old enough to be conversant with Greek mythology."

"I wasn't there, if that's what you mean."

"It had occurred to me. As I was saying, do you remember the myth of Tithonus?"

"As if it were yesterday. Eos, or Aurora, goddess of dawn, loved Tithonus, a mere mortal. She abducted him, then begged Zeus/Jupiter to grant him immortality. The head honcho com-plied, but she forgot to ask for eternal youth. Tithonus grew older and older, more and more dessicated, while she remained young and beautiful. Finally she turned him into a grasshopper.

'And after many a summer dies the swan.

Me only cruel immortality

Consumes; I wither slowly in thine arms,

Here at the quiet limit of the world . . .'

You only have to go back as far as Tennyson for that one, but I still wasn't there."

"I am fully prepared to believe you. But, think a minute, Elinor. I don't want you to be in that situation, stuck looking after an invalid old man. I have infinite confidence in your abilities, but I doubt even you could turn me into a grasshopper."

"Oh, Geoffry, get real. Look at your mother, whom you resemble much more than you do your father. Pardon my candour, but just look at her: smoke-cured, pickled in vodka, and sailing into her nineties. Puh-leese. You're going to be a widower twice over."

"May I remind you, Mistress Richardson, that both your parents are still alive. Our mothers will bury us both."

Elinor laughed. "I guess you're right at that. But since we're conducting the most literary proposal of the decade . . ." she rose and went to the bookcase. "I know you have the plays of Congreve because I checked out your books. Here it is." She thumbed through the pages. "From *The Way of the World* allow me to quote Mrs. Millimant: 'As liberty to pay and receive visits to and from whom I please; to write and receive letters, without interrogatories or wry faces on your part; to wear what I please; and choose conversation with regard only to my own taste; to have no obligation upon me to converse with wits that I don't like, because they are your acquaintance, or to be intimate with fools, because they may be your relations. Come to dinner when I please, dine in my dressing-room when I'm out of humour, without giving a reason. To have my closet inviolate; to be sole empress of my tea-table, which you must never presume to approach without first asking leave. And lastly, wherever I am, you shall always knock at the door before you come in. These articles subscribed, if I continue to endure you a little longer, I may by degrees dwindle into a wife.'"

"I believe that if you read on a little further Mirabell says: 'Then we are agreed.'"

The buzzer announced the arrival of our food.

"Allow me, O Lord and Master." Elinor went to answer the door.

"Bring food, woman. But first I'd like another drink, short and sharp."

"Your wish is my command. How am I doing so far?"

"Pretty well, I'd say. On the day of the ceremony are you going to say, 'This is the third happiest day of my life?' "

"Probably not," replied Elinor as she carried the bags of food into the kitchen. "I'll probably be tempted to say something rude, like 'Up yours, Hedda Gabler!' I hope the whole thing will be very small-scale."

"Minuscule. Let's tell only those people who absolutely have to know, like the minister."

"Suits me," said Elinor. "After all, the real reason for the wedding is to spare me another bout with *Hedda Gabler*."

"And I won't have to sit through another dress rehearsal and performance. Marriage seems like a pretty good trade-off."

"I was sure you would see it my way. Shall we eat?"

"Geoffry, it's Frank, in case you didn't know. Sorry to have missed your call, but I was done in. It was a very long day. What can I tell you. Sally and her husband met me at the airport, and have kept an eye on me since. Temperature is back to normal, but I still feel awfully weak. I hope the recuperation doesn't take too long, as I have to get back into harness pretty soon. Sorry about spoiling the trip, but you were great. I miss you a lot, but that's to be expected. Hope to catch you in next time I phone. Ciao."

Audrey was holding court, an extravagant attitude considering that the only courtiers present were Elinor and I, both dressed in casual, or what Mother would have called "sports" clothes. Small matter; Audrey was on. The fall had failed to knock out the grandeur; she wore a hostess gown not dissimilar to that worn by Hedda in Act I. A turban bore witness that she had not been recently to the hairdresser, and her makeup had the brave, slightly skewed look of lipstick and eyeliner applied with the left hand of a right-handed person. She received us in her bedroom, Hartland having his own rooms down the hall. She could easily have come downstairs to the living room, but that would have denied her the chaise-longue, upholstered in burgundy brocade, on which she half sat, half reclined. Brocade aside, I was reminded of the deck chairs on the *Blue Horizon*, those aluminum-and-vinyl recliners on which Middle America sunned itself around the pool.

"Elinor, Geoffry," she exclaimed, stretching out the hand with the bandaged wrist, "how good of you to come and visit a poor invalid, especially after Geoffry's siege on the cruise. Have you heard from Frank?"

"Only by voice mail. I'll try later today. He's on the mend, but very washed out."

"I've been talking with Elsie," continued Audrey, settling herself in a more upright position now that the supine greetings were over. "She's in much the same condition, better but weak. I suggested she stay close to home, recover her health, and learn her lines. Sincerity is no substitute for talent. Time marches on, and we hope to resume rehearsals next week."

"It's about the performance that we came to see you," began Elinor. "Geoffry and I will be away from Montreal for most of June, so I won't be able to stage manage the production."

All traces of languor fell away as Audrey sat bolt upright and swung her feet onto the floor. "What do you mean you won't be in town?"

"Precisely that," replied Elinor, refusing to be intimidated. "Geoffry and I are to be married, and we will be away on our wedding trip."

"But you can't leave now. Who will look after the back-stage end of things? That Beauchemin woman is quite hope-less. And the rest of the crew are children."

"Audrey," I said quietly, "don't you think perhaps con-gratulations are in order? Elinor has just told you we are to be married. You introduced us, or invited us to the same Christ-mas party. Your matchmaker's dream has come to fruition. And all you can say is, 'But you can't leave!' Watch us."

An opportune interruption arrived with the maid wheeling in a tea trolley. Who but Audrey would still use a tea trolley. On the lower shelf, dominating the sandwiches and pastries, sat another of those intimidating sandwich rolls, glistening with defiance and more difficult to slice than a roast duck. Catching sight of herself in the dressing table mirror across the room, Audrey adjusted her sleeves before pouring tea.

"Congratulations!" she said curtly, passing Elinor a cup. "I hope you'll both be very happy." Audrey fixed me with the same look she would have worn had she found me rifling through her jewel case.

"Thank you," I said.

"Thank you," echoed Elinor as she put down her cup. "There is something else I would like to discuss, Audrey. If the production is scheduled for the fall, I am going to need a re-liable assistant. I started out looking after props and helping with makeup, only to end up as stage manager because Lucille

Beauchemin didn't know how to find the ladies' room. Then at the eleventh hour, Alan asked me to be prompter. It's one thing to help out, another to be saddled with all the joe jobs. I'm going to need some help, and from people who won't do a fade out at the last minute."

Audrey rose to pass the sandwiches, less I suspect from motives of genuine hospitality than for the tactical advantage of standing while the adversaries were seated. "That's perfectly all right, Elinor. You can approach anyone you like to help out. It is for the library after all."

"There you are, Audrey. The buck has landed right back on my desk. You forget I only recently moved back to Montreal from Toronto. I haven't made that many new friends, and such people as I know from the old days are not one bit interested in volunteering for amateur theatricals. You have far more experience in volunteer work than I; you have the network. Surely you can come up with a couple of reliable assistants."

"It would seem that playing the leading role, not to mention recovering from my fall, is enough for me to cope with at the moment."

"With all due respect, Audrey," continued Elinor, "the production was not my idea. I was conscripted, only to find myself in a situation where the sum of the parts adds up to far more than the whole. And to be perfectly candid, I don't much care whether the play goes on or not."

So delighted was I to see Elinor standing up to Audrey I could have hugged her. Instead I came to her defense.

"One thing we have overlooked," I suggested, "is who will come to this production? Will the holders of tickets come back if there is no reception and raffle? Before we commit ourselves to another run at the play, I for one would like to see some figures. How much did we take in through ticket sales and how much did we spend on wine, catering, and expenses for the play, including the rental of Queen Mary Hall. Does it really make sense to play *Hedda Gabler* to a half-empty auditorium if we are going to end up in the red?"

Unsure of what to do, Audrey sat. Having summoned us to dictate terms about the upcoming production, she found herself facing a palace revolt. Audrey is overbearing, but she is not a fool, certainly not when it comes to money. Did she really want to massage her ego through a fundraising scheme that stood to end up in debt?"

"I suppose you do have a point, Geoffry. I'll have Hartland draw up a balance sheet; he's good with figures. In the meantime I don't suppose there's any chance of you changing the wedding plans."

"Not really, Audrey. Elinor thinks it's high time she made an honest man of me."

It was a lame joke, but Audrey had enough sense to turn it to her advantage. "Well, at some point I'll have a little cocktail party for the two of you, perhaps after Labour Day when all the country people have returned to civilization."

"That's very kind of you, Audrey," said Elinor, "but not at all necessary."

"Necessary is not the point," announced Audrey, now back in charge. "It will be fun. Draw up a guest list, say about forty to fifty people. I may ask a few guests on my own, those who bought blocks of seats and donated prizes to the raffle. More tea?"

Elinor and I both declined and, suggesting Audrey not overtire herself so soon after the accident, we eased ourselves away. The sandwich roll still sat, virginal and untouched, on its platter. I felt reasonably confident that Audrey had read the writing on the wall. Hartland is a man who grows obscenely sentimental over babies and kittens; however he is hard-edged and steely-eyed when it comes to figures. After he had calculated expenses over revenues in neat columns and presented the results to Audrey I had small doubt the production would be shelved. I felt a comforting sense of relief. Audrey can be a real pain in the neck, but I did not want to see her exposed to public ridicule, only to learn the production had been a financial failure. To trot out the old saw: discretion truly is the better part of valour.

I arrived home to find a special-delivery letter had been left for me with the doorman. It came from Bob Parkinson and told me he intended to send his father's collection of antique weapons to an auction house in the United States. Would I be kind enough to return the duelling pistols I had borrowed for the play. He concluded by suggesting we get together for a drink really soon and signed off with best wishes.

Without the duelling pistols, could there be a production of *Hedda Gabler*?

I considered the letter a sign from God.

"Frank, Geoff here, your good neighbour to the north. We appear to be playing telephone tag. I thought by calling you early San Fran time I'd catch you in. A good sign, as were you still sick you wouldn't be out. I'm going to marry Elinor. Don't be surprised. After all, it was you who put the idea into my mind. I wish you could be my best man. But I guess you know you already are, here or there. Hope all goes well for you. One of these days we will connect. Wish here were there. À *bientôt*."

Mother looked astonished to see me when I walked into her room followed by Elinor. It was late morning, so Mother was sober.

"Goodness me, Geoffry, I thought you were hundreds of miles away."

"I was, Mother, but now I'm back." Leaning down, I kissed her on both cheeks.

"So I see. And you've brought Elinor. How are you, my dear?"

"Very well thank you, Mrs. Chadwick. You're looking well, I'm glad to say." If Elinor was stretching the truth she did so with the best of intentions. Mother looked as she always does, translucent, insubstantial, slightly out of focus, as though a sudden noise or abrupt movement would cause her to dissolve.

"Did you have a good time—wherever it is you were?" As Mother has always suffered from information underload, she could not be expected to remember I had visited the Caribbean.

"Yes, it was delightful," I lied, telling Mother what she wanted to hear. For me to have taken a cruise and not enjoyed it was permissible, just so long as I did not confess to not having enjoyed it. To admit disappointment showed a want of character. Had Mother and I been sailing on the *Titanic* she would have expected me to go down with the ship.

"I brought you something from St. Thomas." I handed Mother the scarf. "It isn't terribly ethnic, but I thought it perhaps more useful than a necklace and matching bracelet of cowrie shells."

"It's perfectly lovely." Mother shook out the silk square, held it up for admiration, then handed it to Elinor to fold and put away. I knew the gift itself didn't matter much, just so long as I brought her something from the trip. Age imposes rituals.

"We have some news," began Elinor, "although I think Geoffry should tell you."

"Oh, dear, I hope no one has died. I can no longer bear to read the obituary column; always someone I know has gone."

"No, nothing like that," I said. "It's more a case of rebirth; you're about to acquire a daughter-in-law." I paused to let the news sink in.

"How can that be?" demanded Mother. "I have only one son, and he is a terminal bachelor."

"Not any longer. I'm going to marry Elinor."

"Don't tell me. Poor Elinor. Does she know what she is letting herself in for, marrying an older man? It won't be easy."

"Thanks for the vote of confidence, Ma." Above her head I gave Elinor a wink. "I'm going to be perfectly beastly as a husband. I shall lock up the liquor and be stingy with the housekeeping money. I shall be rude to her friends and snore and spend weekends watching sports on TV. And I shall make personal remarks. Poor Elinor indeed!"

"No, but seriously, dear, you are awfully set in your ways. I know you won't be horrid with her. I brought you up better than that, but you have lived by yourself for so long—I think I'd like a little drink."

"Why don't we all have one?" suggested Elinor, riding to the rescue. "So we can toast the happy couple."

I poured three weak drinks, as Mother still had to get through lunch.

"Well, well, here's to happiness for all!" exclaimed Mother, instantly cheered by the feel of a tumbler in her hand. "Where will you hold the ceremony. Not that it matters. I don't expect I shall be able to attend."

"Why don't we get married here at Maple Grove Manor?" asked Elinor. "It's going to be a small wedding, just family and a few friends. Then we can head out for the reception at the Lord Elgin Club. I think I'm still a member. That means Mrs. Chadwick could be present at the ceremony."

"What a lovely idea!" exclaimed Mother, for whom a few swallows of vodka banished all obstacles. "I can simply ride the elevator downstairs."

"Way to go, Mrs. Richardson," I said, giving Elinor a hug. "You know how to smooth out a stony path. Why don't we go downstairs right now and book the room. It's almost time for Mother's lunch."

After a tiny explosion of goodbyes we made good our escape and went down to the director's office. The director turned out to be a helpful, tailored woman who seemed quite taken with the idea of a wedding at Maple Grove. She volunteered the library, the least-used room in the building, and asked for only a few day's notice.

We were crossing the lobby toward the front door when old Mr. Barlowe leaped out of his chair. "Did you hear the one about the two coons who met a cop?" he began.

"I hope the policeman guided them safely across the street," I replied. "Racoons, like most wild animals, are not safe around automobiles."

Momentarily stumped, he rubbed his chin, the brief pause allowing us to push through the front door.

"The resident bore," I offered by way of explanation.

"You handled him very adroitly, I must say."

"No better than you handled Mother. What a stroke of genius to hold the ceremony under her own roof. You have no idea what a large problem that will sidestep."

"I'm more than just an unusually pretty face," said Elinor. "And I have always believed actions speak louder than words. Now if you truly love me—she said moving into her manipulative mode—you will take me someplace expensive and buy me an excellent lunch. We have much to discuss."

"I do truly love you, as only a victim can. What about Chez Claudine?"

"Wow! You really do care. Would you like me to drive?"

"Very much. But I will hold the door."

And away we drove, into our future.

"Geoff, this is turning into a kind of joke. One of these days you will pick up the receiver, and I won't know what to say. I'm off to Santa Fé tomorrow. *Pelléas et Mélisande*, bumped up to the nineteen-twenties. Why must every queen who directs an opera feel he has to reinvent the wheel. I can't believe how much better I feel, although I have to admit that by evening I'm pretty weary. I'm glad for you and Elinor. You have made the right decision. What's more, you have given me hope. If two old farts like us could find a wavelength maybe there's someone else out there. Maybe not, but you don't get to pass Go unless you throw the dice. When I have an address and phone number I'll call and leave them with your service. One of these days we're bound to connect. Give Elinor my love, and keep a little for yourself. Correction: make that a lot. As they say in the comics: 'to be continued.' Ciao."

While Elinor and I were on our honeymoon, exploring the hill towns of Italy and contentedly resigning ourselves to the reassuring boredom of happiness, Frank's Aunt Eileen died. Frank flew into Montreal for the funeral, but did not tarry. When Elinor and I returned to Montreal I went up to the Mount Royal Cemetery to visit Aunt Eileen's grave. She had been buried in a beautiful part of the cemetery. From the hillside where she lies one can see the Laurentian Mountains shimmering in the heat of July. As I stood by her grave, flooded by recollections of childhood, I found myself thinking of Frank. I let my mind wander back over the cruise and thought of that night on deck when, under the inevitable tropical moon, we held one another close. I tried to remember what and how I felt. I tried very hard, but I couldn't. There are times when memory lets us down. And perhaps it's just as well.